Budget Cuts and Midnight Lust

STEM meets Sparks:
A hilarious, steamy teacher romance
where love is the ultimate experiment.

M. Jayne LaDow

This is a work of fiction. Any resemblance to actual persons, living or dead, events, or locales is purely coincidental. Any accidental overlap is purely the result of wild imagination and the occasional awkward situation that just had to be included. The characters, events, and quirky teachers in this book were created for your entertainment and are not to be taken as advice on how to handle your own romantic entanglements, snowstorms, or conference road trips.

Please note that this book contains references to real-world educational struggles, and an obsession with smutty love stories. If this doesn't sound like your cup of tea, you may want to put it down now.

Cover design by M. Jayne LaDow

Published by Writes and Giggles, LLC

For permissions, contact: mjayneladow@gmail.com

To the teachers who fight for field days,
science fairs, and field trips.
And to the kids who don't fit in boxes.

MARCHFIELD, VIRGINIA
FIRE STATION
FIREHOUSE GYM
HIP HAVEN APARTMENTS
MARCHFIELD
HOSPITAL
EGGLECTIC CAFE
SHARKY'S PUB
MRS. BARTLETT'S
PAT'S BAKERY
POLAR VORTEX
CLASSIC CURVES
NAIL NERDS
PIZZA
BARREL
PIE IN THE SKY
FLOWER SHOP
SHARE YOUR BUDS
THE SHOE BOX
MAX'S
MARCHFIELD
MIDDLE
SCHOOL
PARKSON PARK
OZ AND AUDREY'S
KEITH AND RACHEL'S
TO CLOVERFIELD FARM
BOBBY AND MEL'S
EVAN AND VAL'S

Chapter 1: Emma

THE INTERCOM CRACKLED as I took what should have been my first glorious sip of coffee. It was lukewarm because middle school never gives a teacher time to have hot beverages. But that was okay because it matched my enthusiasm for being here on this gloomy Monday morning.

"Ms. Bennett and Dr. Harrison to the principal's office, please."

The squeak of sneakers stopped mid-screech. Basketballs froze mid-bounce. Thirty sweaty kids turned toward me like I'd been called to the gallows. Even Tyler, who'd been two seconds from a layup, stood clutching the ball like it might explode.

A single basketball thudded to the floor and rolled away in the silence.

Great. Nothing good ever comes of a summons to the office. And I knew what this was going to be about.

I set my chipped World's Best PE Teacher mug on the scorer's table and forced a grin. "Don't look so excited. You'll still owe me five laps when I get back."

They groaned in unison, but a few mischievous grins were thrown my way. Seventh graders smelled drama from a mile away, and apparently, I'd just become their main event.

"You're in trouble," Tyler said, spinning the ball on one finger like a show-off.

"Probably," I shot back. "But don't worry. If I get fired, you'll all have to write essays about the history of basketball for your new PE teacher."

A chorus of "Nooo!" rose up, loud enough to rattle the bleachers.

"Maybe they're promoting you," Brianna suggested. "Like... principal or something."

I snorted. "Sure. And you're all getting straight A's on the fitness tests this week."

They groaned again, but my smile couldn't stop the creep of anxiety in my belly. The whispers of budget cuts had been getting louder all week, and if the meeting was about trimming the fat, Field Day was an easy target—at least to someone like science teacher, Dr. Max Harrison.

He'd been parading his glossy PhD credentials and talking up his grand idea for a revamped science fair since last year, wowing admin with fancy proposals and PowerPoints. To him, Field Day was another line item. To me, it was Marchfield's heartbeat.

Waving to Pat Donovan, the other PE teacher wrangling a class in the gym, I slipped out into the main hallway. The squeak of sneakers and the thump of basketballs faded behind me as the heavy doors swung shut, replaced by the distant buzz of fluorescent lights and the faint tang of industrial cleaner that never quite masked decades of middle-school funk.

I ducked into the girls' bathroom for a moment and checked my reflection in the scratched mirror. I looked every bit the part of someone about to be summoned to the principal's office for reasons only partially my fault. My PE polo was rumpled, my cheeks already warming with irritation. But I couldn't help but grin. My purple hair, pulled back in a practical ponytail, caught the fluorescent light and glinted almost silver at the edges. Dyeing it had been the best decision I'd ever made.

And even better, I was pretty sure Max Harrison hated it. Not that I cared what Dr. Max Smarty-Pants Harrison thought. He'd long ago written me off as unprofessional, but the feeling was mutual.

This was war.

I straightened my shoulders, tossed my ponytail back with a little flick, and headed out.

Jogging down the corridor toward the office, my old sneakers slapped against the polished linoleum with every step. Trophy cases lined the walls, their glass smudged with fingerprints and filled with dusty ribbons and faded team photos of Marchfield legends frozen mid-victory, smiling wide as if they knew their glory days still mattered to someone.

I slowed as I passed the 2008 case, the year I'd been an eighth grader here, and my twenty-first school since starting kindergarten. My face wasn't in any of those photos. I'd arrived in January, mid-season, too new to make any of the teams.

But I remembered Field Day that year. Mrs. Carter—back when she still ran PE—had pulled me aside the week before and asked if I wanted to help set up the obstacle course. It was the first time in twenty-one schools that a teacher had given me a job, a purpose, something that made me feel like I belonged.

Coming back here as a teacher had been strange. The building looked the same but felt different. Or maybe I was different. Either way, I'd made Field Day mine—shaped it into something bigger than just another school event. Because I knew what it was like to be on the outside looking in, and I wanted every kid to have what Mrs. Carter had given me: a day where you belonged, where it didn't matter if you were new or popular or struggling. You showed up, you participated, you were part of something.

Field Day had saved me once. Maybe that's why I fought so hard to save it now.

Inside the office, the air was thick with the faint tang of coffee and the scent of polished wood, mixed with the faint mustiness of old carpet. Phones rang in the background, and the administrative assistants darted back and forth, juggling papers and fielding calls. A lost and found table near the door overflowed with backpacks, lunchboxes, and stray sneakers. A few students shifted nervously in seats along the wall, waiting for the assistant principal or guidance counselor.

Of course, Harrison was already there when I arrived, leaning against the wall like he owned the place. His arms were crossed over his chest, and he wore that composed expression that made me want to wipe it off his face with a dodgeball.

Unlike me, he looked perfectly put-together in a crisp button-up and spotless sneakers. Annoyingly, he had one of those faces that belonged in a catalog. His strong jaw had just enough stubble to look rugged and a dimple on the left side, which made it worse somehow.

"Bennett," he said with a nod. "Any idea what this is about?"

I pasted on my best fake smile. "Probably about spring events. You know, the ones that actually matter to students?"

His expression didn't change. "Field Day does have its place. I'm just here to make sure we're thinking strategically about resource allocation."

The corporate-speak dripped off every word. My back teeth ground together. "Right. Because crunching numbers is so much more important than creating memories."

"Memories don't prepare students for college."

"And test scores don't teach them how to be human beings."

Before I launched into a proper argument, the principal's voice boomed from behind the door. "Emma! Max! In here, please!"

Max gestured toward the office, his expression unreadable. I wanted to shove past him, but that would only prove whatever point he was silently making about me being unprofessional.

Principal Kline sat behind his desk, glasses perched on the tip of his nose, a manila folder open in front of him. The creases around his eyes were deeper than usual, and his shoulders slumped like he'd already been through three battles this morning.

"Sit down," he said, voice sharp enough to make both of us flinch. "And please, stop glaring at each other. I can feel the hostility from here."

I bit back a retort while Max settled into his chair looking completely at ease, irritating me more.

Mr. Kline pinched the bridge of his nose. "I'm going to cut right to it. Budget cuts hit us harder than expected. We only have enough funding for one spring event this year. Either the science fair or field day."

The air left my lungs. This couldn't be happening.

"Principal Kline," Max said, his tone measured, "I understand the difficult position you're in. Perhaps we should look at the data. The science fair has measurable academic outcomes—"

"Are you serious, right now?" I whipped around to stare at him.

He met my gaze without flinching. "I'm being practical. The science fair directly supports our STEM initiatives and college readiness metrics."

"Field Day teaches teamwork, perseverance, and community spirit," I snapped. "Things that matter in real life, not just on some standardized test."

"Both matter," Max said.

I hated that his voice stayed level while mine was rising. "But we have limited resources."

"Enough!" Kline slammed a hand on the desk, making both of us jump. "I am not spending the next two months listening to you two argue."

We fell silent, though I felt the frustration radiating between us.

Kline exhaled, rubbing his forehead. "You're both excellent teachers who care deeply about your programs. So here's what's going to happen: you're going to work together. Combine field day and the science fair. One event. One budget. One team."

There was a beat of silence before Max straightened slightly. "You want us to—"

"Work together," Kline finished flatly. "Collaborate. Compromise. All those things adults are supposed to be able to do."

My jaw tightened. Working with Max Harrison would be a nightmare.

"You will plan one event that honors both traditions," Kline continued. "The budget is three hundred and fifty dollars, and if you can't make it work, I'll give the money to the marching band. Do I make myself clear?"

"Yes, sir," we said in unison, though my voice was considerably tighter than Max's.

Kline leaned back in his chair, looking exhausted. "You'll meet on Monday after school to start planning. Four o'clock. Figure out where to meet." He waved us toward the door. "Now get out of my office before I change my mind and cancel both events."

We left in silence, walking back through the office and into the hallway. For a moment, neither of us spoke.

Then Max cleared his throat. "My classroom. Monday at four. We can use the lab tables to spread out materials."

Of course, he was already taking charge. Setting the meeting on his home turf, so he'd have an advantage, but what could I do after Mr. Kline set the parameters?

"Fine."

He studied me for a moment, and I couldn't quite read his expression. "This doesn't have to be a disaster, Bennett. We both want what's best for the students."

"Do we? Because from where I'm standing, you want what's best for your college-prep metrics. I want what's best for the actual kids."

Annoyance flickered across his face. "That's not fair."

"Isn't it?"

"Look," he said, and I heard the effort it took to keep his voice even, "I know we don't see eye to eye on most things, but we're stuck with each other. We might as well try to make it work."

"Right. I'm sure you have a twelve-point plan for that too."

"As a matter of fact—" He stopped himself, jaw tightening. He took a deep breath before saying, "Never mind. Monday. Four o'clock. Don't be late."

He walked away before I could respond, his footsteps echoing down the empty hallway.

I stood there, fists clenched, trying to breathe through the anger. Field Day was mine. I'd nurtured it, protected it for five years. And now I had to share it with someone who thought community and tradition were just line items on a spreadsheet.

WHEN I PUSHED THROUGH the gym doors, thirty pairs of eyes snapped to me like heat-seeking missiles.

"Well?" Tyler called out, still holding the basketball. "Did you get fired?"

"Are we doing essays?" Brianna asked, horrified.

I forced a smile and blew my whistle. "Not today. But we still need to run those laps. Let's go!"

They groaned but fell in behind me as I jogged around the perimeter of the gym.

Tyler caught up with me after the first lap. "What happened, though?"

I thought about Max's measured tone, his assumption that data mattered more than heart, his complete inability to see what Field Day really meant. The way he'd already started organizing our meeting like he was in charge.

"Let's just say," I said as I quickened my pace, "things are about to get interesting around here."

But I knew the truth: this spring was going to be a nightmare.

And I was going to have to find a way to protect Field Day from the one person who had the power to destroy it.

My new partner.

Chapter 2: Max

THE EIGHTH GRADE SCIENCE lab was my sanctuary. Orderly. Predictable. Every beaker in its place, every solution labeled precisely. I'd stayed late to prep tomorrow's lesson on exothermic reactions, finding comfort in the familiar rhythm of measuring and mixing.

My phone buzzed. A calendar reminder: Planning Meeting with Bennett - 4:00 PM - Your Classroom

I checked my watch. 3:57 PM.

Kline had been terse: First collaborative planning session. Monday after school. Make it work.

I'd spent the weekend building a proposal that would satisfy both programs' needs while staying under budget. A hybrid event: "STEM Field Day." Academic stations where students learn physics through relay races, biology through obstacle courses, chemistry through team challenges. It was both educational and community-focused. Emma would have to see the logic.

I pulled up the twelve-page document on my laptop, complete with budget breakdowns, timeline, and implementation strategy. Maybe I should have sent it to her this morning, but I'd wanted to present it properly, walk her through the reasoning. Show her this would work.

Footsteps echoed in the hallway, and Emma appeared in the doorway, in her PE polo, hair pulled back in that purple ponytail. She had a notebook under one arm and an expression that looked almost... nervous?

"Hey," she said, hovering at the threshold like she wasn't sure she was welcome. "Sorry if I'm late. My seventh graders discovered bouncing basketballs in syncopated rhythm, and it took twenty minutes to restore order."

"You're not late." I gestured to the lab stool across from my desk. "I just got here myself."

She wrinkled her nose a little, her forehead furrowing. “In your own classroom? Where have you been all day?”

“I was ah...” I wracked my brain for an answer. “I was in the restroom.”

Emma slid onto the stool and set her notebook on the desk in front of her. I caught a glimpse of hand-drawn diagrams, and what looked like a field layout with stations marked in different colors.

"Okay, I was thinking," she opened her notebook, "about zones. Keep some traditional Field Day stations, but add science demonstrations. Your students would be able to present to an audience of hundreds."

“Outside? In an uncontrolled environment?”

“Well, we could use tents if you think that would be better. Of course, we’d have to rent them...”

"That won’t be necessary." I turned my laptop, so she was able to see the title page: STEM Field Day: An Integrated Educational Experience. "I mapped out the entire event. Look, here's the budget breakdown, the station rotation schedule, the volunteer assignments—"

Emma's expression shifted. The nervousness vanished, replaced by something harder. "You mapped out the entire event?"

"I wanted to have something concrete to work from. A starting point."

She leaned back, crossing her arms. "It looks like you've made all the decisions."

"There are still decisions to be made."

Emma was quiet for a moment. When she spoke, her voice was careful and level, which he suspected was worse than if she'd just gotten angry. "I was told this was a joint project. That we'd have equal footing."

"You do."

"Then why am I sitting here reading a plan I had no part in making?" She tilted her head slightly. "What exactly did you think I was going to contribute?"

Max didn't have a clean answer for that, which was its own kind of problem.

"We can make changes." He slid the papers across the desk and leaned back, watching the set of her shoulders stiffen. Not good, but not unexpected either. "Look this over, and I'll answer your questions."

She didn't touch the pages. She folded her arms instead, like a line drawn in the sand. "Collaborating means we plan together. Not you planning and then presenting me with a finished product."

My jaw tightened. "I spent my entire weekend on this. I thought having a framework would make the process more efficient."

"Efficient," she said the word like it tasted bad. "Right. Because heaven forbid we waste time on something messy like actual conversation."

"That's not what I meant."

"Then what did you mean?" She pulled the laptop closer, scrolling through my document. Her eyes narrowed as she read. "Station One: Physics of Motion. Station Two: Chemical Reactions. Station Three: Simple Machines." She looked up. "Where is the tug of war? The three-legged race? The sack race?"

"I incorporated the principles behind those activities into educational stations. See, Station Four applies the same concepts of force and teamwork—"

"They're not the same, Max." Her voice rose slightly. "A physics lecture about force and motion isn't the same as competing in tug-of-war with your team."

"It's not a lecture. It's hands-on learning." I kept my voice level and reasonable. "Students build catapults and test them. They create chemical reactions. They problem-solve in teams. It's everything Field Day is, just with actual educational value."

Emma's face flushed. "Actual educational value? You think Field Day has no educational value?"

"I think Field Day teaches kids to run in circles and throw balls. This teaches them skills they can use in college. In careers. In real life."

"Real life?" She stood up abruptly, the stool scraping against the floor. "You mean the real life where teamwork matters? Where perseverance matters? Where knowing how to lose gracefully and win humbly matters? Or do those not count because you can't measure them on a rubric?"

"Of course, those things matter—"

"Then why did you eliminate every single activity that teaches them?" She was pacing now, her notebook forgotten on the desk. "The tug-of-war teaches cooperation and strategy. The three-legged race teaches communication and patience. The sack race teaches problem-solving and resilience because when you fall down, you have to get back up."

"And robotics kits teach engineering. Chemistry sets teach the scientific method. Coding tablets teach computational thinking." I pulled up my budget breakdown. "These are twenty-first century skills, Emma. The things colleges look for. The things employers need."

"Not every kid is going to college!" Her voice cracked with frustration. "Not every kid is going to be an engineer or a scientist! But every kid needs to know how to work with others. How to keep trying when things get hard. How to feel like they belong somewhere."

"And they can learn those things while also learning actual content—"

"Field Day is actual content! Just because you can't put it on a standardized test doesn't make it worthless!" She grabbed the laptop and turned it to face me.

"You want to know what I see when I look at this? I see two-thirds of my students sitting on the sidelines watching the 'smart kids' play with expensive equipment they'll never get to touch. I see the girl who struggles in math crying because she can't figure out the catapult calculations. I see the boy with ADHD getting in trouble because he can't sit still during the fifteen-minute rotation."

"That's not—" I started.

"That's exactly what this is." She scrolled aggressively through my timeline. "Fifteen-minute stations. Thirty robotics kits for three hundred students. Tablets that half the kids won't know how to use and the other half will already be bored by. This isn't Field Day, Max. This is a science fair where you've replaced participation ribbons with participation shame."

Heat crept up my neck. "You're being dramatic."

"I'm being realistic! I work with these kids every day. Some of them need to run and move to think. Others shine when they're not stuck behind a desk. And more wait all year for Field Day because it's the one day they get to be the hero instead of the kid who can't keep up." Her eyes were bright with unshed tears.

“Bennett, come on. You’re taking this way too personally.”

“And what about you? Why spend a weekend planning this? What’s in it for you?”

"If you must know, I'm applying for a $50,000 grant. If the board likes STEM Field Day, they might give me enough money to help underprivileged kids get a step up in science and mathematics."

"Yeah, that makes sense. It's all about the money for you."

"That's not fair—"

"Isn't it?" She closed the laptop with more force than necessary. "You need this event to succeed for your grant. Well, I need Field Day to succeed for my students. The ones you apparently don't think matter because they're not going to be scientists."

"I never said they don't matter—"

"You didn't have to. Your proposal said it for you." She grabbed her notebook. "You eliminated every single thing that makes Field Day special. Every tradition. Every game. Every moment of joy that doesn't come with a learning objective attached. You looked at thirty years of community tradition and decided it wasn't good enough."

"Emma, that's not what I'm saying—" It comes out too fast, too sharp. I'm already bracing for the way she stiffens, even though part of me still hopes I can steer this back before it tips out of control.

"Then what *are* you saying?" She turned to face me fully, anger cracking just enough for the hurt to show. "Because from where I'm standing, you spent an entire weekend proving that you're the smartest. That science is more important than physical education. That test scores matter more than kids."

"Kids matter. But I—" The rest of it jammed in my throat. I have spreadsheets, projections, evidence for every choice I made, but none of it seems right for how she's looking at me. For the first time, I'm not sure being right is the same as being understood.

"You didn't build something that honors Field Day." Her voice dropped, became almost quiet. "You took Field Day and turned it into a science fair with better marketing. And you did it without even talking to me."

A heavy and uncomfortable silence stretched between us.

"I created a framework," I said, trying to keep my voice steady. "A starting point for discussion. We can adjust—"

"Adjust what, Max? You've already allocated the entire budget. Assigned all the volunteers. Created the schedule down to the minute. What exactly is left to adjust?"

"The stations. The activities. We can incorporate the traditional events if you feel strongly—"

"If I feel strongly?" She laughed, but there was no humor in it, and the sound scraped straight down my nerves. "I guess you could say that. I've spent five years building this event into something that serves every single student. And you dismissed all of that because it doesn't fit into your neat little boxes of measurable outcomes."

"That's not what I'm doing—" Even as I said it, I knew how hollow it sounded. I'd been so focused on improving what I could quantify that I hadn't stopped to consider what couldn't be graphed.

"Then what are you doing?" She waited, eyes locked on mine, daring me to give her a real answer. But I couldn't. "That's what I thought."

She headed for the door, then stopped and turned back. Her expression had shifted—no longer sharp, just tired. Resigned. That somehow hurt more.

"You know what the worst part is? You think this—" she gestured at my laptop, "—is an improvement. That turning Field Day into science day is progress. But all you've done is prove that you don't understand kids at all."

The words landed heavier than the anger. I opened my mouth, searching for something that wasn't defensive, something that sounded like understanding. "Emma—"

"I need to go. I need to help my aunt with the flower deliveries." She paused in the doorway, her hand on the frame as if she were steadying herself. "But tomorrow I'm going to the PTA meeting to ask for separate funding. The only way to save Field Day is to do it without you."

The door closed behind her, the click final and quiet.

I sat there staring at my twelve-page proposal, every chart and bullet point suddenly feeling less like a solution even though everything in it made sense. It was logical. Efficient. Educational. The grant committee would love it.

The budget breakdown, the station rotations, the volunteer assignments—every piece fit together perfectly. On paper, at least. That had to count for something. It always had before.

Except they didn't fit Emma. Didn't fit her students or whatever Field Day was supposed to be. And somehow, without my meaning to, I'd managed to break something I hadn't even known was fragile.

Some of what she'd said kept circling back, uncomfortable in its familiarity. I didn't dismiss kids. I didn't think test scores mattered more than people. That wasn't who I was. Was it? Still, the doubt lingered in ways I didn't like, pressing at the edges of thoughts I wasn't ready to examine too closely.

But one thing Emma said *was* right. The PTA. We should both go to the PTA to ask for money. I latched onto the idea like a lifeline. A bit more funding and we wouldn't have to choose. We could have two events, two visions. Science *and* Field Day.

It was a clean, practical, solvable compromise. The kind of solution I understood. Even if a part of me suspected it still wasn't the one she'd wanted.

Chapter 3: Emma

I TEXTED MY TEACHER besties on the way to the PTA meeting—Jen from art, who found the bright side of any situation, and Talia from foreign language, who taught me how to curse in three languages when I needed to vent. The two people who'd kept me sane through five years of public school.

Me: Heading into the lion's den. Wish me luck.

By the time I reached the closed door of the chorus room, where the PTA met every other Tuesday night, I had a string of replies.

Jen: You've got this. Remember, you're fighting for something that matters.

Talia: If the PTA says no, we riot. I'll bring the pitchforks.

Jen: Talia, no.

Talia: Talia YES. But seriously, Em... you've got this. Field Day is magic. They'll see it.

I smiled despite my nerves, tucking my phone into my pocket.

After yesterday's disaster of a planning meeting with Max where he presented a proposal that eliminated everything that made Field Day special, I realized I had no choice. If I wanted to save Field Day, I needed funding that didn't depend on him or his grant application.

The PTA had a discretionary fund. Maybe they could allot a hundred dollars to keep Field Day running.

I smoothed down my Marchfield PE polo, took a breath, and pushed open the door.

The chorus room smelled faintly of coffee, old carpet, and stress. A long table claimed the front of the room, where ten parents perched with Styrofoam cups and curious expressions. Mrs. Blakely, the PTA president, gave me an encouraging nod.

I moved to the empty podium in front of the group, set down my cue cards, and gave everyone a big smile.

"Thank you for letting me speak tonight," I began, summoning confidence into my voice. "I wanted to share with you what Field Day means to our community—"

"Oh, I helped with the sack races last year!" Mr. Plainer interrupted, raising his hand. His daughter, Chloe, was in my morning class.

"And I brought three dozen cupcakes," Ms. Chainey chimed in. Her three sons played on the soccer team.

Mrs. Blakely added, with a laugh, "I was on juice box duty. I still have grass stains on my capris."

Warmth spread through my chest as laughter bubbled around the table. These parents remembered. They'd been there.

"Yes, you're all amazing volunteers," I said, letting genuine gratitude show in my voice. "Field Day is the one day every year the whole community shows up for the kids. Grandparents cheer from the bleachers. Neighbors come to watch. The fire department brings their truck. Former students come back to help."

I thought of Mrs. Carter, who'd passed the torch to me five years ago with tears in her eyes. "And it's not about who wins the relay," I continued. "It's about tradition and connection. The kind that makes kids feel like school is more than homework and test scores."

Several heads nodded. Mrs. Thompson's expression had softened, and even Mr. Patel was leaning forward.

"Unfortunately, because of budget cuts, there's a proposal to change Field Day into something else entirely," I said. "To turn it into a STEM exposition where kids rotate through science stations instead of participating in the activities our community loves. I understand the educational value, but—"

The door swung open.

Dr. Max Harrison strode in, juggling a laptop bag, a stack of presentation folders, and a tablet. He wore pressed slacks and a buttoned-down shirt that looked slightly rumpled but only gave him more of a professorial look. A pen fell from his stack and clattered to the floor.

"Sorry I'm late," he said, a little out of breath.

My stomach dropped. Of course, he was here. Of course.

"Dr. Harrison." My voice came out icier than I intended. "I didn't realize you were presenting."

He had the grace to look uncomfortable. "When I emailed Mrs. Blakely earlier, she invited me to share the STEM proposal. She thought the PTA should hear both perspectives."

"Both perspectives," I repeated. "You mean how you want to eliminate Field Day?"

Several parents exchanged glances. Greg Thompson leaned toward his wife and whispered something that made her hide a smile behind her coffee cup.

Mrs. Blakely cleared her throat. "Perhaps we should let Dr. Harrison present his, and then we can discuss both options?"

I stepped aside, gesturing to the podium with exaggerated politeness. "Please. Go ahead."

Max set his materials on the table with his usual precision, adjusting each folder until they were perfectly aligned. Then he began distributing glossy papers to each parent. Full-color charts showed student achievement data, testimonials from former students, and photos from last year's science fair.

I wished I had a grande mocha latte just so I could spill it all over his precious handouts.

"Thank you for allowing me to present," Max began, his voice steady and confident. "The STEM exposition I'm proposing would transform our end-of-year event into a meaningful learning experience. Students would rotate through six stations covering physics, chemistry, coding, and engineering. We'd have quantifiable learning outcomes and measurable skill development."

"As opposed to Field Day," I couldn't help interjecting, "which only teaches meaningless things like teamwork, perseverance, and community."

Max's jaw tightened. "I didn't say Field Day was meaningless—"

"You eliminated every single traditional event from your proposal and replaced them with robotics kits and coding tablets that will break easily."

"These activities provide actual educational value—"

"Field Day provides value!" My voice rose. "Just because you can't measure it on a spreadsheet doesn't mean it doesn't matter!"

Mrs. Chainey raised her hand tentatively. "I'm sorry, but... aren't you two supposed to be working together on this?"

Max and I both stopped. We looked at her. Then at each other. Heat rose up my neck to my face.

"We were assigned to collaborate, yes," Max said stiffly.

"But that implies mutual respect," I shot back. "Not steamrolling over five years of tradition with robotics kits."

"I'm not steamrolling—I'm proposing an alternative that has actual academic merit—"

Heat crawled up my neck before I even realized I'd stepped closer. *Merit.* The word rang like an insult. Five years of scavenged equipment and midnight planning dismissed with a single polished syllable.

"Alternative?" I cut in, my voice sharper than I meant it to be. "You mean a replacement.

"There it is again! That condescending tone suggesting that running around and having fun is somehow less valuable than sitting at a station with a tablet—"

"Students need STEM skills to compete in the modern workforce—"

"Students need to know how to be human beings first!"

"Okay!" Mrs. Blakely's voice cut through our argument. "Why don't we... take a moment. Dr. Harrison, perhaps you would finish your presentation?"

Max's expression was controlled but frustration simmered underneath. He pulled up something on his tablet. "The STEM exposition would require approximately five hundred dollars in materials. Robotics kits, chemistry sets, tablets for coding instruction—"

"The budget was set at three hundred and fifty dollars, and you are already over budget? Field Day only needs two hundred dollars," I interjected. "For an event you and your children already love."

"An event that teaches children to run in a straight line—"

"An event that teaches children they don't have to be perfect at everything to have value!"

From the back row, Greg Thompson leaned toward his wife again. "This is better than cable."

Carla was openly grinning now. "Should we get popcorn?"

Mrs. Blakely looked between us, trying not to laugh. "I can see you both feel very passionately about your respective programs."

"Field Day isn't just my program," I said, forcing my voice to stay level. "It belongs to this entire community. Every parent in this room has participated. Your children love it. Why would we throw that away for—" I gestured at Max's glossy handouts, "—for fifteen-minute rotations with expensive equipment most kids won't even get to touch?"

"Because education should be about growth, not nostalgia," Max said. His voice was quieter now, but there was an edge to it. "Field Day might make people feel good, but feelings don't prepare students for college. For careers. For futures that require actual skills."

Something in his tone made me pause. This wasn't just about the grant or the program. This was personal for him somehow.

But I was too angry to dig into that right now.

"You know what?" I said, turning back to the PTA. "I'm not asking you to choose between programs anymore. I'm asking you to save Field Day. Period. Dr. Harrison can apply for his grant and run his STEM exposition if he wants, but Field Day has been part of this school for thirty years, and it deserves to continue."

Max's expression darkened. "So much for collaboration."

"You killed collaboration when you presented a proposal that eliminated everything I care about!"

"I was trying to create something better—"

"You were trying to replace something you don't understand or value!"

Mrs. Blakely stood up. "All right. I think we've heard enough from both of you." She didn't sound angry, more amused or slightly exasperated, like she was dealing with two squabbling children. "The PTA will discuss both proposals and let you know our decision."

"When?" I asked.

"Shortly. If you could both wait outside for a few minutes?"

Max and I filed out into the hallway, maintaining a careful distance from each other. The door closed behind us, but the sound of muffled discussion filtered through.

We stood in tense silence. I leaned against the wall, arms crossed. Max paced, checking his phone, adjusting his laptop bag—doing anything to avoid looking at me.

"That was—" he started after a minute.

"A disaster," I finished. "Complete disaster."

"I was going to say *unproductive*."

"That too."

My pulse thudded loud in my ears, but the heat ebbed, leaving that awful hollow aftermath. The words I'd thrown at him replayed themselves, jagged and messy. Too sharp. I'd wanted to defend what I built—who I was—but somewhere in the middle of it I'd lost my grip.

Max stopped pacing. "For the record, I didn't come here to sabotage you. I came here to present a viable alternative."

"An alternative that eliminates my program. How is that not sabotage?"

Even as I said it, the fight in my voice lessened. Doubt crept in where certainty had been, quiet and unwelcome.

"I believe—" He stopped himself, jaw tight. "Never mind."

Regret landed heavy in my stomach. What happened to me? I wasn't this person. I was sunshine. I was vibes. Calm, patient, emotionally hydrated. When did I become the kind of woman who snarled like an unhinged raccoon? How did this man unlock that personality in me over and over?

"No, what? You genuinely believe what?"

He looked at me, and something flickered in his expression. "That students deserve better than nostalgia. They deserve programs that prepare them for their futures."

"And you think Field Day doesn't do that."

"Field Day makes students feel good about themselves without challenging them to grow."

The words hit harder than I expected. "You really believe that?"

"I do."

Before I responded, the chorus room door opened. Mrs. Blakely stepped out, looking apologetic. "Would you both come back inside?"

We followed her back inside. The parents studied us with expressions ranging from sympathetic to entertained.

Mrs. Blakely folded her hands on the table. "First, I want to thank you both for your passionate presentations. It's clear you both care deeply about your students."

A small flutter of hope trembled inside me.

"However," she continued, "I'm afraid the PTA has already allocated all of our discretionary funds for this year."

My heart sank. "All of it?"

"We purchased gold-colored pencils for the honor roll students," she said with an apologetic grimace. "The superintendent requested it. Apparently, it's part of a district-wide recognition initiative."

I blinked. "Gold-colored pencils."

"Four hundred dollars' worth," Mrs. Blakely confirmed. "They arrive next week."

Next to me, Max had gone very still. "You spent four hundred dollars on pencils."

"Gold ones," Mr. Patel added helpfully.

"We're very sorry," Mrs. Blakely said. "We wish we could help. Both programs sound wonderful—well, when you're not arguing about them. But there's simply no money left in the budget."

“But why did you let us come to present?” Max asked, running a hand through his hair and mussing it.

Mrs. Blakely sighed. “Because budgets change, grant money falls through, and sometimes we don’t know where we stand until the very last meeting. We wanted to be informed before making anything official. It wouldn’t have been fair to shut either of you down without hearing what you’ve built.”

The meeting adjourned shortly after, parents filing out with sympathetic looks and whispered conversations. I caught fragments as they passed:

"Shame we can't help—"

"Those pencils were such a waste—"

"Maybe they'll figure out how to work together after all—"

"Or kill each other. Could go either way."

I stood there, bag in hand, feeling numb. No money. No funding. Nothing.

Max was already packing up his materials, his movements sharp and controlled.

"So that's it," I said. "No help from the PTA."

"Looks that way." He didn't look at me.

"What are we supposed to do now?"

He met my eyes, and his expression was carefully blank. "I don't know, Bennett. Run your Field Day on whatever budget you can scrape together. I'll figure something else out."

"I don't believe you."

"Believe it or not." He closed his laptop with more force than necessary. "You made it pretty clear tonight where you stand."

"Because you made it clear yesterday when you gutted my entire program!" My voice echoed in the empty chorus room. Losing my temper again was pointless.

Suddenly, a noise shattered the silence—a grotesque mashup of a humming engine, a frog's croak, and a cat's scream. My ears protested. Max froze mid-step.

"YEEEEEEOOOOWWWWW—"

We both froze as the low sound grew louder, wobbling and twisting in a way that made my teeth ache.

The door burst open and Henry Larkins, the chorus teacher, entered—his Mongolian throat chant ending in a high, startled squeak the moment he saw us. He was all angles and lanky limbs, towering in an almost unsteady way, with a long, narrow face and sharp, darting eyes that bounced between Max and me.

"Oh! Oh my! I didn't realize anyone was in here!"

I pressed my palms to my cheeks, trying to cool them. "Hi, Henry," I said, my voice breathless, "We were just leaving."

"I'll step outside for a minute while you finish up," Henry said, disappearing out the door—and the wobbly, off-key note began again, rattling my ears and making me flinch.

Max and I stood there, eyes locking for a long awkward beat. His expression was half-apologetic, half-exasperated.

"Guess we... tried our best," he muttered.

"Tried our best?" Was he seriously acting like our efforts were somehow on the same level? Like five years of planning and implementing successful field days could be compared to his shiny little robotics kits?

I wanted to scream, to argue, to make him understand everything I'd built, but the words stuck in my throat, tangled with exhaustion and disbelief. Not tonight. It wasn't worth it.

So, I pressed my lips together, stiffened my shoulders, and left with my head held high. The hallway swallowed me, Henry's chant echoing faintly behind me.

I tried to convince myself that I hadn't lost. Survival meant knowing when to escape before I lost my sanity. And honestly... who had the energy to fight a broke PTA, a cheerful chaos-chorus teacher, and Max all at once? Not me. Not today.

It wasn't defeat. It was a tactical retreat. Strategic withdrawal. Or if I was being honest with myself, it was a full-blown, socially awkward, dramatic exit worthy of a viral GIF.

Somewhere deep down, though, I knew I'd be back. Because I always came back. And next time? Maybe I'd have a better plan... or at least earplugs.

Chapter 4: Max

THE DAY AFTER THE PTA disaster, I stayed late, ostensibly to grade some student work, but mostly I'd been staring at my laptop screen where my STEM exposition proposal mocked me with its perfect formatting and complete irrelevance.

Twelve pages. Color-coded budget spreadsheets. Station rotation schedules down to the minute.

All of it was useless.

I closed the laptop harder than necessary and scrubbed my hands over my face. The fluorescent lights buzzed overhead, and somewhere down the hall a locker slammed. Normal sounds. A normal Tuesday afternoon.

Except nothing felt normal anymore.

I kept replaying the PTA meeting. Mrs. Blakely's apologetic face. The parents' sympathetic looks.

But mostly I kept seeing Emma.

The way her purple ponytail had caught the light when she'd turned to argue with me. How her cheeks had flushed when she talked about Field Day belonging to the community. That crack in her voice when she'd said "You don't get it, do you?"

I didn't, but I was starting to realize that was the problem.

My chest tightened, anxiety swirling in my gut.

Of course, I was nervous about the grant. Without a science-based event to showcase, there was no chance of winning the $50,000. The butterflies inside me had nothing to do with the way Emma's whole face changed when she was passionate about something. Or how she'd looked at me like I was a problem she couldn't solve.

Grabbing my pen, I forced myself to focus. There had to be a solution. Some way to appease Emma and the grant review board. I just had to organize my thoughts and create a framework—

"Hey, man. Working late again?" Eli leaned against the doorway, his forehead furrowed and eyes narrowed on me.

Dante was right behind him with an identical expression of concern.

"What's wrong?"

Dante sauntered in, his gaze sweeping over the papers on my desk. "Why do they have two scores on them?"

I looked down. He was right. "I was just—"

"Re-grading papers," Eli shook his head, walking forward and setting a few cans of soda on the lab table. "This is an intervention."

"What?" I spluttered. "Why?"

"You look like you haven't slept in days." Dante passed me a soda. "You are wearing two different shoes today."

"I am not," I blustered before looking down at the one black and one navy shoe. "Well, damn. That's why my back hurts."

I accepted the can and flicked it open. "Fine. Intervene."

Eli settled onto a lab stool and spun it once with his foot. It squeaked in protest. "So. The PTA meeting."

"Was a disaster," I said.

"Scale of one to ten?" Dante asked as he dragged another stool closer.

"Eleven. Possibly twelve." I took a long pull from my soda. It tasted citrusy and suited my mood. "We argued in front of the parents. There's no money anyway. And Emma walked out."

Eli winced. "Oof. Walked out walked out?"

"Door slam. Dramatic exit. Very effective."

Dante nodded. "Okay. So what now?"

"I don't know." The words came out quieter than I liked, which annoyed me. I stared at the table instead, at a coffee ring shaped like a doomed planet. "My grant application is due in four weeks."

Dante's eyebrows jumped. He glanced at Eli, and they did that silent guy thing where a full conversation happened without sound.

"What happened when you showed Emma your plan?" Dante asked.

"She hated it." I rubbed my face and let my hands drop. "Which was ironic, because I thought she'd be relieved."

"For what?" Eli asked, grinning.

"Because I did the hard part for her."

The second it left my mouth, I knew I'd stepped on a landmine.

Dante tilted his head. "You're saying Emma—Emma *Bennett*—doesn't work hard?"

"No. No." I straightened. "She's smart. She's capable." Annoyingly so.

"And pretty," Nolan added without looking up from his phone.

I closed my eyes. Of course she was.

"I wanted to—" I stopped. The end of that sentence sounded like it came with handcuffs.

"Control everything?" Eli supplied.

"No." I shrugged, though my shoulders were basically welded to my ears. "I need it to work. If we can't have a traditional science fair, then the STEM exposition has to work."

Dante leaned back. "So you worked around her instead of with her."

"No," I said, setting my soda down a little too hard. "I built a proposal that combined both programs—"

"Without her," Eli said. "That's not teamwork. That's you playing SimCity with real people."

I hated that he was right. "It was efficient. This grant is fifty thousand dollars. That's real money for kids who need it. Kids like me." I swallowed hard. I had to make this work.

"So you eliminated variables," Eli said. "Including Emma."

Silence settled in, thick and uncomfortable. I searched for an argument and came up empty.

"She cares as much as you do," Dante said. "Just in a different direction. Field Day isn't nostalgia for her. It's personal."

I thought of Emma's face when she talked about Mrs. Carter. About being the fat kid. About finally belonging.

My chest tightened, which I didn't appreciate.

"Max," Eli said, quieter now, "you can't spreadsheet your way into trust."

I scowled. "People are unreliable. And occasionally terrible. Trusting them is how things fall apart."

Dante grinned. "Buddy, you trust us."

"That's different."

"How?"

I opened my mouth, then closed it.

"Look," Dante said, standing. "You're one of the smartest guys I know. So figure it out. Maybe start with an apology. Preferably one that doesn't include a PowerPoint."

Of course that was their advice. Apologize. As if I hadn't spent my entire adult life optimizing situations specifically to avoid that outcome.

Eli nodded. "And maybe don't call her a variable."

"...I didn't say that out loud." I crossed my arms, defensive. In my head though...

They both stared at me.

I hated that they were right. I hated that I'd reduced Emma to a problem to solve instead of a person to work with. It was easier that way. Variables didn't get hurt. Variables didn't walk out of rooms looking disappointed.

The silence stretched. It pressed against my ribs, waiting.

Before they nagged at me further, a sound echoed from the hallway.

Someone was crying.

We all froze.

"Is that—" Eli started.

The three of us stepped into the hallway to find Lynda Peterson, the school librarian, leaning against the wall near the library entrance down the hall. Her phone was pressed to her ear, tears streaming down her face.

"Yes, I understand," she was saying, her voice shaking. "I'll get the first flight out. Tonight, if possible. Just—just tell him I'm coming."

She ended the call and pressed her palm to her forehead, visibly trying to compose herself.

"Lynda?" I approached carefully. "Is everything all right?"

She jumped, startled to find us there. "Oh. Max. I—" Her voice cracked. "My father had a heart attack. He's in the hospital in Florida. I need to leave immediately."

"I'm sorry," Eli said. "Is there anything we can do?"

"I don't even know." She wiped at her tears with shaking hands. "I need to pack, get to the airport, call Principal Kline—" She stopped suddenly, her eyes widening. "Oh God. Darcy."

"My parrot." Fresh tears welled in her eyes. "He's in the library, and I can't take him with me. My father's in the ICU, I don't know how long I'll be gone—" She was spiraling, words tumbling over each other. "Mrs. Kline is allergic to birds, Coach Reeves has three cats, the custodians hate him, but I can't leave him—"

"We'll figure it out," I heard myself say. "Don't worry about the parrot right now. Focus on your father."

She looked at me with desperate gratitude. “He can’t be left alone for long because he gets sad. I can’t afford to hire a live-in sitter for him.”

"Understood. The three of us will figure it out."

"Thank you." She grabbed my hand, squeezing it. "Thank you so much. He's—he's very dear to me. His name is Darcy. After Mr. Darcy, you know, from *Pride and Prejudice*."

I had no idea who that was, but I nodded. "Darcy. Got it."

"I need to go. His supplies are in the library. I need to—" She was already hurrying down the hall, still crying, fumbling with her phone to call someone else.

We stood there for a moment in the empty hallway.

Then Dante and Eli both turned to look at me.

"No," I said. "Absolutely not."

"You volunteered," Eli pointed out.

"I volunteered all three of us to make sure he was taken care of. Not to personally take care of him."

"Max." Dante's grin was insufferable. "You're the science guy. You love animals."

"I love studying animals. From a distance. In controlled environments. Not in my classroom with students who will teach it to swear."

"It's temporary," Eli said. "How hard can a bird be?"

"Birds are basically dinosaurs. Did you know that? Literal descendants of velociraptors."

"All the more reason for you to take him." Dante was already walking toward the library. "Come on. Let's go get Darcy."

I wanted to argue. To point out all the logical reasons why this was a terrible idea. But Mrs. Peterson's tear-streaked face kept flashing in my mind, and I couldn't let her parrot end up neglected, or worse.

The library was dim, most of the lights off for the evening. But from the back corner, near Mrs. Peterson's desk, came a voice.

"HELLO! HELLO GORGEOUS!"

We rounded the bookshelf to find a large cage sitting on a rolling cart. Inside was a magnificent scarlet macaw, all brilliant red and blue feathers, with a knowing gleam in his round black eyes.

"Holy crap," Dante breathed. "That's not a parrot. That's a small dragon."

Darcy tilted his head, studying us. Then, in a perfect imitation of Mrs. Peterson's voice: "SHH! THIS IS THE LIBRARY."

"Oh man." Dante was outright grinning now. "Max, you're doomed."

Despite everything, I felt my lips twitch.

I approached the cage slowly. Darcy watched me with suspicion. "Hey there, Darcy."

"DARCY!" the parrot announced. "DARCY IS GORGEOUS!"

"Modest too," Eli observed.

I spotted a notebook on Mrs. Peterson's desk, titled "Darcy Care Instructions." Inside were three pages, single spaced, with subsections.

"He eats fresh fruits and vegetables, special pellets, and the occasional nut," I read aloud. "Requires at least four hours of out-of-cage time daily. Highly social and bonds with people. May become depressed or aggressive if left alone or neglected. Vocabulary of approximately eighty words, still learning new ones."

"Eighty words?" Dante leaned toward the cage. "What else can you say, buddy?"

"DAMN IT!" Darcy squawked cheerfully. "DAMN IT, DARCY!"

We all burst out laughing.

"Mrs. Peterson definitely didn't teach him that," Eli managed.

I kept reading. "Dislikes loud noises, sudden movements, and ceiling fans. Loves music and cartoons. Will throw food if displeased."

"So he's a feathered eighth grader," Dante said.

"I'M PRETTY!" Darcy announced.

"He's not wrong," Eli admitted.

I sighed and started looking for the cage supplies. Mrs. Peterson had everything neatly organized—food containers, spare perches, toys, cleaning supplies. A smaller travel cage sat folded against the wall.

"Help me move this stuff to my classroom," I said. "If I'm doing this, I'm doing it properly."

"There's the Max we know and love," Dante said. "Can't take a parrot without systematically organizing the parrot acquisition."

"Mock me all you want. This bird is terrifying."

"TERRIFYING!" Darcy shrieked.

It took us twenty minutes to move everything to my classroom. Darcy provided running commentary the entire time, alternating between "CAREFUL!" and "DAMN IT!" with occasional declarations of his own bravado.

By the time we had the large cage set up by my desk in the classroom—away from the windows, as per the instructions, I was starting to regret every life choice that had led to this moment.

Dante collapsed into a chair. "You know what's funny?"

"Nothing about this situation?"

"You can't control a parrot." He grinned. "Maybe that's what you need right now."

I looked at Darcy, who was busily rearranging his perches with his beak and making grumbling sounds that definitely sounded judgmental.

"First step: admit you have a problem," Eli added. "Second step: get a parrot. You're halfway there."

"I hate you both."

"HATE YOU!" Darcy contributed. "HATE YOU!"

Despite everything, laughter bubbled up in my chest. "This is insane," I said.

"Yep." Dante stood and clapped me on the shoulder. "But hey, at least you won't be lonely while you figure out how to fix things with Emma."

I stiffened. "It never rains, but it pours."

They both stared at me.

"What?" I demanded.

"Man," Eli said. "You don't see it, do you?"

"See what?"

Dante shook his head. "Never mind. You'll figure it out eventually."

"Figure out what?"

But they were already heading for the door, still grinning like they knew something I didn't.

"Good luck with Darcy!" Eli called. "And Max? Maybe text Emma? Apologize for being a steamroller. See what happens."

"I wasn't—"

The door closed behind them.

I stood alone in my classroom, surrounded by the wreckage of my perfect plans and one scarlet macaw named after a literary character I'd never read.

Darcy tilted his head. "PRETTY BIRD?"

"Yeah," I muttered. "You're a pretty bird."

I pulled out my phone, scrolling through my contacts and stared at Emma's name. My thumb hovered over the message button.

What would I even say? Sorry I tried to bulldoze your program? Sorry I don't know how to work with people? Sorry I kept thinking about the way your eyes lit up when you talked about the kids?

Where had that come from? That wasn't relevant. That wasn't helpful. That was my brain reaching for distractions when things got uncomfortable.

Emma and I were professional colleagues. That's all.

I lowered the phone.

The tightness in my chest clenched harder. If I messaged her now just to feel better, that would be selfish. I didn't deserve relief. She deserved respect.

"Damn it," I muttered.

"DAMN IT!" Darcy echoed, thrilled.

I picked up my phone again and typed, then deleted, then typed again. This time I forced myself to stop rewriting it into something clever or defensive. No explanations. No justifications. No attempt to manage the outcome.

Just the truth.

ME: I'm sorry for how I handled the PTA meeting.

I hit send before I could talk myself out of it.

Delivered. Read.

Nothing.

I set the phone down and turned back to my laptop, the apology sitting there between us, unanswered, but at least honest.

Behind me, Darcy whistled something that sounded vaguely like Mozart. I hadn't realized how tense I was until my shoulders loosened.

Then he stopped.

"PRETTY EMMA."

I turned slowly. "No."

"PRETTY EMMA!"

"You're a menace."

"DARCY IS GORGEOUS!"

I covered my face, laughing despite myself.

My phone buzzed.

Emma: Fine. Tomorrow after school. I'm picking the location.

Not friendly. Not forgiving. But not a no.

"Deal," I typed.

"PRETTY EMMA!" Darcy announced.

"Stop," I said, still smiling.

Tomorrow, I'd listen instead of solve. I'd work with someone instead of around them.

I picked up Darcy's travel case and a box of supplies. He stared back, smug.

"Don't get used to this," I told him.

"DAMN IT," Darcy said.

Yeah. That was about right.

Chapter 5: Emma

MY APARTMENT ABOVE Share Your Buds always smelled like freesia. Stella claimed it drifted up from the shop below, and maybe it did, but the scent felt older, like it had followed me through years of borrowed rooms and half-packed boxes.

Sure, the walk-up was cramped and the stairs creaked like they were personally offended by anyone over a hundred pounds, but it was mine. Well, technically Stella's. She owned the building and rented the place to me at what she called the family rate, said with a casual shrug that dared me to argue. On a teacher's salary, it was the only way I could afford to live alone. It wasn't the first time she'd made sure I landed on my feet.

I dropped my keys into the little basket by the door, a habit I'd picked up years ago, and kicked off my shoes. The main room served as living room, dining room, and kitchen all in one. Exposed brick on one wall—original to the building and probably the only thing holding the place up—was covered in framed pictures of the people and places I loved. Stella showed up in more than a few of them, always smiling like she was keeping a quiet promise. The couch was a thrift-store find she'd helped me reupholster one long weekend, teaching me patience in the same steady way she always had. Mismatched throw pillows I'd collected over the years were piled at both ends, none of them matching, all of them familiar.

A bay window overlooked Main Street, letting in golden late-afternoon light. My reading nook was tucked into the alcove with an oversized chair, a floor lamp, and a stack of books that never seemed to grow smaller. Plants crowded every available surface, all gifts from Stella, because she believed greenery fixed more things than people gave it credit for.

The buzzer rang.

"Hello?" I called into the ancient intercom system that was more crackle than communication.

"It's us!" Jen's voice came through, barely audible over static. "We have pizza!"

"And chocolate cake!" Talia added.

I buzzed them in and opened the door, listening to the familiar symphony of complaints as they climbed the stairs.

"Why... do you... live... so high up?" Jen panted, appearing in the doorway with two pizza boxes stacked precariously in her arms. Her curly hair was staging a full escape from its bun, and her paint-splattered overalls said she'd come straight from school.

"For the glutes," I said, taking the boxes. "Free workout. Builds character."

"I hate character," Jen wheezed, staggering inside like she'd survived a natural disaster.

Talia followed, unbothered by the climb, holding a bakery box overhead like a prize. "Chocolate cake from Pat's. The good stuff. Because crises deserve premium carbs."

"Who said I was having a crisis?" I asked.

"You texted 'Can you come over? I need pizza and distraction,'" Talia said, setting the cake down and crossing her arms. She was small, sharp, and terrifyingly observant. "That's not a request. That's a flare gun."

"Could've been a bad day."

"Emma," Jen said, rummaging through my cabinets. "We've known you for two years. You don't spiral over bad days. This is about Dr. Tall, Dark, and Spreadsheets."

"Who?" I frowned. "Max?"

Talia's eyes lit up. "Ohhh. First name usage. That's new."

"It's literally his name."

"You've called him many things," Talia said, counting on her fingers. "Dr. Smarty Pants. The Spreadsheet Menace. Control Freak with a PhD[1]. Several creative curse words. Never Max."

Heat crept up my neck. "Can we please just eat pizza?"

"After you tell us everything," Jen said, flopping onto the couch with two slices already stacked on her plate. "Start with the PTA meeting. We want tone, volume, and whether anyone cried!"

---

1. http://phd.fr

I grabbed a slice and collapsed into the armchair, curling my feet beneath me. "It was a disaster. A full-scale, train-off-the-tracks disaster."

Talia nodded, satisfied. "Excellent. Continue."

I took a bite, letting the cheese and grease comfort me for a moment before saying, "It seemed like a good plan, but then Max interrupted and presented his STEM day proposal. And we argued. In front of the entire PTA. Like children."

"What kind of arguing?" Jen asked.

"The kind where I interrupted his presentation, wagged my finger like an unhinged heckler, and raised my voice to a level normally reserved for rowdy classes." I set my pizza down, suddenly not hungry.

"His plan is ridiculous. So many holes you could sail a battleship through them, and it kills the Field Day vibe."

"Okay, but—" Talia held up a hand. "Devil's advocate for a second. Is his plan that bad? Like... maybe the science stuff could be fun?"

I shot her a look sharp enough to cut cheese.

"I'm just saying! I don't know anything about PE. Maybe there's middle ground?"

"There's no middle ground when someone tells the entire PTA your program is pointless," I said, sharper than I meant. "He declared Field Day scientifically worthless."

Jen winced. "He said that?"

"Not verbatim, but yes. That was the vibe." I grabbed my pizza and took a pointed bite. "And the worst part? I tried to collaborate. I brought ideas, compromises, solutions. But he had already written a twelve-page proposal without so much as a 'hey, can we talk?'"

"Twelve pages?" Talia's eyebrows shot up. "For a school Field Day?"

"With color-coded budget spreadsheets, a minute-by-minute timeline, and volunteer assignments," I confirmed. "He'd planned everything before the meeting even started."

"Control freak," Jen muttered.

"Massive control freak," I agreed, slumping back. "And now I have no idea how to fix this without... murder."

"You could kiss him," Talia suggested, reaching for another slice.

I choked on pizza. "What?"

"Oh, come on," she said, grinning. "He's Marchfield's own McDreamy."

"He's got that crooked grin of his and that whisper of stubble you love."

"I love it on Ryan Reynolds! Not on Dr. Max Harrison, science prude and irritant."

"Come on, you have to admit, he's your type."

My friends smirked at each other.

"Em." Talia leaned forward. "Healthy professional rivalry does not include texting us at eleven PM about how his stupid dimple shows up when he's being condescending."

Jen sighed. "Or complaining that someone so annoying has forearms that are... criminally nice."

I froze. "I have never—"

Jen pulled out her phone and grinned. "April fourteenth. You texted: 'Why does the universe give good forearms to terrible people? It's not fair.' Want me to read more?"

"I wasn't even talking about him!"

"Are you sure? 'Cause I remember you saying something else..."

"Jen, I swear—"

"— about his stupidly nice eyes for someone with such terrible opinions."

I grabbed a throw pillow and hugged it like armor. "Okay! He's cute. Annoying people can be objectively attractive. It's not a crime."

"It's not a crime," Talia said, leaning back in the armchair, arms crossed, one eyebrow raised. "But it *is* interesting. Especially since you're so defensive about it."

"I'm not defensive!" I snapped.

They both stared at me, unblinking.

I deflated. "Fine. Maybe I'm a little attracted to him. Physically. In a purely aesthetic way that has nothing to do with my feelings about him as a person or a colleague."

"Uh-huh," Jen said, tilting her head. "And how do you feel about him as a person?"

I chewed the inside of my cheek. "He's infuriating."

"And?"

"Condescending."

"And?"

"He thinks data is more important than people."

"But?" Talia prompted, leaning forward like she was digging for treasure.

I picked at a loose thread on the pillow. "But... he cares. About the grant and the students it would help. When he talks about building programs for kids who need them, he means it. It's not about credentials or his resume. It's personal."

"Did he say why?" Jen asked, tilting her head in curiosity.

"No. But the way he said it..." I trailed off, remembering Max's expression in that first meeting with Principal Kline. The flash of something raw before he locked it down. "I think maybe he was one of those kids. The ones who needed someone to show them a way out."

We ate in silence for a moment. The apartment was filled with the soft scrape of forks, distant traffic from Main Street, and the quiet hum of evening life.

"So... what are you going to do?" Jen asked, breaking the quiet.

I shrugged, staring at the pizza box like it held all the answers. "I don't know. Keep fighting for Field Day. Try to make this collaboration work somehow. Fail spectacularly." I gave a weak smile. "The usual."

My phone buzzed on the coffee table. All three of us looked at it.

"If that's him—" Talia started.

"It's not him. Why would it be him?" I said, though my stomach flipped as I reached for the phone.

I picked it up. The contact at the top of my list: Dr. Doom.

I froze. Perfect. That's exactly how I labeled him in my contacts. Immature of me? Maybe.

The message preview appeared:

Dr. Doom: I'm sorry for how I handled the PTA meeting.

I blinked. My thumb hovered over the screen. My chest tightened. That word 'sorry' was... sincere. And yet, I still wanted to scream at him, lecture him, maybe hug him. I had no idea which impulse I was supposed to follow.

"It's him, isn't it?" Jen was practically vibrating with curiosity. "What did he say?"

"He apologized." I read the message again to make sure I hadn't hallucinated it. "He actually apologized."

"What are you going to say?" Talia asked.

"I don't know." My thumb hovered over the keyboard. Part of me wanted to ignore it. To let him stew. To make him feel a fraction of the frustration and hurt I'd been feeling.

But the part of me that remembered the raw look in his eyes when he'd talked about the grant, and I wanted to give him a chance.

"Say yes," Jen said.

"To what? He just apologized. He didn't ask—"

"He will. And when he does, say yes."

"Why?"

"Because you can't work together if you're not talking," Jen said reasonably. "And because you want to."

My phone buzzed again.

DR. DOOM: Can we try again?

"I don't—"

"Emma." Talia's voice was gentle now. "You care about Field Day. He cares about his grant. You're both fighting for students. Maybe if you talked to each other—like people, not opponents—you might find some actual middle ground."

I looked at the message again and responded before analyzing it to death

ME: Fine. Tomorrow after school. But I'm picking the location this time.

I hit send before I could overthink it.

Three dots appeared immediately. Then:

Dr. Doom: Deal. Where?

I was going to have to change his name on my phone...

Me: I'll let you know.

Because if we were going to do this, and try to work together, it needed to be on neutral ground.

"What did you say?" Jen asked.

"We'll talk tomorrow. I'm picking the place."

I'd barely finished speaking when the apartment door flew open.

Aunt Stella stood in the doorway, holding a massive arrangement of white roses and purple irises. But it was her knowing grin that made my stomach drop.

"Sweetheart!" She swept in like she owned the place—which, technically, she did. "I heard voices and thought I'd bring up this arrangement. Mary Ellen ordered it for an engagement party this weekend, and I need somewhere to store it that's not cluttered with the spring inventory."

She was lying. The shop had plenty of storage space.

"Hi, Stella," Jen and Talia chorused.

"Girls, how wonderful to see you." Stella set the flowers on my tiny kitchen counter, taking up most of the available space, and turned to survey us with sharp gray eyes that missed nothing. "So. What are we discussing? The look on Emma's face suggests boy trouble."

"Aunt Stella—"

"Is it that science teacher? The one with the chiseled jaw like Superman?" She didn't wait for an answer. "Bob mentioned there was quite a show at the PTA meeting when I stopped by the hardware store. He said you two were going at it like cats in a bag."

I dropped my head into my hands. "How would he know? He doesn't even have kids."

"His sister does. He was babysitting for Greg and Carla." Stella perched on the arm of the couch. "So? What's the verdict? Are you going to work it out?"

"Still deciding," I muttered.

"Work it out," Stella said. "That boy's got good bone structure. Shame to waste it on a rivalry."

"Stella!"

"What? I'm just saying. I saw him in the coffee shop last week. Tall. Serious. Nice hands. You could do worse."

"We're barely even colleagues. We're professional adversaries forced into collaboration by budget cuts."

"Uh-huh." Stella's grin widened. "And how's that working out for you?"

"Terribly, thanks for asking."

"Enemies to lovers, right, girls?" She winked at Jen and Talia. "You're both fighting for students, right? Same team. Different positions."

"He wants to eliminate Field Day—"

"He wants funding for science programs. You want funding for Field Day. Neither of you is wrong, sweetheart. You're so busy being right that you can't see the middle ground."

I wanted to argue, but the words stuck in my throat. Because maybe she had a point.

"Besides," Stella continued, standing and brushing invisible dust from her overalls, "life's too short to waste on hating attractive men. Just have sex."

She headed for the door, then paused. "Oh, and Emma? When you meet him tomorrow, wear the purple sweater. Brings out your eyes."

"How did you—"

But she was already gone, the door clicking shut behind her, leaving the scent of roses and irises in her wake.

The three of us sat in silence for a moment.

"Are you going to wear the purple sweater tomorrow?" Talia's grin was back.

"Absolutely not."

"But you are going to talk to him tomorrow."

I thought about Max's message. About the apology and Aunt Stella's voice in my head, far too pleased with herself.

"Yeah," I said. "I'm going to talk to him."

"And try to find middle ground?" Jen asked.

"And try not to throw anything at him," I amended. "Baby steps."

Talia stood and grabbed the bakery box. "Then we need cake. Peace negotiations require chocolate."

We ate until the plates were empty and the conversation drifted, but my phone stayed on the coffee table, Max's message right at the top. Tomorrow pressed at the edges of my thoughts.

Where I'd take him.

What I'd say.

Whether it was possible to work with someone who drove me insane and made my stomach do that stupid, fluttery thing.

"You're thinking about him," Jen said.

"I'm thinking about Field Day."

"While thinking about him."

"He's part of the problem."

"Or part of the solution," Talia said. "if you let him be."

I glanced at the flowers Aunt Stella had left, all soft petals and terrible implications. At my friends. At the life I'd built here.

Field Day mattered.

But maybe there was room for more.

"I'm going to regret this," I said.

"Probably," Jen agreed.

"But it'll be interesting," Talia added.

They were right.

I picked up my phone. Two messages. An apology and an agreement. Not much—but enough to start.

Tomorrow I'd find out if there was any middle ground, and I was wearing the purple sweater.

Damn Aunt Stella.

Chapter 6: Max

THE PERCOLATOR WAS tucked between the hardware store and the bookshop on Main Street. The old, mismatched furniture looked like it was aiming for artfully casual and landing somewhere closer to structurally questionable. String lights crisscrossed the ceiling, and chalkboard menus covered one wall in elaborate script that took too long to decode when all I wanted was black coffee.

I'd never been here before. My caffeine came from home or the teacher's lounge, but Emma had picked this place, so here I was.

With a macaw.

Because apparently my life had become a situation comedy I hadn't auditioned for.

"We're meeting someone," I told Darcy through the mesh of his travel cage. "Please behave. Please don't say anything embarrassing. Please don't bite anyone."

"DARCY IS GORGEOUS!"

"Yes, you're very pretty. Can you be quiet?"

"DAMN IT!"

Two older ladies turned to stare. My face heated.

This was a terrible idea. I should have left him in my classroom. Or with Eli. Or outside the coffee shop. How was I supposed to convince Emma Bennett that I was a reasonable collaborative partner with Darcy intervening?

But Darcy had screeched the moment I'd tried to leave him at school. Not a warning squawk, a full-volume, sustained alarm that echoed down the hallway and drew concerned looks from three teachers and one security guard. Twenty straight minutes of it. No pauses. No mercy.

I'd tried ignoring him. I'd tried bribery with apple slices. I'd even tried reasoning with him. Nothing worked. The second I stepped toward the door, he screamed like he'd been personally betrayed.

Darcy, it turned out, had abandonment issues that rivaled my own, which were both ironic and deeply inconvenient. By the time I gave up and wheeled his travel cage out with me, my ears were ringing, my patience was gone.

So now Darcy was with me, glowering from his cage, feathers fluffed in smug victory, because the alternative was public humiliation and a noise complaint.

I pushed through the door, the little bell jingling overhead, and immediately wanted to leave. The place was packed with the afternoon crowd: college students with laptops, parents with strollers, elderly couples lingering over crossword puzzles. Every table seemed occupied.

"Can I help you?" The barista with impressive tattoos and an eyebrow piercing looked from me to the travel cage with concealed amusement.

"Coffee. Black. Large." I paused. "And is there somewhere I could... sit? With the..."

"Bird?" He grinned. "Yeah, man. We're pet-friendly. Corner booth in the back is open. I'll bring the coffee over."

"Thank you."

I navigated through the crowded shop, trying to ignore the stares and whispers. The corner booth had a high back that offered some privacy, a small table scarred with cup rings, and a view of the door, so I could see when Emma arrived.

I set Darcy's cage on the bench beside me and pulled out my phone. 4:47 PM. She'd said four forty-five.

Maybe she wasn't coming.

Maybe she'd changed her mind.

Maybe—

The bell over the door jingled, and Emma walked in.

She wore jeans and a purple sweater that made her eyes look impossibly bright. Her violet hair was loose around her shoulders instead of pulled back in her usual ponytail. She scanned the coffee shop, spotted me, and something flickered across her face.

Surprise? Annoyance? I couldn't tell.

She wove through the tables toward me, and I stood awkwardly.

"Hey," she said, sliding into the booth across from me. "Is that Darcy? I heard Ms. P asked you to watch him."

"I tried to leave him. He... protested. Loudly. For extended periods."

Her lips twitched. "Separation anxiety?"

"Apparently." I sat back down. "I'm sorry. I know this is unprofessional. I can take him back to—"

"HELLO GORGEOUS!" Darcy announced.

"Hi, Darcy," she crooned, extending a finger toward the carrier.

“Don’t touch him!” I barked, extending my hands which were covered in band-aids.

Seventeen of them, to be exact. Bright blue, because that's all the drugstore had at seven AM when I'd finally admitted I needed them. Darcy had discovered that my fingers made excellent chew toys, and my attempts to discourage this behavior had been met with enthusiastic defiance.

I was a man of science, holder of a PhD, applicant for a prestigious NASA grant.

And I'd been defeated by a three-pound bird.

“Keep your fingers away,” I gestured at the cage. "He’s vicious."

She laughed. “Darcy and I are on good terms. He’s never bitten me.”

Fearlessly, she reached through the narrow opening and scratched Darcy on the side of the head.

“PRETTY EMMA!” the macaw blared, loud enough to turn a few heads in the café.

“Pretty Darcy,” she corrected, giving me a sideways smirk.

My stomach dropped. Fantastic. Exactly what I needed. The damn bird was flirting with her like a feathered Casanova.

“Darcy, please stop talking,” I begged, half-laughing, half-mortified.

“DARCY IS GORGEOUS!” the macaw announced. “EMMA IS GORGEOUS!”

I pressed a hand to my face. “I swear I didn’t teach him that,” I muttered, which of course sounded like something a pervert would say.

Great. Just great.

Emma laughed, the sound bright and genuine in the crowded coffee shop. "Oh, Darcy has been calling me gorgeous since I dyed my hair. He thinks I'm a bird."

Some of the tension in my shoulders ease. "I volunteered to help Lynda and ended up with temporary custody."

"That was nice of you." Emma studied me, and I shifted in my seat, feeling like an amoeba under the microscope.

"Dante and Eli were in my classroom when she got the call about her dad, and I said I'd make sure Darcy was taken care of."

"Let me guess. You didn't realize that meant taking him home?"

"I thought someone else would volunteer." I held up my bandaged hands. "I was wrong."

Emma's eyes widened. "He did all of that? He's always been so affectionate."

"He shows his love through minor violence." I pulled my hands back, self-conscious. "It's fine. They're just scratches. Well, bites. Small bites."

"Max." Her voice had gone softer. "That's a lot of band-aids."

"Seventeen. Two fell off during fourth period when Michael Flannigan's microscope accidentally fell off the lab table."

"Michael is a mess." She shook her head. "Destruction follows in his wake."

The barista appeared with my coffee and paused when he saw Emma. "Hey, Em. What can I get you?"

"Caramel latte, please. Extra shot. Thanks."

She waited until he left before turning back to me. "So you're being mauled by a parrot you didn't want while applying for a grant that depends on an event you can't plan because we can't agree on anything."

"When you put it that way, it sounds bad."

"It is bad, Max." But she was almost smiling. "Your life is a disaster."

"DISASTER!" Darcy agreed. "DAMN IT!"

A woman at the next table shot us a disapproving look.

"Sorry," I called over. Then spoke quieter to Emma: "This was a mistake. I should have met you without the bird."

"No." Emma leaned forward, and I caught a whiff of her delicious scent—citrus and vanilla. "This is perfect. This is the most human I've ever seen you."

"Human?"

"Yeah. You're always so..." She gestured vaguely. "Controlled. Perfect. Like you've got everything figured out. But right now you look like you haven't slept, your hands are covered in band-aids, and you brought a parrot to a coffee shop because you couldn't say no to a crying librarian. It's... endearing."

My brain stuttered over that last word. "Endearing?"

"Don't let it go to your head." But her smile was genuine. "Look, I've been thinking about what you said. About the grant. About why it matters to you."

"Emma—"

"Let me finish." She wrapped her hands around the coffee cup the barista had just delivered. "I was angry. I'm still a little angry. You steamrolled me with that proposal, and it felt like you were saying everything I care about doesn't matter."

"That's not what I meant—"

"I know." She met my eyes. "And I might have let my defensiveness get in the way of listening."

I looked at Darcy, who was preening contentedly in his cage as I set my cup down. "I was controlling and obstinate. I have trust issues."

"You do?" she asked.

"I never learned how to work with people. Growing up, I moved around a lot. Foster care. Different homes, different schools. The only person I could count on was myself, so I learned to do everything alone. To control every variable."

Emma's expression shifted. "Max—"

"And then I got to college, and graduate school, and I kept doing it that way because it worked. I published papers. I won grants. I got hired at Marchfield." I forced myself to meet her eyes. "But public school teachers rely on one another, and I don't know how to do that."

"That sounds lonely."

The observation hit harder than I expected. "It's safe."

"Is it?" She tilted her head. "Because from where I'm sitting, you look pretty miserable."

"I'm sleep-deprived and bullied by a parrot. That's different."

She snorted. "Is it?"

Before I answered, Darcy let out a piercing whistle. Not his usual squawk, but a clear, musical note that cut cleanly through the café noise. A few heads turned.

Then, as if that weren't bad enough: "KISS KISS!"

Emma's cheeks flushed pink. "Did he just—"

"What the hell?" Heat rushed straight to my face as every eye in the room became aware of us. "Lynda probably kisses him. Constantly. It's a bird thing. It doesn't mean—"

"KISS KISS PRETTY EMMA!"

I stared at the cage, horrified. The bird puffed up, delighted with himself, rocking like he was conducting a social experiment.

"Oh my God," I muttered. This was not happening. This was not how this meeting was supposed to go. I'd brought spreadsheets. I had talking points. I had not prepared for avian matchmaking.

Darcy leaned forward, black eyes bright. "KISS!"

"Darcy," I said through clenched teeth, "please stop talking forever."

He whistled again, long and triumphant.

Emma bit her lip, trying—and failing—not to smile.

I considered, briefly and seriously, abandoning science altogether and letting the bird have my job.

Emma was laughing now, really laughing, her shoulders shaking. "Oh my God. You should take him to a bar. Darcy is a great wingman."

"Ha ha. He's a feathered chaos agent." My lips twitched despite my mortification.

"Here, let me take him out of the cage," Emma suggested.

"He bites."

"I see that." She gestured at my hands. "But I'm willing to risk it."

I hesitated, then carefully unlatched the cage door. "If he draws blood, you should go to urgent care and get a tetanus shot."

"Birds don't carry tetanus, but deal."

I opened the door slowly. Darcy tilted his head, studying Emma with one bright eye. Then, moving with surprising gentleness, he stepped onto her extended hand, shimming up her arm.

"Good boy," I murmured. "Be nice. Please be nice."

Darcy ruffled his feathers, preened for a moment, then perched on her shoulder, leaning in against the side of Emma's head.

"Hey there, handsome," Emma crooned.

"PRETTY," he said, but quietly this time. Almost sweet.

"You are very pretty," Emma agreed. "Very handsome. Much more polite than your caretaker."

"I'm sitting right here."

"I know." But she was smiling, gently scratching the top of Darcy's head with one finger. The bird closed his eyes and made a blissful sound.

"He never does that with me," I said before I could stop myself.

"Maybe you're not scratching the right spot."

"Maybe he just likes you better."

"PRETTY EMMA," Darcy confirmed, leaning into her touch.

And she was.

No, I took that back. Emma was beautiful.

Her hair was down, framing her face and brushing her shoulders, which softened her in a way that felt unfair. Her eyebrows didn't quite match—one lifted a little higher than the other—and I noted it because it made her expressions easier to read, a small tell I was already filing away.

Her smile wasn't perfect either. It pulled crooked on one side, like she was always on the edge of laughing at something the rest of the world had missed. That imperfection made it better. Made it hers.

Even now, leaning toward Darcy with her attention fully engaged, she looked alive—so present it seemed to brighten the entire coffee shop. Realizing I was noticing all of this, cataloging it without meaning to, unsettled me far more than the bird ever could.

Darcy yanked the paper straw out of Emma's latte with his beak.

The moment shattered. Coffee sloshed, Emma gasped, and I lurched forward on instinct, all lingering thoughts about her smile evaporating as my brain slammed back into crisis management mode.

"Darcy—no," I said, grabbing for the bird, ready to stuff him into his carrier. Darcy was flapping feathers angrily and tossing the wet straw at me,

"It's fine," Emma said as Darcy nipped my knuckle, making me jerk back to examine my bleeding knuckle.

I pressed a napkin to the cut and watched as Emma distracted Darcy with a seed stick from his carrier.

"We should talk about the new plan while he's distracted."

"Okay."

"I can't do it your way. All STEM stations, no traditional Field Day elements. That's not a compromise."

I took a breath. "What if we started over? Find a way to combine what we both want."

She looked up. "What do you mean?"

"You want Field Day to be a place where every kid feels included. Where the ones who don't fit the academic mold get to shine. Where community matters." I ticked the points off on my bandaged fingers. "Right?"

"Right."

"I want to build a STEM program that gives kids opportunities they wouldn't otherwise have. That shows them science can be a way forward. That education can change lives." I met her eyes.

Emma was quiet for a moment, absently stroking Darcy's feathers. "What if it's not either-or? What if it's both-and?"

"What do you mean?"

"Field Day that teaches science. Or a science fair that feels like Field Day. Something that has the fun and community driven with the learning and opportunities of the other." She leaned forward, and Darcy protested softly at the movement. "What if we stopped trying to defend our separate programs and started building something new together?"

The idea hung between us, fragile and potentially brilliant.

"That would require me to trust you," I said.

"Yes."

"And you to trust me."

"Also yes." She smiled slightly. "Terrifying, right?"

"Absolutely terrifying."

"TERRIFYING!" Darcy contributed, the mangled straw falling from his beak. "DARCY TERRIFYING!"

We both laughed, and some of the tension broke.

"Okay," I said. "Let's try again. No more solo proposals. No more steamrolling. We plan together. Equal input. We make all the decisions together."

"Agreed." Emma held out her hand. "Partners?"

I looked from the parrot to her extended hand. At the woman who'd called me out on my control issues. Who might be the first person I could trust.

I took her hand. Her grip was firm, callused from years of handling athletic equipment. Warm.

"Partners," I agreed.

"KISS KISS!" Darcy announced.

A ripple of laughter swept through the coffee shop. People paused mid-sip, heads lifting like prairie dogs sensing drama.

A pair of college girls at the corner table froze, straws halfway to their mouths, grinning like they'd just been handed front-row seats to a live-action rom-com. Near the window, a woman in a beanie whispered something to her friend and nudged her with an elbow, eyes bright with expectation. Even the barista leaned over the counter, chin in hand, openly enjoying the show.

Did they seriously think I was going to kiss her?

I dropped Emma's hand like it burned me. "That's not—we're not—he just says things—"

"Pretty girl like that," an older man called out from his armchair in the corner, one leg crossed over the other, newspaper forgotten on his lap, "You'd better kiss her before someone else does."

A few people applauded. Someone whistled. The whole café smelled of coffee, cinnamon pastries, and nosy optimism—like the entire room had collectively decided it knew how our afternoon should end.

Meanwhile, my ears were on fire, and Emma looked torn between mortified and amused.

Emma's cheeks were pink again, but she called out, "Thanks, everyone. Nothing to see here but a nosy parrot."

When the noise level returned to normal, I asked. "When do we want to start?"

"Monday? After school? We could—"

"Max? Emma? Is that you?"

I looked up to find Oz standing next to our table, holding a toddler on his hip who looked between Emma and Darcy with wide eyes. Behind him stood Audrey, a petite woman with red hair.

"Hey, Oz." I tried to sound casual. "Audrey. This is—"

"Emma Bennett. We've met, Max. Remember, we all teach at the same school." Audrey's eyes were twinkling.

"Hi, guys." Emma's smile was genuine. "Liam, do you want to pet the bird?"

Liam's eyes went wide. "BIRD!"

"BABY!" Darcy announced, leaning toward Liam with interest.

"His name is Darcy," Emma said, angling the parrot, so Liam could see better. "Can you say Darcy?"

"Darcy," Liam attempted. "Darcy bird!" I winced as his chubby fingers stretched toward the red feathers on Darcy's wing, but he patted it gently.

"PRETTY BABY" Darcy agreed, leaning closer. Apparently, he only hated me.

Oz looked between me and Emma again, his grin widening. "So. Coffee meeting? Work stuff?"

"Yes," I said quickly. "Just planning for the combined event. We're collaborating."

Why did I feel so awkward? Like I'd been caught by my parents?

"Collaborate. Right." Audrey fought back laughter. "That must be... intense."

"It's fine," Emma said, a little too brightly.

"And the parrot?" Oz asked as Darcy bobbed up and down on Emma's shoulder, dancing with Liam.

"Max is taking care of him for Lynda. He's very sweet."

"The bird or Max?" Audrey asked with a sly grin.

"The bird," Emma and I said simultaneously, then looked at each other.

"Well," Oz said, trying not to laugh. "We should let you get back to your... planning. Max? I'll see you on Wednesday at basketball. You're going to have so many questions to answer."

"This is just work."

"Uh-huh." He picked up Liam, shifting the boy to his other hip. "Have fun. Nice seeing you, Emma. You too, Darcy."

"BYE BYE!" Darcy called after them.

They left as Audrey whispered something to Oz that made him bark out a laugh.

Emma and I sat in silence for a moment.

"Well," she said with a helpless shrug. "That's going to be all over school by Monday."

"What is?"

"That we were here. Together. With a bird. Looking very un-work-like."

"We are working. This is work."

"Max." She met my eyes. "We're in a coffee shop. You brought a parrot. I'm wearing my nice sweater. This looks like a date."

My brain short-circuited. "A date."

"I'm not saying it is one. I'm saying that's what people will think."

"But it's not."

"Obviously, it's not," she said firmly. "We're colleagues. Partners on a project. That's all."

"Right. That's all."

"KISS KISS!" Darcy suggested again.

"Darcy, I swear to God—" I started.

Emma laughed, and the tension broke. “Darcy’s determined to make this awkward."

"He's succeeding spectacularly." I ran a bandaged hand through my hair. "I'm sorry. This isn't how I thought this would go."

"How did you think it would go?"

"Professional. Organized. We'd discuss logistics and create a framework and establish clear parameters for collaboration."

"And instead you're covered in band-aids, the parrot is starting rumors, and half the school is going to think we're dating by Monday morning."

"Exactly."

I thought about my twelve-page proposal. My color-coded spreadsheets. My desperate attempts to make everything perfect and predictable and safe.

And then I thought about Emma's laugh. Darcy's contentment on her shoulder. The warmth of her hand when we'd shaken on being partners.

Nothing about this was safe, but it somehow felt right.

Emma checked her phone. "I should go. I told Stella, my aunt, I'd help with the evening flower deliveries."

"Your aunt is a florist?"

"Yeah, I live above Share Your Buds. Stella is the owner." She stood, and my heart flipped a little. I realized I didn't want her to go. "Monday after school? Your classroom or my office?"

"Yours?" I offered. "Mine smells like chemicals and apparently houses a judgmental parrot now."

"Mine it is." She transferred Darcy back into his carrier and closed it up, then reached out to scratch Darcy one more time. "Take care of this guy. And Max? Put antibiotic ointment on those bites."

"I will."

"And... don't let the rumor mill get to you. People are going to talk. Let them talk."

"That doesn't bother you?"

"It bothers me less than cancelling Field Day would." She shouldered her bag. "See you Monday, partner."

"See you Monday."

I watched her weave through the crowded coffee shop and out the door, purple hair and sweater bright against the gray afternoon.

"PRETTY EMMA," Darcy said, almost wistfully.

"Yeah," I agreed. "Pretty Emma."

I packed up Darcy and his supplies, very aware of the looks we were getting from other customers. The rumor mill was definitely going to be spinning by Monday, but as I carried Darcy back to the car, his travel cage swinging. I found I didn't care.

Emma Bennett was my partner.

And if my traitorous brain kept replaying the way she'd laughed, the softness in her voice when she talked to Darcy, the warmth of her hand on mine—

Well, that was something I'd deal with later.

Much later.

Preferably never.

"KISS KISS," Darcy said from his cage.

"We are not discussing this."

"PRETTY EMMA KISS KISS!"

"I'm going to teach you thermodynamics. And the periodic table. And how to be quiet forever."

But Darcy ruffled his feathers, looking smug.

Apparently everyone, including Darcy, knew something I was still trying to deny.

This was going to be so much more complicated than I'd planned.

Chapter 7: Emma

IT WAS 2:47 PM ON WEDNESDAY afternoon when the fire alarm shrieked through the school. My seventh graders were in the middle of a particularly intense dodgeball tournament.

"Everyone out!" I shouted over the wailing siren, gesturing toward the gym doors. "Leave the balls! Go!"

Thirty sweaty twelve-year-olds scrambled for the exit where Pat and his class were leaving. Their voices rose with a mixture of excitement and annoyance that their game had to wait. I did a quick head count as they filed past, then jogged toward my duty station to help clear the hallways.

Halfway down the main corridor, I spotted Max herding his sixth-grade class outside, the tiny eleven-year-olds like a flock of startled pigeons, eyes wide, hands clasped over their ears against the alarm's wail.

Max's shirt was half untucked, his hair sticking up in wild directions like he'd just lost a fight with static electricity. He clutched his emergency folder and class roster in one hand, using the other to shoo students ahead of him.

Under the flickering emergency lights, he had a determined but distracted energy, like he was thinking three steps ahead and none of them involved self-preservation. His lab coat was gone, and there was a faint smudge of something on his sleeve.

He looked nothing like the cool, composed man I usually saw, and somehow that made him more appealing. The cracks in his armor, hesitation in his eyes, the tension he didn't bother hiding made my chest tighten in a way I hadn't expected.

And instead of pushing me away, that vulnerability drew me in, tugging at something instinctive and soft inside me. I wanted to step closer to let him know he didn't have to hold himself together so tightly all the time. Seeing him like this made him feel more real, more human, and the closeness that followed was inevitable, as if I were being pulled into his orbit without resistance.

"Dr. Harrison!" I called, my voice carrying over the alarm. "You really should warn the school if you're going to set it on fire."

His students giggled as they passed me. He rolled his eyes, though I caught the faint curve of a smile.

"It's not me," he said. "Your jump ropes overheated. Friction can do that."

I laughed, surprised by myself. What was I doing? It wasn't even that funny—and yet the way he said it, that wicked gleam in his eye, gave me butterflies.

He tried to step past me, but I shifted into his path, tilting my head.

"Did you forget someone?"

He blinked, looking back over his shoulder for stragglers, confusion knitting his brow. "No."

One of my eyebrows lifted. "Where's Darcy?"

He frowned. "It's a drill. He'll be fine."

"Max." I crossed my arms. "This isn't a pre-scheduled practice drill. There could be an actual fire somewhere in the building. You should bring him just in case."

He looked down at his hands, every finger still wrapped in those bright blue bandages, and sighed. "Damn bird."

"Hey, Marnie," I called to the sprightly teen-living teacher as she passed. "Can you take Dr. Harrison's folder and check on his students? He needs to go back for Darcy."

"Sure can," Marnie said, giving me a quick wink. "Good luck, hero."

Max groaned and turned back toward his classroom.

The rational side of my brain told me to step back and let him deal with the bird while I finished clearing the hall, then get outside with the rest of the staff. That was the sensible thing to do. The responsible thing.

But another part of me, quieter and far less reasonable, leaned toward him instead. I wanted to follow him, to stay close, as if Darcy was something we should face together. The idea of turning away and leaving him alone with it made me restless. I told myself it was concern, professionalism, anything but what it really felt like—this instinctive need to be near him.

Before I overthought it, my feet were already moving after him.

We turned off the main hall, taking a shortcut to the back entrance of his classroom. The corridor narrowed as we moved deeper into the building, the ceiling lowering. The concrete floor and bare walls amplified the pulse of the fire alarm and made it echo as we hurried toward the rear of the science wing.

He opened a solid wood door, ushering me through into the science storage area. Metal storage shelves crowded both sides, stacked with dusty textbooks, outdated lab equipment, and half-labeled boxes.

At the other end of the small rectangular room was a wooden door with a large window. I knew it would open into the back of Max's classroom, so I grabbed the handle and twisted.

It didn't budge.

I tried again, harder this time, the metal biting into my palm. "Do you have a key?"

"Umm." He patted his pockets while looking through the window in the door. "I think it's in my lab coat."

He pointed to the white coat hanging off the back of a tall chair by Darcy's cage. Following his gaze, I could see the tail of his lanyard hanging out of the pocket.

"Okay. Fine. We'll just go back the way we came and—"

But behind us, the door we'd entered through began to close, slowly, almost lazily, as if it had all the time in the world. The gap of light narrowed inch by inch, and with it, the alarms faded, their sharp urgency dulled into a distant, muffled pulse. The air seemed heavier, the corridor tighter as if the walls were inching closer.

For a heartbeat, I stared. Then I spun and lunged for it. My fingers closed around the cold and unforgiving handle as the door clicked shut. I twisted hard, but nothing happened. I tried again, bracing my foot against the concrete floor, wrenching with everything I had. The handle refused to move, solid and final, confirming what I'd already known.

We were locked in.

"This can't be happening," I muttered, pulling harder.

Max set down the travel cage he'd grabbed somewhere along the way and tried the handle himself. His movements were methodical, calm, completely at odds with the panic starting to claw up my throat.

"It's locked, too," he confirmed.

"I can see that, Max."

"LOCKED!" Darcy announced from his cage inside Max's room. "LOCKED LOCKED LOCKED!"

I pressed my forehead against the cold metal door, the chill seeping into my skin. "This is my fault. I'm sorry. I should have just let you handle it yourself. Now we're trapped and—"

The words tumbled out, guilt knotting tight in my chest. My pulse hammered as worst-case scenarios stacked up one after another, each more vivid than the last. I hated that I'd dragged him into this, hated even more that a small, traitorous part of me was glad to be with him, even now. The thought only made the shame burn hotter as I stood there, forehead pressed to the door, wishing I could rewind the last few minutes and choose differently.

"Hey." Max's hand touched my shoulder, warm and steady. I turned to face him, and the emergency lights painted him in alternating shadows and red. "It's fine. Someone will find us."

"During a fire drill when everyone's supposed to be outside?" My voice rose despite my best efforts to stay calm. "Max, we might be stuck here for—"

"Fifteen minutes. Twenty, tops." His voice was so reasonable, so steady. "They'll do a head count. They'll realize we're missing. They'll search the building."

"And if there's an actual fire?"

"Then we'll smell smoke. We'll break the window in the door if we have to." He kept his eyes on mine, grounding me. "But there's no smoke. No heat. This is just a drill."

I took a shaky breath, then another. He was right. Of course, he was. The logic of it settled in my head even as my body refused to calm down.

Being trapped in this narrow space with Max did strange things to my senses. I was hyperaware of how close he stood. Warmth radiated from him and I heard the steady rhythm of his breathing beneath the lingering alarms. Every small movement amplified the heat inside me: the shift of his shoulders, the brush of air on my face when he exhaled.

The space between us seemed to hum with unspoken awareness. I found myself wondering what it would feel like to lean into his steadiness, to let the chaos fade until the only thing that existed was this charged closeness.

The thought sent a flutter through me, one I quickly tried—and failed—to ignore.

The confined corridor left nowhere for my nerves to go, nowhere to put the energy thrumming through me. It wasn't fear driving my pulse though. It was the way his presence filled the space, grounding and unsettling all at once.

It was adrenaline. The stress of being locked in during a drill.

But I couldn't ignore that being this close to Max stripped away my distance and composure.

Every glance, every shift of movement felt charged, as if the air between us had thickened. My heart raced for reasons I wasn't ready to admit, and that realization unsettled me far more than the fact that we were stuck.

He stepped closer. Not enough to touch, but close enough that the heat of him seeped into me. His shoulders were tense, coiled with a kind of restless energy he usually kept hidden beneath cool control. Now it radiated off him, sharp and aware.

His eyes flicked to mine, then down to my mouth, then back, so quick I might've imagined it if my heart didn't stutter in response.

One hand braced against the wall beside my head, palm splayed, as if he was trying to steady himself or maybe trying very hard not to reach for me.

I pressed a little closer to the cool metal shelves, keeping my voice low, almost breathless. "Is it me, or did this hallway get smaller?" My words wavered, but there was a trace of flirting.

"Understandable reaction," he murmured, his eyes flicking up to mine. "Most people can only handle me in open spaces."

I swallowed, my pulse thudding loud in my ears. "Max."

At the sound of his name, his jaw flexed, a subtle but deliberate motion, like he was fighting an instinct he didn't trust. The space between us seemed to tighten, the air heavier, every breath charged.

Then, abruptly, the alarm cut off, leaving a ringing silence that was somehow louder than the noise had been. It left just the two of us, locked in together with the narrow corridor pressing in and every small movement amplified.

Max's voice cut through it, low and steady, yet closer somehow than it should have been. "Drill's over. They'll find us soon." His words brushed against me, the proximity of him making my pulse hitch despite the warning in his tone.

My legs were shaky, so I slid down to sit on the floor. "Might as well get comfortable then."

Max hesitated, then sat down beside me.

Unable to see us through the window, Darcy called out, "PRETTY EMMA?"

I couldn't help but smile as I reassured him. "Hi, Darcy. Having fun?"

"DRAMA QUEEN!"

"He learned that today," Max explained, and there was something almost sheepish in his expression. "Along with approximately seven other phrases I wish he hadn't."

"Such as?"

"Butt is the most recent addition."

I laughed, the sound echoing in the narrow space and easing some of the tightness in my chest. "Lynda's going to love that when she gets back."

"I'm starting to think she's never coming back." Max adjusted his position, trying to get comfortable on the hard floor. "And she's laughing because she left Darcy with the least-skilled person to care for him."

"You have skills."

"I have equations and spreadsheets. It's different."

"Oh, come on." I pulled my knees up to my chest, studying him in the red emergency lighting. "You came back for your bird during a fire drill."

"My basic human decency is a low bar."

"You'd be surprised how many people can't clear it."

I was painfully aware of how close we were, our shoulders nearly brushing. Every slight movement he made sent a flicker of heat across my skin, as if the air itself bent around him.

I felt the subtle rise and fall of his chest with each steady breath. He seemed so calm, and I wondered if I was the only one feeling this impossible attraction, or if he noticed it too.

But when his eyes flicked toward me, the space between us seemed to charge with energy. One careless inhale, one careless shift, and the distance might collapse entirely. The thought both thrilled and terrified me.

"Thank you," I said, struggling for composure. "For Monday, at the Percolator. For listening and trying to understand why Field Day matters."

"You don't have to thank me for that. I should have tried listening first."

"You aren't alone." I picked at a loose thread on my sneaker. "Most people assume it's just games."

Max was quiet for a moment. "You're right, I did think that. But I was wrong." He turned to look at me, and the sincerity in his expression made my chest tight. "What you do, making kids feel seen, giving them a place to belong, that's not less important than what I do. It's probably more important."

"Max—"

"I mean it." He shifted slightly, and our shoulders brushed. Neither of us moved away. "I've been thinking about what you said. About being the kid who didn't fit. About Mrs. Carter seeing something in you."

He paused, then continued, "I was that kid too. The one who didn't belong. But instead of finding it in PE, I found it in science class. Mr. Bednarz saw something in me that nobody else did. Gave me extra lab time, helped me apply to college, and wrote recommendation letters for me. He's why I'm here and why I care so much about the grant."

"To be that person for other kids," I said, understanding clicking into place.

"Yeah." He looked down at his bandaged hands. "I know I'm not good at community building and making everyone feel included. That's your superpower, not mine. But I am good at showing kids that science can be a way forward. That education can change everything."

My heart squeezed at the thought of the young boy he once had been, even as it raced for the man he had become.

His dark eyes found mine, steady and intense, and for a moment the world narrowed. His lips parted, as if he were about to speak, but no words came. A faint pink crept up the side of his neck, subtle and unguarded, and he shifted, angling his body toward me.

His hand rested near his knee, and I caught it twitch, like he wanted to close the space between us but was holding himself back, afraid of crossing some invisible line. My own pulse thrummed in response, making every subtle shift feel magnified.

And then his knee brushed mine. The contact was brief, but electric, and it echoed through every nerve in my body. The room seemed impossibly small, the air too thick, and for a moment, I couldn't tell where he ended and I began.

I leaned in and closed the tiny, aching space between us. My mouth brushed over his lips. He tasted of coffee and chocolate, and I sank into the richness of his flavor.

His hand slid to my cheek, gentle but certain, and he kissed me back with a longing that surprised and delighted me.

Inside his classroom, Darcy sang something light and cheerful, but it barely registered. My attention was hijacked by Max: the way he moved, the faint crease of concentration between his brows, the subtle warmth radiating from him. Every small touch and kiss seemed amplified.

My pulse quickened at the brush of his arm at my waist and the low timbre of his growl of pleasure. His presence seemed to bend the space around me, setting my senses ablaze, with every nerve ending alive. I was lost, caught entirely in Max.

Footsteps echoed in the hallway beyond the locked door. Then a jangling of keys.

"Hello?" a deep voice called. "Anyone in there?"

I jerked away from Max and scrambled to my feet, barely noticing him doing the same.

"Yes!" we shouted.

The door swung open to reveal Charlie, lead custodian, looking between us with obvious amusement. "There you are. Principal Kline sent me to check the service corridors. Everyone's been looking for you two."

"The door locked behind us," I explained, trying not to look flustered. "And Max didn't have his key."

"Huh. That shouldn't happen." Charlie knelt by the lock mechanism, frowning. "I need to fix that. Would be a real problem if there'd been an actual fire."

Max nodded, looking calm and collected, while I was about to melt into the floor. My pulse betrayed me, my cheeks flushed, and a wild tug of energy ran through me, making me hyper-aware of every glance, every movement. I was completely out of control and far from composed.

"Agreed," I said, forcing my voice steady, but tighter than I intended. I couldn't stop my eyes from flicking to Max, and I tried not to notice the easy way he exuded control while I fumbled.

Charlie unlocked Max's classroom door, and I ushered Darcy into the main hallway, hoping for a moment of quiet as the students and staff began to filter back into the building. The drill was over, and we'd been trapped for—I checked my watch—nearly twenty minutes.

"HELLO," Darcy announced, oblivious to my mortification as the first students came into view. "HELLO GORGEOUS!"

"Found them!" Charlie called out cheerfully from behind me, his voice booming down the corridor. "Stuck together in the science closet!"

I groaned. Did he have to shout it out?

Several teachers turned, eyebrows raised, and my face heated instantly. I tried to shrink back, wishing I could disappear into the walls.

Darcy, undeterred, leaned forward and chirped, "KISS KISS!"

A few students nearby giggled, Val and Audrey exchanged amused, knowing glances, and I caught Eli trying—and failing—to hide a smirk behind his hand.

Begging for the floor to swallow me whole, I dashed toward the gym with Darcy still clinging to my shoulder. My heart hammered in my chest, part embarrassment, part frustration at being completely exposed, and part... something else I wasn't ready to name.

Dante appeared around the corner. "There you are! We were taking bets on whether you'd gotten lost or just decided to skip the rest of the day." His grin was insufferable.

"Got stuck," I said, though I knew my red face gave me away. "Doors locked."

Dante's eyes were twinkling. "That's... unfortunate."

"KISS KISS!" Darcy announced to the hallway at large. "MAX AND EMMA!"

Dante's face flushed as he tried—and failed—to hide his laughter. "Did the bird just out you?"

"Here," I said, shoving Darcy toward him. "Take him back to Max."

Talia and Jen appeared at the end of the hallway, drawn by the commotion. Jen's eyes landed on my bright pink cheeks, and her expression instantly shifted to a knowing, mischievous smile. Talia raised an eyebrow, as if silently asking what had happened.

"We heard you were stuck with Max in a closet during the fire drill." Jen grinned, eyes sparkling with mischief.

"KISS KISS!" Darcy added from Dante's arm.

"Stop spreading rumors, Darcy," I admonished the bird, a blush creeping up my neck.

"He's just stating facts," Dante laughed, barely able to keep a straight face.

"Okay, show's over," Principal Kline's voice cut through the gathering crowd. "Everyone back to class. We've got fifteen minutes left in the period. Every minute counts."

He shooed my friends reluctantly away, though I caught Jen's and Talia's gaze with my own, silently promising that there would be explanations later.

As the hallway emptied and the echoes of laughter faded, I exhaled, letting the tension slip from my shoulders.

My heart was still racing, my cheeks still warm, and I knew, despite the embarrassment, the teasing, and the chaos, something had shifted between Max and me.

The tension that had always lurked beneath our interactions, the unspoken push and pull, had transformed. We were no longer adversaries in subtle battles of wit and control. An undercurrent of closeness, of awareness, of possibilities replaced it.

And I wasn't rushing to escape it.

Chapter 8: Max

I TRUDGED DOWN THE long corridor from the science wing toward the gymnasium, my laptop bag heavier than usual and my pulse doing something complicated every time I thought about seeing Emma.

The kiss. The fire drill. Emma pressed against me in the darkness, her hands fisted in my shirt, the way she'd looked at me with wide blue eyes afterwards like maybe I wasn't the complete disaster she'd initially thought I was.

I'd spent the weekend trying not to think about it. Failing spectacularly.

I passed a few classroom doors that stood open, teachers packing up or hunched over their computers. A few students lingered by lockers, the stragglers heading to after-school clubs and sports.

I nodded at Pat Donovan as I passed the main gym entrance. He and Dante were setting up cones for what looked like intramural basketball practice.

"Harrison!" Dante called out, jogging over with that grin that meant trouble. "Wanna play with us?

"I have a planning meeting with Emma."

Pat and Dante exchanged a look that made my neck heat.

"If we hear yelling, we'll bust in to rescue you," Dante said, grin widening.

"Pretty sure I can handle Bennett on my own," I said, regretting the phrasing.

I wished I had held my tongue because their laughter followed me down the hallway.

Rounding the corner past the locker rooms, I found the small hallway that led to the PE offices. Emma's was tucked at the end, door slightly ajar. Through the gap, I could see her bent over her desk, purple ponytail swinging as she sketched something in her notebook, lower lip caught between her teeth in concentration.

My heart made an arrhythmic stutter that I'd normally attribute to excessive caffeine or a concerning cardiac event.

Except I knew what was causing it.

Emma Bennett.

And she was completely unaware that she'd rewired my entire nervous system in the span of one frantic kiss.

I knocked on the doorframe, and she looked up. Her face transformed. Uncertainty melted into a smile that felt like sunlight on the cold earth of my heart, thawing something I hadn't realized was frozen until this moment.

"Hey," she said, setting down her pen. "Come on in."

"Okay." I stepped inside, taking in the cramped space. One wall was covered in Field Day photos from previous years—kids mid-relay race, parents cheering, teachers beaming beside students clutching ribbons. Emma's desk was buried under equipment catalogs and hand-drawn station layouts. A coffee mug that served as a paperweight declared "I Teach PE. What's Your Superpower?"

The door had a lock.

I immediately hated that I'd noticed. This was a professional meeting.

Get a grip, I told myself. You're not cataloging possibilities. It's an office; offices have locks. I lined up the reasonable explanations—privacy, compliance, security.

Not assignations. Not affairs.

"Sit down," she gestured at the small table shoved against one wall as she moved to join me there.

"Okay," I said, kicking myself for the cleverless response. Heat crept up my neck, traitorous and fast.

I stepped forward and my heel caught the edge of a dented trash can and sent it skittering across the floor with a hollow clatter. I muttered an apology, nudging it back into place with more care than necessary.

We sat shoulder to shoulder at the table, closer than the room required, and my arm brushed hers—just enough contact to register. I adjusted my chair, then adjusted it again, as if the right angle might steady me.

"Is it warm in here?" I asked, too quickly, already regretting it.

Her cheeks flushed. "The heating system in this wing is terrible. Always either freezing or..." She gestured vaguely between us. "Not freezing."

She reached across the table for a thick manila folder that had been sitting beside a stack of equipment catalogs. Flipping it open, she pulled out a hand-drawn map of the football field and track.

The field was divided into color-coded sections, each labeled in her neat handwriting: Relay Start/Finish, Tug-of-War Station, Three-Legged Race Course, Sack Race. Small arrows indicated traffic flow, and she'd even noted where parent viewing areas were and volunteer locations.

"This is what we've used the last few years," she said, smoothing the paper flat between us.

“Right.” I became hyper-aware of how small the space was. Emma’s office could fit inside my classroom twice over. My knee bounced once before I stilled it, fingers worrying the edge of my notebook until the paper bent. I swallowed, suddenly conscious of my own breathing.

“How was your day?” I asked, my voice landing a half-beat later than I meant it to.

“Fine. Good. The rumor mill is grinding already. Pat tried to start a betting pool on whether we’re dating.” Her cheeks deepened to crimson. “I shut it down. Obviously.”

My stomach dropped in a clean, traitorous swoop. I let out a laugh that came out too loud, too fast, and dragged a hand over the back of my neck. My collar was suddenly tighter than it had been a moment ago.

“Of course,” I said, nodding a little too much. I shifted in my chair, which chose that moment to squeak against the tile. Perfect. I pressed my foot flat to the floor to still it, willing my face back to neutral while my pulse thudded in my ears.

Desperately, I pulled my phone from my pocket and snapped a photo of the map, just to give my hands something to do. A second later it bloomed open on my laptop, bright and unnecessary. I nodded at the screen like it had rescued me.

“Bobby asked me about it too. I told her we’re colleagues working on a project.”

“Which is true.”

“Completely true.”

The silence stretched. I became acutely aware of the faint hum of the lights, of the way my foot had crept halfway onto the rung of her chair without my noticing. I pulled it back, too fast.

For a beat, we stared at each other, long enough for me to register everything at once: the way her mouth was set like she was holding back a comment, the faint crease between her brows, the color still high on her cheeks. She didn't look away. She just watched me, steady and unreadable, the weight of her attention settling in my chest, tight and electric, as if any movement might snap it.

"So, planning. We should plan." Emma set her notebook on the table with more force than necessary.

"Yes." I drew in a slow breath and straightened, rolling my shoulders back like I was shrugging off a weight no one else could see. I turned my laptop to face her, deliberately, carefully, anchoring my hands on its edges until they stopped fidgeting. The familiar posture settled in—teacher, presenter, professional.

"I notice you have the area separated into six zones on the map."

"Too many zones and the kids don't finish. Too few and they get crowded." Emma leaned forward, to point to the map, her shoulder brushing mine in the cramped space. "What are you thinking?"

I tried to focus on the screen instead of how close she was, my fingers drumming an anxious rhythm against my knee beneath the table. "How about a physics relay race? Some kids run while others use the data to learn about speed and air resistance?"

I waited for her to find fault, to argue, to tell me I was still missing the point. Her face stayed blank, unreadable, and my stomach dropped. Too complicated. Too much science. I'd done it again—

"My students could run the station and use the data to complete their projects after the event," I added, the words tripping over each other now. "It might work out for both of us."

For a split second, she didn't move, and my mind filled the silence for her. Was I overreaching again? I braced myself, already rehearsing how I'd walk it back.

Then her expression shifted, slowly enough that I tracked it: her eyebrows lifting first, surprise softening the line of her forehead. Her eyes widened as skepticism gave way to consideration, and then to excitement.

"Max, that's brilliant." Her whole face lit up, animated in a way that made my chest tight. "That honors both programs."

The knot in my stomach eased, replaced by a cautious, flickering hope. "You think so?"

"I do! The tug-of-war teams could measure force." She was already sketching modifications in her notebook. "What if we add heart rate monitors on them for the sack race? The kids could track their own data."

"That's perfect." I pulled up a new document, typing quickly.

"Volunteers would monitor the equipment," Emma added, jotting down notes in the folder.

"Have you ever done an Egg Drop Challenge?"

"I have. That might be a great activity in this section closest to the school." She leaned forward, pointing to a spot on her map, and I caught the faint scent of her shampoo—something citrus and clean. "Maybe the firemen could drop the eggs from their hook and ladder?"

I pulled my laptop closer, already typing notes, trying to ignore how aware I was of her proximity. "How about Balloon-Powered Cars? The kids could build and race the cars and chart speed and distance."

"That can go with the long jump in this area." Emma pointed toward the back section of the field, her shoulder brushing mine as she shifted the map between us. Neither of us pulled away.

God, don't overthink this. Just focus on the map, not on her shoulder.

"The track is really smooth back there," she finished, and for a moment, I couldn't remember what we were talking about.

Get it together, man.

"Students can use the data to test hypotheses on projectile motion." My hand moved to adjust the paper at the exact same moment as hers, and our fingers collided. A jolt ran up my arm, sudden and stupidly electric. I froze for half a second before I pulled back, heat rushing up my neck like a signal flare.

"Right. Yes. As long as it isn't projectile vomiting..." Emma laughed, quick and breathless, like the room exhaled with her. Warmth filled the small office in a way I hadn't noticed was missing until that sound. She shook her head, grinning, and the corners of her eyes crinkled.

Her joke landed, and I realized I was grinning too. For a moment, I watched her—the way her eyes sparkled when she teased, the small tilt of her head, the quick, playful lift of her shoulders as she leaned back slightly. I had to remind myself to breathe, to focus on the meeting, not the way her presence made the office feel impossibly small.

We fell into a rhythm after that, trading ideas and building on each other's suggestions. I'd gesture at my screen, and she'd lean in close enough that I could see the faint freckles across her nose. She sketched changes in her notebook, her hand moving confident and quick, and I found myself watching, caught between wanting to look away but not wanting to miss a single motion.

Every so often our knees brushed under the table or our elbows collided, and we both froze for a heartbeat, aware of the contact, the tension pulling and tugging between us. But neither of us reacted.

"Station four," Emma said, tapping her pen against her notebook. "What if we combine the traditional three-legged race with some kind of physics component? Balance? Center of gravity?"

"Teamwork and applied physics." I was already pulling up a new document, fingers flying across the keyboard. "Partners could measure their combined center of gravity before and after being bound together. Test different binding positions to find the most stable configuration."

"So they're problem-solving while racing." Emma's eyes lit up. "Figuring out the science makes them faster."

"Exactly. And it uses materials we already have—rope, stopwatches, measuring tape. Keeps costs down."

"And every kid gets to participate. No one's just watching;" She met my eyes, and her expression softened. "You're listening."

"I'm trying to." The admission felt vulnerable.

"I appreciate that." Her voice dropped lower. "This is good, Max. What we're building. It's good."

The words hung between us, layered with meaning that had nothing to do with STEM Field Day.

The moment broke when the gym door banged open in the distance and voices echoed across the space. Emma tensed, glancing toward her open office door.

"That's Pat's basketball intramurals," I said, standing to close the door.

I returned to the table in silence, my hands lingering on the edge a moment longer than necessary. The noise from the gym faded to a distant thump of basketballs and scattered shouts, as if it existed in another world. The office shrank, becoming tighter, more intimate, the space between us charged in a way that made my stomach twist.

I was hyper-aware of every movement. Her pencil tapping lightly against the notebook, the subtle rise and fall of her shoulders as she breathed, the faint brush of her sleeve against mine, and I wanted to lean closer. But my brain screamed to stop, retreat, pump the brakes.

"We should keep the door open," Emma murmured. "For... professional reasons."

"Probably," I agreed, but neither of us moved to open it.

Emma's pen froze mid-stroke, and her lips parted, a careless curve that made me suck in a breath. The flush creeping down her neck vanished beneath the collar of her polo, but I saw it, and my hands itched, trembling, wanting to trace that line.

Her eyes locked onto mine, pupils wide and bright in the dim office light, and I felt it like a hot, electric punch to the chest. A lock of violet hair escaped from her ponytail, brushing her cheek. I wanted to tuck it behind her ear. I wanted to let it slip through my fingers. I wanted to close the six inches between us and kiss her. My hands twitched, fingers curling and uncurling against the table.

Her tongue darted out to wet her bottom lip, and my lungs betrayed me when I took in too much air.

I coughed. Wheezing, an awkward rasp escaping me like a nervous, sputtering fool. Perfect, I thought, internally groaning. Nothing says "professional colleague" more than choking on air because your coworker's hair is purple.

Emma blinked at me, one eyebrow lifting, and I gave her a small, sheepish shrug. "Uh... the air," I said. "It's... dry."

I was such an idiot.

I should look away. Focus. Be professional.

I didn't. I couldn't.

I leaned in just a fraction—enough to feel the space shrink even more—and then my brain screamed at me.

Stop. Focus.

I pulled back, heart hammering, pulse racing, hands gripping the edge of the table for support. The air between us still hummed, electric and alive, daring me to try again, daring me to stay frozen, daring me to let her see how much of me she had captured.

Her gaze stayed locked on mine, eyes wide and bright. She swallowed, the motion small but deliberate. A faint flush crept along her neck, disappearing under her shirt.

She leaned back enough to put a little distance between us, tilting her head as if to regain composure, but her shoulders stayed slightly forward, betraying her curiosity.

Her eyes flicked away for a fraction of a second, then back to mine, as she fought for control. The smallest, reluctant smile tugged at her lips before she masked it with a deep breath.

"Right," Emma said, her voice breathless, rough around the edges with emotion she didn't fully hide. "Station layouts. Where were we?"

We worked for another hour, occasionally interrupted by particularly loud shouts from the gym. Emma's phone buzzed around five-thirty, and her expression shifted as she read the message.

"Kline just emailed. We are down to a hundred and fifty dollars because he's hiring a motivational speaker for the next faculty meeting."

"One hundred and fifty?" I pulled up our current budget spreadsheet. "That's—"

"Impossible," Emma finished. "It will barely cover basic supplies."

I stared at the numbers, mind racing through calculations. "What if we borrow equipment instead of buying? Ask local businesses for donations?"

"We're already borrowing from all of our feeder schools." Emma was already making notes. "But we could ask for donations."

"Maybe a fundraiser."

We looked at each other, and despite the setback, I grinned. "We can work through this."

"Yeah," Emma agreed, smiling back. "We can."

The next hour flew past. We divided tasks, assigned responsibilities, created backup plans for our backup plans.

Emma spread her diagrams across the table without apology. I added purple highlighter to my color-coding system without realizing I'd done it.

The sounds from the gym faded as Pat's practice ended, replaced by the distant echo of the custodial staff on their evening rounds.

When my stomach growled audibly around six-thirty, Emma didn't even look up from her sketches.

"Pizza?" she suggested.

"Is there a place that delivers here?"

"Mario's. They know the school address by heart." She was already pulling up the number on her phone. "What do you want?"

"Whatever you're having is fine."

She gave me a look. "Max. You're allowed to have preferences."

"I know. I just..." I shrugged. "I'm not picky about food."

"Everyone's picky about pizza," she set her phone down, studying me with that particular intensity that made me feel simultaneously seen and exposed. "What do you like?"

The question felt heavier than it should. What did I like? Not what was easiest, not what avoided conflict, not what let me fade into the background of whatever foster home I'd been in that month.

What did Max Harrison, human being, actually want?

"Pepperoni," I said. "And mushrooms. But if you don't like them, I don't have to —"

"I love mushrooms." Emma's smile was warm. "See? That wasn't so hard."

She ordered while I cleared space on the small table, moving our planning documents to her desk. When the pizza arrived twenty minutes later and buzzed Emma's phone, she went down to get it, and we ate straight from the box, grease staining our fingers.

"Tell me about Mr. Bednarz," Emma said between bites. "Your mentor teacher. The one who helped you."

I set down my pizza, surprised by the question. "What do you want to know?"

"Everything. What made him different?"

I thought back to my junior year of high school, which was the third school I'd attended within two years. "He was my chemistry teacher. I was failing because I never did my homework. I couldn't focus in any of my foster placements; they were too chaotic. But I aced every test, every lab. He noticed."

"He saw you were smart."

"He saw I was struggling." The distinction mattered. "He started letting me do homework in his room after school. He started keeping healthy snacks in his classroom closet. He never made me feel bad about it. I was a student worth investing in."

Emma's eyes had gone soft. "He sounds wonderful."

"He wrote my college recommendation letters. Helped me apply for scholarships. Came to my high school graduation." My throat tightened. "He's why I'm here. Why I care so much about the grant. That fifty thousand dollars would help kids like me. Kids who just need someone to see them."

"Max." Emma reached across the table, her hand covering mine. "That's beautiful. I'm sorry I dismissed it."

"You didn't dismiss it. You pointed out its flaws." I turned my hand over, lacing our fingers together. The contact sent electricity up my arm. "I was so focused on academic outcomes that I forgot about the actual kids. You reminded me that both things matter."

"We're better together," Emma said softly.

"Yeah." I squeezed her hand. "We are."

Her hand stayed in mine, thumb tracing slow, deliberate circles against my palm. Heat radiated up my arm and pooled in my chest, my heart hammering in a rhythm that was too fast and too slow.

Her breathing was shallow, quick, each tiny inhale stirring something tight in my stomach. Her pulse fluttered at the base of her throat, that delicate hollow where her neck met her collarbone, and my fingers twitched, wanting to follow the line of her arm, but I froze, aware of how close we already were.

She shifted, leaning a fraction closer, and her sleeve brushed mine. My own arm reacted before my brain, hairs rising, muscles coiling. Her thumb pressed a little harder against my palm, tentative, testing the line between comfort and something more carnal. It echoed through me, that subtle pulse of intent, and my chest tightened again.

Her eyes flicked to mine, then down, then back, as if she were struggling to stay composed while still letting me see her. Her lips parted for a breath she didn't take, and I imagined how soft they might feel against my skin. Every movement, every brush of contact, every small sound she made amplified the tension until the air itself snapped. I wanted to lean in and close the six inches between us.

But I didn't.

"Max," she said, my name barely more than a whisper.

"Yeah?" My voice came out rougher than intended.

"Should we finish..." She swallowed, not finishing the sentence, but she wasn't pulling her hand away either.

I turned my hand over slowly, deliberately, lacing our fingers together. Her breath caught. The small sound went straight through me.

"Should we what?" I asked, even though I knew what she meant. We should focus on work. Remember we were colleagues in her office at school.

Emma's gaze dropped to our joined hands, then back to my face. Her cheeks were flushed now, her eyes dark. "I don't know anymore... Max?"

"Yeah?"

"About Wednesday. When we—" She gestured vaguely. "When we kissed. I don't want to pretend it didn't happen."

My pulse thundered in my ears. "I don't want to pretend either."

"But we're working together. And if we—if this—" She made another helpless gesture. "I don't want to mess up our working relationship."

"Neither do I." I took a breath, letting her hand go and forced myself to think rationally. "We should keep things professional. At least until after STEM Field Day."

"That makes sense." Emma nodded, but she looked as disappointed as I felt. "Professional. Colleagues. Partners on a project."

"Exactly."

"So we agree?"

"Completely agree."

I was glad we'd talked it out. Now we could move forward. It was logical. Necessary. The sensible outcome of two adults addressing a problem instead of letting it fester. I told myself that meant the tension would ease, that the air would thin back out, that my pulse would slow and everything would fall neatly back into place.

That was how it was supposed to work.

But even as I clung to the comfort of that reasoning, I was aware of how close she still was, how her hand hadn't quite let go of mine, how the room hadn't expanded the way logic said it should. Moving forward didn't mean moving away. And the realization sat there quietly, unsettling and undeniable.

I leaned closer.

"Max," Emma whispered. "We said—"

I paused millimeters from her mouth, close enough to feel her breath against my lips. The pink softness called to me in a way I couldn't resist, couldn't rationalize, couldn't control.

My voice came out rougher than intended. "I know what we said. Tell me to stop, and I will."

But instead of pulling back, she closed the distance. Kissing me softly at first. Her mouth warm against mine. Emma's free hand came up to cup my jaw. I tasted the cherry chapstick on her lips, heard the slight catch of her breath when I traced the seam of her mouth with my tongue. She opened for me with a soft sound that went straight to my gut, and suddenly tentative became desperate.

Our joined hands tightened, knuckles white with the force of it. My other hand found her waist, pulling her closer across the small table. Papers scattered. Something clattered to the floor. Neither of us cared.

Emma's tongue met mine, and I was drowning in the taste of her, the feel of her, the small needy sounds she was making against my mouth. This was nothing like our kiss in the science closet. This was deliberate. Conscious. A choice we were both making with full awareness. No matter the consequences.

But I didn't care. Couldn't care. Not when she was kissing me like I was oxygen and she'd been holding her breath for weeks.

Emma pulled back just far enough to breathe, her forehead resting against mine. "We're bad at the professional thing."

"Spectacularly bad." I ran my thumb along her jaw, marveling that I was allowed to touch her like this. "We should stop."

"We absolutely should." She kissed me again, deeper this time.

I stood, the chair scraping against the floor. Emma rose with me, and suddenly we were pressed together in the tiny space between the table and her desk. Her back hit the edge of the desk. My hands found her waist. She made a sound low in her throat that shot straight through me.

"Max," she breathed against my mouth.

"Emma." I kissed along her jaw, down her neck. She tilted her head back, giving me access, her fingers threading through my hair.

"The door is unlocked," she managed.

I pulled back enough to look at her. Her lips were swollen, cheeks flushed, eyes dark with want. She was the most beautiful thing I'd ever seen.

"Lock it," I said.

Emma stared at me for a heartbeat. Then she moved past me to the door, flipping the lock with a soft click that sounded impossibly loud in the quiet office.

She turned back to face me, leaning against the door. "This is a terrible idea."

"The worst." I crossed the small space to her. "We work together."

"Yes." Her fingers found the top button of my shirt.

"We're planning a major school event." I let her work the button free.

"We are." She moved to the next one.

I braced my hands on either side of her head, caging her against the door. "And we just agreed to keep things professional."

"We did." Her hands slid inside my open shirt, pushing it off my shoulders.

"Tell me to go, and I will." I found the hem of her polo, my fingers grazing the bare skin beneath.

Emma's hands came up to grip my shirt, pulling it down my arms. "Don't go."

I lifted her polo slowly, breaking eye contact only long enough to pull it over her head. She reached for my belt as I tossed the shirt aside, her breath coming faster. My hands found the button of her jeans while she worked my belt free, our movements growing more urgent even as we maintained that careful choreography—professional colleagues who'd stopped pretending.

The kiss this time was desperate. Hungry. Weeks of tension and arguing and trying not to notice each other exploded out of control.

The practical, hot pink sports bra she wore devastated me. My mouth went dry.

"You're staring," Emma said, but she was smiling.

"You're beautiful."

Her smile softened into something more vulnerable. "Max—"

I kissed her before she could second-guess this, before either of us remembered all the reasons this was complicated. My hands mapped the curve of her waist, the softness of her skin, the strength in her shoulders. She was a contradiction—tough and soft, confident and uncertain, everything I hadn't known I needed.

Emma's fingers dug into my shoulders, pulling me impossibly closer. I lifted her onto the desk in one motion. Papers scattered. Neither of us cared.

She wrapped her legs around my waist, the friction making us both gasp. Her hands found my belt, working at the buckle with urgent fingers.

"This is insane," Emma breathed. "We're in my office. At school."

"I know." I kissed down her neck, across her collarbone, feeling her pulse racing against my lips. "Want me to stop?"

"God, no." She got my belt undone, her fingers fumbling with the button of my pants, each brush of her knuckles making me harder.

I reached behind her, unhooking her bra with hands that shook. When I pulled it away, I had to look for a moment. Emma flushed under my gaze, starting to cross her arms.

"Don't," I said, catching her wrists. "You're perfect."

"I'm not—"

"Perfect," I repeated, lowering my mouth onto her breast. She tasted like salt and something sweet, and when I circled her nipple with my tongue, she arched into me with a moan she quickly muffled with her hand.

Right. We had to be quiet. The gym was empty now, but custodial staff were in the building. Charlie made rounds around seven.

I glanced at my watch. Six forty-five.

"We don't have long," I murmured against her skin, my breath making her shiver.

"Then stop talking." Emma's hands were urgent now, pushing my pants down my hips, her palm grazing me through my boxers in a way that made my vision blur.

I helped her with her athletic shorts, pulling them and her underwear off in one motion. The sight of her, flushed and wanting, and spread out on the desk for me, almost made me lose it right there.

"Wait," I managed, voice strained. "I don't have—do you have—"

"Desk drawer." Emma's cheeks flushed deeper. "Left side, under the sticky notes. Don't ask why."

I reached over, fumbling through the drawer until my fingers found the small box. "Emma Bennett. Prepared for everything."

"Shut up." But she was smiling, breathless, her hand wrapping around me and making me forget whatever smartass comment I'd been about to make. "I'm a PE teacher. We have to teach health class sometimes. They give us samples for—just hurry up."

I made quick work of it, hands shaking as Emma's fingers traced patterns on my thighs that were going to drive me insane.

I pulled her to the edge of the desk, and she guided me with urgent hands, her eyes locked on mine. "Please, Max."

I kissed her as I pressed into her, swallowing her gasp. We both froze for a moment, the sensation overwhelming—the heat, the tightness, the intimacy of it.

"Okay?" I managed, barely holding still when every instinct screamed at me to move.

"More than okay." Emma's legs tightened around me, her heels digging into my lower back. "Move. Now."

I did. We found a rhythm quickly, desperately, both of us chasing something that had been building since that first disastrous meeting in Kline's office. Emma's nails raked down my back. I buried my face in her neck to muffle the sounds I couldn't quite control, tasting the salt on her skin.

"Harder," she gasped, and I complied, changing the angle, hitting deeper.

"Emma—fuck—" I couldn't form coherent sentences anymore.

"Max," Emma gasped, her inner walls starting to flutter around me. "I'm—oh God—"

"I know. So do I." I changed the angle, and she made a sound that would've been loud if she hadn't bitten down on my shoulder to stifle it, her teeth sinking in hard enough that I knew I would feel it tomorrow.

We came together, her body clenching around me in waves as I pulsed inside her, both of us clinging to each other and shaking with the force of it. For a moment, there was just breathing and heartbeats and the smell of her shampoo mixing with sweat and sex.

Reality crashed back in slowly.

We were in Emma's office. At school. Where we'd had sex on her desk like teenagers who couldn't wait.

I started to pull back, but Emma's arms tightened around me. "Don't. Not yet."

"Okay." I pressed a kiss to her temple, her cheek, her lips—soft and slow this time. "You okay?"

"I'm..." Emma laughed breathlessly. "I have no idea what I am. That was..."

"Yeah." I stroked her hair back from her face, still trying to slow my racing heart.

"We can't do this again."

"Definitely not."

"Someone could've heard or tried the door."

"I know."

Neither of us moved.

Finally, Emma loosened her grip, and I stepped back. We both winced at the loss of contact, then started the awkward process of finding clothes and getting dressed in the cramped space.

Emma pulled her polo back on inside-out. I reached out, catching her hand before she could grab her shorts.

Misunderstanding, she kissed me—hot and deep and making me want to say screw the custodian and take her again right there.

"Emma. Your shirt."

"I'm not taking it off again for you." She smiled then glanced down, saw the tag sticking out at her neck, and turned scarlet. "Oh my God."

"Here." I helped her pull it off and turn it right side out, trying not to get distracted by the flash of her sports bra again, by the marks I'd left on her breasts. Failed completely.

Emma caught me looking and shook her head, a smile tugging at her lips even as her pupils dilated. "Focus, Harrison."

"Trying." I handed her the corrected shirt and looked away while she dressed, forcing myself to find my own clothes and not think about how she'd felt wrapped around me.

Her hair had come free of its ponytail, falling in waves around her shoulders. I didn't look much better—shirt wrinkled, lips swollen, visible bite mark on my shoulder that I'd have to explain to Eli somehow.

We looked like exactly what we were: colleagues who'd lost control.

"So," Emma said, once we were dressed, "Professional partners."

"Nailed it," I agreed.

She laughed, then clapped a hand over her mouth. "We're disasters."

"Complete disasters." I reached out, unable to resist touching her, my fingers grazing her jaw. "But I don't regret it."

"Me neither." She leaned into my touch. "We clearly can't keep doing this here, though. But..." Her eyes met mine. "I don't want to pretend this didn't happen."

A smile spread across my face. "Neither do I."

"So let me take you to dinner. Properly. Friday night?"

"Friday's four days away." She stepped closer, her body brushing mine and making me want her all over again. "That's a long time to pretend we're just colleagues planning a field day."

"True." I caught her hand, pressing a kiss to her palm, then her wrist, feeling her pulse jump. "But it gives us time to figure out how to not be complete disasters about this."

"Also true." She looked up at me, and something soft crossed her face. "Okay. Friday. Pick me up at seven?"

"I'll be there at 6:55."

"Of course you will." She was grinning now. "Let me guess, you'll have the whole evening planned down to the minute?"

"I'll try to leave room for spontaneity."

"Dr. Max Harrison? Spontaneous? I'll believe it when I see it."

A bang from somewhere in the building made us both jump. Footsteps in the hallway—Charlie was starting his rounds.

"We should go," Emma said. "Separately. You first. I'll clean up here and leave in ten minutes."

"Okay." I hesitated at the door, then pulled her in for one more kiss—slow and deep and full of promise. "Emma?"

"Yeah?" She was breathless again.

"This—what we're doing—I don't take it lightly. I need you to know that."

Her expression softened. "I know. Me neither."

I unlocked the door, checked that the hallway was clear, and slipped out. My car was on the opposite side of the building from the gym. I walked quickly, trying to look like a teacher leaving after a normal planning session.

My phone buzzed as I reached the parking lot.

Emma: Forgot to mention—you left a hickey on my collarbone.

I typed back: **You bit my shoulder hard enough to leave teeth marks. Worth it.**

Her response was immediate: **Friday feels very far away.**

Me: Want to meet for lunch tomorrow? Two colleagues discussing STEM Field Day over sandwiches.

Emma: You're going to be terrible at keeping this quiet, aren't you?

Me: Probably. See you tomorrow, Emma.

Emma: See you tomorrow.

I sat in my car for a moment, trying to process what had happened. I'd had sex with Emma Bennett. My colleague. The woman I was rapidly falling for despite every rational reason to take things slow.

But instead of feeling panicked or regretful, I felt... good. Right. Like I'd done something that wasn't carefully calculated and controlled.

Four days until Friday. I could make it four days.

Maybe.

Chapter 9: Emma

I NOTICED THE WARM, bitter scent of Max's morning brew mixed with the natural smell of aged wood and brick as we entered his house on Friday night.

We'd spent three hours at Baci and Basilico, a small Italian place just outside Marchfield where we'd talked about everything except Field Day. His childhood in Boston, my summers with Mom. His decision to teach instead of doing research, my realization that coaching was more fulfilling than competing. The conversation had flowed so easily that I'd barely noticed the restaurant emptying around us until the owner had gently suggested we might want to continue our evening elsewhere.

"INTRUDER!" Darcy's voice echoed from the kitchen as we entered. "STRANGER DANGER!"

"Darcy," Max said. "It's me."

“DR. DOOOOOOM!” the parrot shrieked, followed it with a few notes of Darth Vader’s theme song.

We moved through a wide archway separating the living room and the kitchen, which flowed past butcher block counters, to a large window overlooking the street below. Next to the window sat an elaborate cage.

"Hi, Darcy," I laughed.

The parrot tilted his head, considering. "EMMA! KISS KISS!"

While I patted and crooned at Darcy, Max poured two glasses of wine, and we went back to the living room. It was a little messy but comfortable. Lived-in. The kind of place where you wanted to relax instead of worrying about messing something up.

The space still held traces of its past life as a train station. The exposed bricks showed the outline of where old signage had hung. The windows were tall and arched. They would have once looked out onto platforms where commuters rushed to catch their trains. Now they overlooked a quiet residential street, but the vintage glass still had that slight waviness that came with age.

The floors were scarred and weathered but beautifully maintained, creaking softly as we walked. Above us, the tin ceiling tiles created geometric patterns, painted white now but showing their ornate pressed designs. I imagined the echo of footsteps and announcements that once filled this space.

Max had made it a home, though. The built-in bookshelves were crammed with a chaotic mix of science texts, novels, and what appeared to be an entire collection of *Calvin and Hobbes*. Papers were stacked on the coffee table next to a forgotten mug. A throw blanket was bunched up on one end of the deep black leather couch.

"It's not much," Max said, handing me a glass. "But it's home."

"It's perfect," I said, turning in a slow circle to take it all in. "An old train station. That's amazing. When was it converted?"

"1920s building, renovated about ten years ago. The owners kept as much of the original character as possible." He gestured to the ceiling. "Those tin tiles are original. So are the floors and the brick. They rented it to me when they moved back to Richmond. They'd let me buy it, but I'm not sure if I'm staying in Marchfield long term."

My stomach did an uncomfortable flip, the kind that came from old instincts I'd never quite shaken. Of course. Max was brilliant, ambitious, MIT-educated. Marchfield Middle School was a stepping stone to something bigger, and I knew he wanted that grant. People like him didn't stay put. They passed through.

Just because I was planning to teach in this town until they carried me out in a box didn't mean Max would want the same thing.

"Makes sense," I said, keeping my voice light, the way I'd learned to when the ground felt unsteady. "Keep your options open."

"You know how it is," he said. "If you want to make a real difference, you have to go where you're needed."

It was the same thing he'd said at dinner when I'd asked why he chose teaching. Then, it seemed noble. Now is was a warning—like the first crack in something I hadn't realized I was bracing myself against.

“Of course.” I forced a smile, wrapping both hands around my wine glass, anchoring myself to the cool weight of it. “I’m lucky. Marchfield is where I’m needed.”

Something flickered across his face—surprise, maybe?—but he didn’t push. He nodded and settled onto the couch, leaving space for me to join him. I sat on the opposite end, leaving space between us. Easier to exit if I needed to.

“Maybe I should go,” I said. I didn’t want to, but the warmth from dinner, the easy conversation had gone brittle. Or maybe that was just me, already rehearsing how to leave before someone else decided to.

“Emma.” Max set down his wine glass. “I didn’t mean—” He ran a hand through his hair, frustrated. “I’m terrible at this. I meant I don’t own the place, not that I’m actively planning to leave. And definitely not that I want you to leave right now.”

The honesty in his voice stopped me from standing. It took a second for my body to catch up, to believe him.

“I’ve been in Marchfield for three years,” he continued, “And yeah, part of me always thought it was temporary. But...” His eyes met mine. “Lately I’m not so sure what I want anymore.”

The knot in my chest loosened, though it didn’t disappear. Uncertainty had never been neutral to me—it was something that could turn on you if you weren’t careful.

“Lately?” I echoed, quieter this time.

"Since about Monday afternoon." A small smile tugged at his mouth. "When a certain PE teacher kissed me in my classroom and completely upended everything I thought I knew about my plans."

“We should talk about that.”

"We should," Max agreed. He set down his wine glass and turned to face me fully. "I'll go first. I like you, Emma. A lot. More than I ever expected I would—especially after we spent two years barely tolerating each other."

I looked at him in surprise. "I never—"

"You absolutely did." His smile was soft, almost teasing. "Remember that faculty meeting where you suggested part of the science department's budget should be redirected to actual physical education?"

"I only said that because you said gym class was organized recess." I set my wine glass down with more force than necessary, feeling heat creep up my neck.

"And you told me I couldn't run a mile without stopping." He was grinning now, leaning back against the couch like he enjoyed this.

"Could you?" I challenged, with a grin.

"That's not the point." He leaned forward. "The point is, we've been circling each other for two years, convinced the other person was the enemy. And maybe at first we were—we wanted different things, we had opposite approaches to everything."

He rubbed the back of his neck, a gesture I was learning meant he was working through something difficult. "But somewhere in the last few weeks, that changed. The arguments stopped feeling like battles and started feeling like... I don't know. Like the best part of my day."

His eyes met mine, direct and honest. "I know we work together. But I don't want to pretend Monday didn't happen, or that I don't want to see where this goes."

I slid closer, reached out and took his hand. "I'm not great at this, Max. Relationships. I tend to get too focused on work or too competitive."

"Emma." He squeezed my fingers, his thumb tracing circles on my palm. "In case you haven't noticed, I'm the same way."

"Okay, so we're both disasters."

"Complementary disasters." He tugged me closer. "Look, I'm not expecting perfect. I'm not even expecting easy. But I think we are good at figuring it out together."

I looked at our joined hands, his thumb still moving in those slow circles. "What if we're terrible at it? What if we fight all the time?"

"We already fight all the time," he pointed out. "At least now we can make up properly."

He leaned into me, his free hand coming up to cup my jaw, tilting my face toward his. His thumb brushed across my cheekbone, and I felt the warmth of his breath against my lips as he closed the distance between us. The kiss started gentle, tentative, like we were still figuring out this new territory. Then his fingers threaded into my hair at the nape of my neck, and I melted into him, my hand sliding up his chest to grip his shoulder.

"KISS KISS!" Darcy announced from the kitchen.

We broke apart, laughing. The parrot had perfect timing.

"I'm going to cover his cage," Max muttered.

"Don't you dare. He's our chaperone."

"Our extremely loud chaperone." But Max was smiling as he kissed me again, deeper this time.

My hands found their way to his hair, then his shoulders, then under the hem of his shirt. His skin was warm under my fingers, and when he made a soft growl against my mouth, power surged through me.

"Emma," he breathed. "We should—"

"Bedroom?" I suggested.

"Yes. God, yes."

He stood, pulling me up with him, and led me down a short hallway. The bedroom walls were more exposed brick, this time painted a deep charcoal gray. A vintage reading lamp with a brass base sat on the nightstand with a pile of books. Two tall windows were covered with gauzy linen curtains in soft white that would filter the morning light perfectly. A thick charcoal colored duvet was smoothed across a queen-sized bed.

No random pile of laundry on the floor, no mismatched furniture. Just clean lines, warm textures, and the kind of space that makes you want to spend an entire Sunday tangled up in those sheets.

And suddenly I was nervous.

It was different from before. That had been impulsive. Frantic tension snapped. This was deliberate. Chosen. A door we were walking through together with full knowledge of what it meant.

Max seemed to sense my hesitation. His hands settled on my hips, steadying but not pushing. "Hey. Where'd you go?"

"I'm just..." I forced a laugh. "This is different. Monday was—"

"Impulsive?"

"Yeah. And this is..."

"A choice." He said it gently. "One we're both making. But, Emma, if you want to slow down—"

"I don't." The certainty in my voice surprised even me. "I really don't."

But he still took his time. His hands slid under my shirt, warm against my ribs, and when I shivered, he paused. "Cold?"

"No. Definitely not cold."

He pulled my shirt over my head slowly, deliberately, his eyes never leaving mine. There was something different in his gaze tonight, not the frantic need from Monday, but something deeper. Intent.

His mouth traced a slow path down my neck, across my collarbone, lower. I arched into him, my fingers tangling in his hair. His hands mapped my sides, my back, learning the curve of my spine, and I moaned out loud as he explored my sensitive breasts.

When he reached behind me to unhook my bra, he did it slowly, one hook at a time as he continued to press kisses against my nipples. And when the fabric fell away, I gasped, my nails digging into his shoulders as his lips claimed me, his fingers tracing patterns on my skin.

I couldn't tell if I wanted him to go faster or never stop.

And somewhere in the deliberate slowness, in the way he looked at me like I was something precious—not wanted but valued, not just desired but cherished—the last of my nervousness transformed into something else entirely.

And gave me power.

The realization that I made this brilliant, composed man completely come undone with a touch. I ran my hands down his chest, feeling his muscles tense under my fingers, the rapid beat of his heart beneath my palm. His skin was warm, smooth over hard muscle, and I took my time exploring. The ridges of his abs. The hollow at the base of his throat where his pulse jumped.

When I traced the line of his collarbone with my tongue, he sucked in a sharp breath, his hands tightening on my waist. I did it again, slower this time, and he trembled.

"Emma." It wasn't quite a plea, but it was close.

I kissed along his jaw, feeling the scratch of stubble against my lips. Found the spot just below his ear that made him grip me harder. Bit gently at his earlobe and he shuddered, his fingers digging into my hips, pulling me closer until every inch of him was pressed against me.

His control was fracturing. In the tension of his shoulders, in the way his breath came faster, and in the low sound he made when I rolled my hips against his.

"God, Emma—" My name came out strangled, desperate.

I smiled against his neck, enjoying this too much. The power of knowing exactly what I was doing to him. The heat building between us, slow and deliberate and so much better than Monday's frantic rush.

I smiled against his neck, pressing my body flush against his, and was rewarded with a low groan that I felt as much as heard.

My fingers worked the button of his pants and lowered the zipper carefully over the bulge. His pants fell to the floor, followed by his boxers. And there he was. Magnificent, proud, and big enough to make my knees weak.

Teasing the head of his cock with my tongue, I slowly spread my lips over him before taking him deep into the back of my throat.

A rough sound tore from Max's chest, and I smiled around him at the sound, his pleasure becoming mine. Easing back a little, I drew him out of my mouth only to take him deep again.

His fingers caught in my hair, and he tugged the clip that held it back off, wrapping the strands about his hands. I could feel him losing control. The growl in the back of his throat became more urgent until he lifted me off my knees, and we staggered the few paces to the bed.

Pushing him onto his back, I straddled him, my eyes on his. His hands flew to my hips, gripping hard enough to leave marks, steadying and urging at once. The control he'd been maintaining, that careful deliberateness, was starting to crack.

Good.

"Let me," I said, echoing his earlier words. My hands were already at work, stroking his chest and bringing his shirt up with me. He ripped it over his head, and I let myself look.

He was all lean muscle and golden skin in the lamplight. Broader through the shoulders than I'd realized, with that defined chest that tapered down to a narrow waist. A light dusting of dark hair across his pecs, trailing down his stomach in a line that disappeared into his jeans. The kind of body that came from someone who actually moved—running, playing basketball, living—not from vanity hours at a gym.

"Where have you been hiding this six pack, Dr. Harrison?" I teased, running my fingers along the defined lines of his abs.

He laughed, a little breathless. "Under button-downs and lab coats, apparently."

"Criminal." I traced the V of muscle that disappeared into his waistband. "Absolutely criminal. Do the other science teachers know about this?"

"Pretty sure Bobby suspects. We play basketball sometimes."

"And you never thought to mention it?" My hands explored the broad plane of his chest, the curve of his shoulders.

"Didn't think you'd care." His voice had gone rough. "You made it pretty clear you thought I was a nerdy science teacher who couldn't run a mile."

"I was wrong." I pressed my palm flat against his stomach. "So wrong."

"Emma—" He reached for me, but I leaned back, just out of reach.

His hands dropped, fisting in the sheets beside him. "You're killing me."

"Good."

"Yes." The word came out rough, almost desperate. "God, yes."

He did. His hands fell away, letting me set the pace, even though the tension grew in every muscle as he held himself still. Waiting. Watching me with an intensity that should have made me self-conscious but instead made me feel powerful. Wanted.

I took my time, learning what made his breath catch—my nails dragging lightly down his sides. What made his fingers dig into the sheets—my teeth grazing the sensitive skin above his hip bone. What made him say my name like a prayer—when I kissed along that defined V of muscle, lower and lower.

When his hands found my waist, fingers sliding to the zipper at my side, he dragged it down, his knuckles brushing my skin. I backed off him and let the skirt fall in a whisper of fabric around my feet. I stepped out of it, standing before him in just my granny panties, and saw his eyes go dark.

"Beautiful," he breathed.

I glanced down at the unsexy cotton underwear. "Really? Because these are my comfort-over-style panties."

He laughed, pulling me back toward him. "I don't care if they're from a discount bin at Target. You're still the sexiest woman I've ever seen."

"They literally might be from a discount bin at Target."

"Even better." His hands slid up my thighs. "Practical. Functional. Very you."

"Stop using my own words against me," I said, but I was grinning as I stepped out of the panties and pushed him back onto the bed.

He rolled to the side and tucked me in close. Pressing against me skin to skin, I moaned at the feel of him, his arms around me. The bulge of his need, pressing hard against my pelvis.

I lifted my leg, crooking my knee over his hip and aligning my wet pussy with his cock. Both of us held our breath.

"I saw the doctor on Wednesday..." we both started and then laughed.

"I'm clean and on the pill," I said.

"I'm clean, too. Does that mean?"

"Yes."

I gasped as he surged into me, filling me up and driving me mad with pleasure. His fingers dipped to circle my clit as his hips continued to stroke slow and smooth. I wrapped my arm around his shoulders and kissed him hard as pleasure washed over me.

The world narrowed—his breath against my neck, my name on his lips as we moved together. Every touch built on the last, slow and deliberate until neither of us held back anything.

Rolling to his back, he took me with him until I was straddling him again. My body arched up, his hands on my breasts, then slipping down to where we were joined. I rolled my hips, once, twice. Feeling the pleasure tightening inside me, bordering with pain before flashing like lightning outward.

Continuing to move together, he made a low sound in the back of his throat as I kissed him, deep and claiming. His body grew taut, every muscle tensing as we chased the edge together.

"Emma—" My name broke on his lips.

"I've got you," I whispered against his mouth. "Let go."

And he did. We both did.

WE SPENT THE REST OF the night learning about each other. What made him gasp, what made me arch, the rhythm we found together that was clumsy at first but quickly became something perfect. I'd expected good, based on the chemistry that had been sparking between us for weeks. But this was something more.

It was Max's laugh when we had to pause because my knee cramped—the way he massaged the muscle while pressing kisses to my ankle, my calf, my inner thigh, distracting me so thoroughly I forgot to be embarrassed.

It was the playful competition of switching positions, taking turns on top and grinning at each other with delight after each flip.

It was the way he looked at me as we moved together, like I was the answer to every question he'd ever asked.

And then he slipped a hand to the back of my knee and tickled the warm flesh there. I shrieked, laughter bursting out of me, the sound filling the room and mingling with his own delighted chuckle.

"STRANGER DANGER!" Darcy's voice shrieked from the kitchen. "INTRUDER! CALL 911!"

We froze, before dissolving into breathless laughter.

"That bird," Max managed, his forehead pressed to mine, "has the worst timing."

"He's jealous," I said, running my hands down Max's back. "DARCY, WE'RE FINE!"

"FINE! FINE! EVERYTHING'S FINE!"

"See?" I grinned. "He's reassured."

Max hugged me close, and when I mentioned heading home, he whispered against my shoulder, "Stay."

I pulled back just enough to see his face, finding his eyes soft and hopeful in the dim light. "I'd like that," I said, settling back into his arms.

I WOKE TO SUNLIGHT streaming through Max's bedroom window and his arm draped over my waist. For a moment, I lay there, savoring the weight of him against my back, the soft sound of his breathing, the unfamiliar but wonderful feeling of waking up in his space.

Then reality crept in around the edges of contentment.

What time was it?

A quick glance at the clock on the nightstand showed 9:47. Saturday morning. No school, no immediate obligations. Just... this. Us. The whole day stretching ahead with possibility.

The realization should have been relaxing, but instead my brain started spinning. What was the morning after protocol? Was I supposed to leave? Stay? Suggest breakfast? Wait for him to suggest it?

"I can hear you thinking," Max mumbled into my hair. "S'too early for thinking."

"It's almost ten."

"Lies. False. Morning doesn't start until..." He pressed a kiss to my shoulder. "At least noon on Saturdays."

Despite myself, I laughed. "That's not how time works."

"Should be." Another kiss, this one on the back of my neck, sending shivers down my spine. "Could make it a thing."

I turned in his arms, finding him rumpled and stubbled and somehow even more attractive than he'd been last night. "Good morning."

"Best morning," he corrected and kissed me.

Thirty minutes later, after we'd thoroughly christened his shower and used up all the hot water, I stood in Max's kitchen wearing one of his MIT t-shirts and nothing else, watching him attempt to make breakfast while Darcy provided running commentary.

"TOAST! BURN TOAST!" the parrot announced as smoke rose from the toaster.

"It's not burned," Max protested, popping up two decidedly dark pieces of bread. "It's well-done."

"CALL THE FIRE DEPARTMENT!"

We ate the burnt toast standing at his counter, stealing bites from each other's plates and trading lazy kisses that tasted like butter and coffee and Saturday morning freedom.

"So," Max said, setting down his mug. "What are your Saturday plans? Besides standing in my kitchen, looking unfairly good in my shirt."

I glanced down at the oversized MIT tee. "I should go home at some point. Change. Maybe pretend to be a responsible adult."

"Or," he said, pulling me closer by the hem of the shirt, "you could stay. Be irresponsible adults together."

"What does that look like?"

"I don't know. Farmers' market? Or order takeout and avoid all responsibilities." His hands settled on my hips. "Whatever you want."

What I wanted was to stay in this bubble where Field Day drama and budget cuts and the complicated reality of dating a coworker didn't exist. Where it was only us, figuring this out.

"Farmers' market sounds nice," I said. "But I really do need to go home and change first. I can't walk around town in your t-shirt and last night's underwear."

"Why not? I think it's a great look."

"Max."

"Fine." He pressed a kiss to my forehead. "But you're coming back, right? This isn't a polite exit?"

The vulnerability in his voice made my chest tighten. "I'm coming back. Give me an hour."

An hour later, I was back at my apartment, standing in front of my bathroom mirror in fresh clothes, trying to figure out if a scarf in May would look ridiculous.

Because there, right there on my neck just below my ear, was a purple mark that no amount of concealer was going to hide.

I pulled out my phone.

Emma: So. You gave me a hickey.

The typing bubble appeared immediately.

Max: Oh god. Really? I'm so sorry.

Emma: Don't apologize. I'm trying to decide if I can pull off a scarf at the farmers' market.

Max: In 75-degree weather?

Emma: Exactly my dilemma.

Max: Wear your hair down?

Emma: My hair is never down.

Max: I noticed. I like it down.

I looked at myself in the mirror again—hair loose around my shoulders, hiding the evidence of last night. It looked... different. Softer, maybe. Like someone who'd spent the night with a guy she liked instead of someone who was always buttoned-up and in control.

Emma: Fine. But you're buying me coffee at the market as compensation.

Max: Deal. And Emma?

Emma: Yeah?

Max: I'm not actually sorry.

I smiled at my phone, my reflection smiling back.

Neither was I.

Chapter 10: Max

FORTY-EIGHT HOURS.

That's how long Emma and I had existed in our own private bubble. Saturday at the farmers' market, where I'd caught her smelling every variety of heirloom tomato before making her selection, then bought her bright yellow sunflowers that matched the glow she'd had all morning.

We spent Sunday tangled up on my couch with kung pao chicken and fried rice, her feet in my lap while she tried to convince me that *Return of the Jedi* was better than *Empire*. I loved watching her argue—the way she got animated, using her chopsticks for emphasis, building her case about redemption and hope like she was defending a doctoral thesis. She was wrong, obviously, but I wasn't about to tell her that.

Now it was Monday morning, and the grant application was due by Friday. I should regret that I hadn't worked on it at all over the weekend. This grant was important, potentially the most important professional opportunity I'd had since moving to Marchfield. Fifty thousand dollars to develop a new curriculum would make a difference in so many ways.

But every time I'd considered opening my laptop this weekend, Emma had been there. Saturday morning, stealing my coffee and making Darcy sing show tunes. Sunday afternoon, napping with her head on my shoulder.

I didn't regret that. I wouldn't.

Though I was definitely going to regret it Friday at 11:59 PM if I didn't start writing now.

The cursor blinked at me from the blank document, mocking my complete inability to form a coherent sentence.

Describe how this grant will enhance STEM education at your school.

Right. STEM education. Renewable energy. Student outcomes. All the things that had seemed critically important on Friday afternoon, before

Emma had smiled at me across a plate of pasta and asked about my life in Boston.

I'd spent three years building toward this. Collecting student engagement data, attending every professional development workshop the district offered, refining my renewable energy curriculum until I could teach it in my sleep. It had all been leading to this grant, to bigger opportunities, to a career that mattered beyond Marchfield.

Except somewhere between Friday night and Sunday afternoon, I'd started wondering if leaving was really what I wanted anymore.

I typed: "The funds will allow us to expand our—"

My mind supplied: *expand our relationship beyond just weekends at my house*

Wrong answer, Harrison.

A knock interrupted my train of thought.

"Mr. Harrison?" Bethany Chen stood in my doorway, grinning like the Cheshire Cat. "Ms Bennett asked me to give you this." She handed me a sticky note with Emma's handwriting: *We need three more volunteers for the obstacle course. Ideas?*

"Thanks, Bethany."

"You're welcome." She didn't leave. "So... are you and Ms. Bennett, like, dating?"

"Bethany."

"Because everyone says you are. Maya saw you leaving together last Friday, and Tyler said—"

"Don't you have class?"

She giggled and disappeared down the hall.

I returned to the application.

The funds will allow us to expand our hands-on learning opportunities through—

"Yo, Max!" Eli appeared in my doorway, eating an apple. "Quick question. Are you banging Emma Bennett?"

I closed my laptop. "Who's watching your class?"

"Kendra is doing a guidance lesson with them. And you didn't answer my question."

"Because it's none of your business."

"So yes." My idiotic friend took another bite of the apple. "Interesting. Because I told you she was hot, like three months ago, and you went all self-righteous about professionalism."

Three months ago, Emma Bennett was my professional nemesis who'd made it her mission to undermine me every chance she got. Three months ago, I hadn't known what she looked like when she laughed, or how she took her coffee, or the sound she made when—

Focus, Harrison.

"I'm writing a grant application."

"You're writing an application while thinking about Emma Bennett naked. I can see it on your face."

"EMMA!" Darcy shrieked from his cage where he'd been feasting on seeds and fruit. "KISS KISS! EMMA KISS!"

Eli's grin turned predatory. "Even your bird knows."

I glared at Darcy. "Traitor."

They weren't wrong though. I'd tried to draft the section about collaborative teaching three times this morning, and every version somehow turned into a love letter about Emma's organizational skills, her laugh, the way she'd felt in my arms two nights ago—

I frowned. "Get out."

"You've got it bad, man." Eli tossed his apple core into my trash can from across the room. "Just saying."

After he left, I managed another paragraph before my planning period ended and class began. Eighth graders tumbled in noisily, and I dove into a lesson on chemical bonds that kept all of us occupied.

When the bell rang, students flooded into the hallway. I was erasing the whiteboard when I heard it.

"MAX AND EMMA SITTING IN A TREE!"

I froze.

"K-I-S-S-I-N-G!"

That was definitely Darcy, but why did he sound so far away?

I spun around. The parrot's cage door hung open, and Darcy was perched on the top of the door, ruffling his feathers with obvious pride.

"Darcy. Get back in your cage."

"FIRST COMES LOVE!"

"Darcy—"

"THEN COMES MARRIAGE!"

Students gathered, phones out, already recording.

"THEN COMES BABY IN A BABY CARRIAGE!"

I grabbed a chair and lunged for him, but Darcy shrieked with delight, launching into the air, swooping over my head and out into the hallway.

"SOMEBODY'S GETTING LAID!"

Oh God.

I chased him down the hallway, past a gaggle of freshmen who dissolved into hysterics. Darcy landed on a locker, tilted his head at me, and squawked, "MAX IS A TOTAL SNACK!"

"Where did you even learn that?" I growled as I made another grab for him.

This time he flew toward the auditorium wing. I followed, very aware that half the school was parading along behind me.

I rounded the corner as Emma appeared from the opposite direction.

"I heard shouting," she said, her voice breathless. "Was that—"

Darcy perched high up on top of one of the hallway clocks. "MAX LOVES EMMA!"

She looked at me. I looked at her.

"He escaped," I said.

"I can see that."

Darcy landed on the trophy case, preening. "EMMA AND MAX K-I-S-S-I-N-G!"

"Okay, that one's actually accurate," I muttered.

Emma's mouth twitched. "Focus, Harrison."

We moved in tandem, approaching from different angles. Darcy watched us with one beady eye, enjoying himself.

"On three," Emma whispered. "One... two..."

Darcy launched himself toward the auditorium doors before we reached three. We ran after him, pushing through into the dim space. The stage was empty, but Darcy's telltale squawks came from backstage.

"Dressing rooms," Emma said, pointing.

We slipped through the stage door into the narrow hallway lined with dressing rooms for the drama productions. Darcy's voice echoed off the walls: "PRETTY PRETTY PRETTY!"

"He's in there." Emma indicated the last door on the left, slightly ajar.

We crept forward. I could see Darcy through the crack, perched on the makeup counter, admiring himself in the mirror.

"You go left, I'll go right," I breathed.

Emma nodded. We eased the door open and split up, moving slowly, so we wouldn't spook him.

Darcy bobbed his head at his reflection. "SEXY BEAST!"

I was close enough to grab him when Emma's phone buzzed loudly in her pocket.

Darcy exploded into motion. I dove, Emma lunged, and somehow—miraculously—my hands closed around his feathery body.

"Got him!"

"POLICE! HELP!" Darcy shrieked.

Emma laughed, slightly breathless. "Nice catch."

"Thanks." I tucked Darcy securely against my chest, where he continued to protest loudly. "Though I think he's going to hold this against me."

We headed back through the auditorium, and I tried very hard not to notice how good Emma looked disheveled from the chase, or how close we were walking, or how easy it would be to drop the bird and—

"Mr. Harrison! Ms. Bennett!" Val Bellini's voice rang out across the hallway. "Did you catch the fugitive?"

"Got him," I called back, holding up Darcy.

The crowd of students and teachers cheered, all looking entertained by the chaos.

"I WANT A LAWYER!" Darcy yelled.

The crowd laughed, and I carried my dramatic parrot back to my classroom, Emma walking beside me.

"You know," she said as we reached the science wing, "Darcy has sealed the deal. Everyone knows or at least suspects now."

I looked down at the parrot, who blinked up at me innocently. "Yeah. He's thorough like that."

"I guess we stop pretending?" I met her eyes. "I mean, we weren't doing a great job of it anyway."

"No, we really weren't." She smiled. "Okay. No reason to pretend."

"No more pretending," I agreed. Then, because the hallway was still empty, and we were done being careful: "Can I kiss you goodbye?"

"In the science wing? Max Harrison, you rebel."

"You're a bad influence."

"The worst," she agreed, and kissed me quickly on the cheek before hurrying back to the gym.

Chapter 11: Emma

TUESDAY NIGHTS AT THE Barrel were ladies' night—half-price wine and appetizers, which made it the unofficial teacher decompression spot. I'd missed the last few get-togethers. Actually, I'd missed all of them since moving to Marchfield, always finding a reason to decline. Tonight's reason was laundry—I was down to my last clean sports bra and had a pile of clothes that really couldn't wait another day.

But Jen had cornered me after school with Talia in tow, and apparently "I have laundry" wasn't an acceptable excuse.

"You can do laundry tomorrow," Jen had said, linking her arm through mine like we'd been friends for years instead of polite colleagues for months. "Tonight, you're coming out with us. No more excuses."

"We've been asking for weeks," Talia had added, falling into step on my other side. "At this point, we're starting to take it personally."

"I'm not—it's not personal," I'd protested. "I've been busy—"

"With Max Harrison," Talia had finished with a knowing grin. "Yes, we know. Everyone knows. But even lovebirds need to come up for air occasionally. And we need details."

So here I was, walking into The Barrel after school, following Jen's bright pink cardigan through the crowd of teachers and townspeople who apparently also knew that Tuesday was the night to be here.

The place smelled like wood smoke, craft beer, and the kind of comfort food that made you forget you had a meal plan. Exposed brick walls were decorated with vintage farming equipment and local art. A row of ax-throwing lanes lined one wall, separated from the dining area by chain-link fencing. Classic rock played just loud enough to fill the space without drowning out conversation.

"There!" Jen pointed to a high-top table near the back, already claimed with jackets and purses. "Perfect spot. We can see everything from here."

"So," Talia said, flagging down a server with the confidence of someone who'd done this a hundred times. "First round's on me. Emma, what are you drinking?"

"Um, whatever's cheap is fine."

"Wrong answer." Talia grinned. "This is ladies' night. We're getting the good wine. Jen, back me up."

"She's right," Jen said, scanning the wine list. "We're celebrating."

"Celebrating what?" I asked.

"Surviving Monday?" Talia laughed.

"It's Tuesday," I pointed out.

"We survived Monday *and* Tuesday. That deserves celebration."

The server appeared—a college-aged guy who clearly knew them both—and took our order. As he walked away, Talia leaned forward conspiratorially.

"Okay, so. Ground rules for ladies' night. One: no talking about school after the first round. Two: no checking work email. Three: what's said at The Barrel stays at The Barrel."

"Very Vegas," I said.

"Exactly." She clinked her water glass against mine. "Also, rule four: you have to tell us everything about you and Max Harrison."

"Come on, Emma. The whole school knows you're together. Give us the details."

"He's... surprisingly romantic," I admitted. "Like, he bought me sunflowers at the farmers' market because he noticed me looking at them. And he remembers how I take my coffee—which sounds small, but he pays attention to the details, you know? Most people don't."

Jen said warmly. "That's so sweet. You two are cute together."

"You're crazy about each other, which is lovely to watch."

Our drinks arrived, giving me a moment to breathe.

"Oh god," Talia said, her eyes going wide as she looked past me toward the entrance. "Incoming."

I turned to see Max walking in with Eli and Dante, the three of them scanning the room. Max spotted us immediately, his face lighting up in a way that made my stomach flip.

"I thought this was ladies' night," I said.

"It is," Jen confirmed. "But the guys show up around now and then. They pretend it's a coincidence."

"It's never a coincidence," Talia added. "They literally have a group chat called 'Barrel Tuesdays.'"

Max reached our table first, his hand finding my shoulder in that casual, comfortable way that still made me hyperaware of his touch. "Hey. Didn't know you were coming out tonight."

"Jen and Talia didn't give me a choice."

"Smart women." He looked at my nearly empty wine glass. "Having fun?"

"Getting there."

Eli appeared at Talia's other side, already flagging down the server. "Ladies. Looking lovely this evening. Are we doing appetizers or going straight to the good stuff?"

"We already ordered," Talia said. "You're on your own."

"Harsh. I thought we were friends."

"We are friends. That's why I'm not enabling your jalapeño popper addiction."

Dante pulled up a chair next to Jen, quiet as always, but his eyes were already scanning the room with that guidance counselor awareness that noticed everything.

"Busy tonight," he observed.

"Tuesday special brings them out," Jen said. "Half-price everything gets people through the door."

"Speaking of people—" Dante nodded toward the far corner near the windows. "Is that Val Bellini?"

We all turned to look, with varying degrees of subtlety.

Val was one of Marchfield's social studies teachers, and she was engaged to Evan Shurger, the tech ed teacher. They had fallen in love a few years before I started teaching in Marchfield, but I'd heard it had been a whirlwind romance.

Two older women sat with them, and even from across the restaurant, the tension was palpable. One woman wore an expensive silk blouse, had the same dark hair as Val, and was gesturing at something on her phone. The other woman had a smile pasted on her face. She had warm brown skin, high cheekbones, and long dark hair pulled back in a simple braid.

Val looked frustrated, and Evan appeared to be slowly dying inside.

"Are those their mothers?" Jen asked.

"Yep," Eli said. "That's definitely Mrs. Bellini. I'd recognize her 'I'm very important' energy anywhere."

"The other one's Evan's mom," Dante added. "She's sweet but don't count her out. Yona told me she has nerves of steel."

"Yona?" I asked. "The full-time substitute?"

Dante nodded. "Yeah, she and Evan go way back."

Mrs. Bellini turned her phone toward the table, clearly showing them something. Wedding venues? Invitation designs? Val's expression grew more strained. Evan looked like he wanted to bolt.

"God, imagine having your mom that involved in your relationship," Eli said. "That would be a nightmare."

"I don't know," Jen said. "My mom has opinions about everything I do, but at least she cares, you know? Some people don't have that."

"There's caring and then there's..." Talia gestured toward Val's table. "Whatever that is."

"Helicopter parenting taken to a terrifying extreme," Eli finished.

Jen groaned, "My mom keeps setting me up with her friends' sons. It's mortifying, but she wants me to be happy. To settle down, have a family."

"Did you tell her to back off?" Talia asked.

"Eventually. But it took a while. She means well, but she has this vision of what my life should look like, and sometimes it's hard to push back against that."

I took a long sip of wine, trying to ignore the uncomfortable tightness in my chest. The casual way they all talked about their parents, their families, made me wonder what Max was thinking? I snuck a look out from under my lashes at him.

"What about you, Max?" Talia asked. "Your parents give you relationship advice?"

The question hung in the air for half a beat too long.

"No," Max said, his voice carefully neutral. "That's not really their style."

The answer was smooth, practiced. Emma felt him shift beside her, the subtle tightening in his shoulders, the way his smile arrived a second too late. It wasn't avoidance so much as self-preservation, and she recognized it instantly. Some truths weren't meant for a table full of half-listening people and clinking glasses.

She wanted to reach for his hand under the table, to ground him, but her own fingers stayed curled in her lap. Because the truth was, she'd built the same reflex. Learned how to keep answers light, unremarkable. Learned how to make herself easy to sit with.

"Lucky you," Eli said, oblivious. "My mom calls every Wednesday. And I'm expected at dinner on Sunday night. It's exhausting."

"At least she asks," Jen said. "My dad won't even acknowledge that I date. As far as he's concerned, I'm still twelve and think boys are icky."

They all laughed. Max smiled when he was supposed to, but his eyes stayed guarded.

Emma took another sip of wine, the warmth spreading without quite reaching the knot in her chest. Listening to them talk about parents—too involved, not involved enough—made her feel suspended between categories, like there wasn't a box for the kind of family she had.

Across the table, Dante met her gaze. He didn't look curious. Just steady. Like he'd noticed the space she kept around certain words. He knew there was a story she was actively not telling.

"Emma," Talia said, turning to me. "You've never told us much about your parents."

My throat went tight. "Hands-off, definitely. My parents were arrested when I was ten. Drug charges. I was raised by my Aunt Stella."

The table went quiet for a beat. I took a sip of wine to fill the silence, trying to make it sound casual, like it didn't matter. Like I hadn't just dropped a bomb into the middle of their easy banter.

It wasn't the whole truth, but it was enough. Enough to deflect without revealing the messier parts—the different schools, the way I'd learned to pack light because we might move at any time. I'd learned early that needing people meant eventually being disappointed by them, so it was safer not to need anyone at all.

"It's okay." I gave them all a smile. "Aunt Stella was wonderful. She welcomed me in and hugged me tight, giving me a safe place to live."

"I love Stella." Talia took my hand and squeezed. "I'm buying her a gift the next chance I get because my mother is an evil harpy."

Across the restaurant, Val stood abruptly and headed toward the bathrooms. Mrs. Bellini's expression turned thunderous.

"Yikes," Eli muttered.

"That's going to be a fun conversation later," Talia said.

"More like a fight," Jen corrected.

The server arrived with our appetizers—wings, loaded fries, jalapeño poppers—and the conversation shifted to safer topics. But I couldn't shake the unease that had settled over me.

Max's hand found mine under the table, his thumb tracing circles on my palm. The gesture was comforting, and I wondered if he was thinking about how similar we were.

We'd spent hours together—talking, laughing, falling into bed. I knew about his past, but not the things that mattered. I knew he'd been in the foster program and gone to MIT. That he'd taught in Boston before coming to Marchfield, and he wanted the grant to help kids like him in the STEM program.

"You okay?" Max murmured, leaning close enough that the others couldn't hear.

"Yeah. Fine."

But I wasn't fine. Because I'd realized that what we were doing—this relationship, this thing between us—it was built on surface-level attraction and easy chemistry. We'd never gone deeper than that.

And I didn't know if we could.

Chapter 12: Emma

THE CONVERSATION MOVED on, and Jen and Dante steered it toward safer topics, something about a terrible movie they had seen. But the easy warmth from earlier had evaporated, replaced by something strained.

I took a long sip of wine, trying to settle the tightness in my chest. I shouldn't have said anything. Should've kept it light, deflected better. Now they all knew that I came from the kind of background people pitied, the kind that made them look at you differently. I could already feel it, the subtle shift in how everyone was looking at me. Not with judgment, which would've been easier to handle, but with that careful sympathy that made me feel like something fragile that might break if they said the wrong thing.

This was why I didn't share. Why I kept things surface-level and easy. Because once people knew your damage, they either treated you like you were broken or they ran. And I didn't know which was worse.

Across the restaurant, Val returned from the bathroom, said something short to the table, grabbed her purse, and walked out. Just left. Mrs. Bellini looked stunned. Evan half-stood, looking torn, then sat back down heavily.

"Well," Talia said, breaking the tension. "Who wants to throw some axes? Indulge in therapeutic violence?"

"Yes," I said. "Absolutely. Let's go throw sharp objects at things."

Perfect. Physical violence was what I needed right now. Something concrete and simple where the only goal was to hit the target and not kill anyone No emotional processing required. Just me, an ax, and a wooden bullseye that wouldn't look at me with sympathetic eyes.

"I'm in," Max said, standing up.

We migrated toward the back of the restaurant where the ax-throwing lanes were set up behind chain-link fencing. The space was significantly louder with music, laughter, and the solid thunk of axes hitting wooden targets.

Talia grabbed lanes for the group, and the attendant gave us a quick safety demo that mostly boiled down to: don't throw until the person in front of you has retrieved their ax and try not to kill anyone.

"Very reassuring," Max muttered.

I picked up an ax, testing the weight. It was heavier than I expected—maybe three pounds, the balance point somewhere near the middle of the handle. My coaching brain automatically kicked in, analyzing the mechanics of it. The throw would be all in the wrist and follow-through, similar to a free throw but with rotation. The attendant had made it look easy, but I could already see how technique would matter more than strength.

"You look like you're about to murder someone," Jen observed.

"Therapeutic violence, remember?" I stepped up to the line, gripped the ax the way the attendant had shown us, and threw.

It spun through the air and embedded itself in the outer ring of the target with a satisfying thunk.

"Not bad for someone with deep-seated abandonment issues," Talia called out.

"Too soon!" Jen swatted her.

"What? We're all thinking it. I'm just saying it out loud."

Max stepped up beside me, retrieving my axe and then grabbing his own. "Want to share a lane? We can take turns pretending we're okay."

Despite everything, I laughed. "That sounds healthy."

"Extremely healthy." He threw his axe. It hit closer to the center. "See? I'm processing my childhood trauma through sport."

"That's basically what all PE is."

"Explains a lot about dodgeball."

I took the axes from him. "Did you play any sports at MIT?"

"No, MIT students prefer intellectual competitions. Like who could go the longest without sleep during finals week." He watched me throw. The ax hit closer to the center this time. "I won sophomore year. Forty-three hours. Hallucinated that my physics professor was a sentient equation. Do not recommend."

"Forty-three hours? That's horrifying."

"It was MIT. Everything was horrifying." He retrieved both axes. "But at least no one asked about my family. Too busy asking about my theoretical framework for quantum mechanics."

"Is that why you came to Marchfield? To escape theoretical frameworks?"

"That and the Boston winters. Also..." He paused, lining up his throw. "I wanted to teach somewhere that actually needed good science teachers. Boston had plenty. Marchfield didn't."

"The noble educator," I said, throwing my ax. It bounced off the target entirely and clattered to the ground.

"I'm just a guy who wants to make a difference," he corrected, retrieving my runaway ax. "Also, that was a terrible throw."

"I'm emotionally compromised."

"Fair point." He handed me the ax. "Want to try again, or should we acknowledge that we're both disasters and call it a night?"

"We can be disasters who throw axes."

"I like that plan."

We threw in silence for a moment, the background noise of the restaurant providing cover. Eli and Talia were arguing about scoring. Dante was quietly correcting Jen's form. It was loud enough that we could talk without being overheard.

"So," Max said, retrieving our axes. "We have more in common than I originally thought."

The casual way he said it made my chest hurt. "Max—"

"It's fine. I'm fine. We're both well-adjusted." He threw his ax. It hit dead center. "See? Therapy through sport."

"You're really going to joke about this?"

"Would you prefer I cry? Because I can do that too, but it's less fun at a bar." He looked at me, his expression softening. "Emma, I learned a long time ago that if you don't laugh about the shitty stuff, you just end up drowning in it. So yeah, I'm going to joke. It's how I cope."

I understood that. God, did I understand that!

"My mom used to say the same thing," I said, lining up my throw. "After we'd move to a new place, she'd make me say one good thing about the move. Even if it was 'the new apartment has better water pressure' or 'the school mascot is less terrifying.'"

"What was the most terrifying mascot?"

"A fighting pickle. I'm not kidding. The Mooresville Fighting Pickles."

Max laughed, the sound genuine. "That's amazing."

"It was deeply unsettling." I threw my ax. It stuck this time, right near the center. "But Mom would turn everything into a game. She'd say 'we're not running away, we're running toward something better.'"

"Was she right?"

"No." I retrieved both axes. "The stakes just got higher, we were in so much debt. Scary men were coming after my dad, and then the police."

"My first family sent me back after three months because I didn't fit in with their biological children. The second one forgot to feed me regularly—that was fun. The third one..." He threw his ax harder than necessary. It embedded deep in the target. "Had a teenage son who thought I was a punching bag."

"Jesus, Max."

"I was moved out after six months. But I learned a valuable lesson: don't trust people to stick around." He retrieved his ax, then mine, handing it back to me. "And definitely don't need them. Because needing people means getting hurt when they inevitably leave."

"So what are we doing?" I asked. "If neither of us knows how to need people?"

"I have no idea." He leaned against the barrier between lanes. "But I like you, Emma. Which is terrifying and completely against my usual policy of emotional unavailability. So clearly you've broken me."

Despite everything, I smiled. "I'm pretty sure you broke me first."

"We can both be broken. We're an excellent matching set."

"The most dysfunctional matching set."

"Hey, at least we're self-aware about it." He stepped closer. "Look, I don't know what this is. I don't know if I'm staying in Marchfield long-term. The grant could change everything. But I know I don't want to lose this. Not yet."

"Even though we're both disasters?"

"Especially because we're both disasters. At least we're disasters together."

I threw my ax. It hit right next to his, dead center.

"Would you look at that," Max said. "We make a pretty good team."

"For two people with massive trust issues."

"The best kind of team."

From across the lanes, Eli shouted, "Max! Tell Talia that the bullseye counts for extra points!"

"It does not!" Talia yelled back.

"That's not how scoring works!" Jen added.

"Dante, back me up!" Eli called.

Dante just shook his head, staying out of it.

"We should intervene before someone gets hacked to bits," Max said.

"Probably." But I didn't move. "Max?"

"Yeah?"

"For what it's worth, I'm really glad you're here. Even if we're both terrible at this."

"Same." He bumped his shoulder against mine. "Now, let's go save Eli from Talia's wrath."

"You think we can?"

"Absolutely not. But it'll be fun to watch."

Chapter 13: Max

THE SPREADSHEET MOCKED me from my laptop screen. I'd color-coded everything. Green for confirmed expenses, yellow for possible cuts, red for essential items we couldn't eliminate. The problem was that almost everything was red, and our budget was $547 over a $100 limit.

Even if we eliminated prizes entirely and borrowed equipment, we were still screwed.

I took another sip of cold coffee and adjusted my calculations for the third time that hour. Maybe if we reduced the number of activities from eight to six?

My phone buzzed with text from Emma: **You awake?**

Of course, I was. I wasn't asleep because my brain refused to shut off, replaying the evening and everything I'd learned about Emma. And it left me with a warmth in my chest I didn't quite know what to do with.

I responded to her: **Unfortunately.**

Emma: Me too.

I'm trying to work on the budget for STEM Field Day,

Three dots appeared. Disappeared. Appeared again.

Emma: We'll figure it out. Go to sleep, Harrison.

You go to sleep, Bennett.

Emma: I will if you will.

I smiled despite myself and set down my phone. My mind kept replaying Emma's words. She'd had it rough, but she'd chosen at some point not to let it poison her attitude. Instead, she'd chosen to be happy and to help others.

The warmth in my chest from our conversation refused to fade, and the more I tried to focus on sleep, the louder the spreadsheet in front of me seemed to laugh. Every formula, every red-highlighted expense, felt like it was daring me to relax.

I stared at the ceiling for a long minute, my thoughts ping-ponging between logistics and her smile, and realized that maybe it wasn't the caffeine keeping me awake. Maybe it was that familiar mix of hope and worry, the way she made me want to do better, even in the small, impossible things. And somehow, just thinking about her—about her voice, her confidence, the way she'd leaned into me when we'd thrown axes—made every unsolvable number feel a little less threatening.

I sighed.

Sleep wasn't coming. But neither was panic.

BY THE TIME I DRAGGED myself to school the next morning, I'd slept maybe ninety minutes and consumed enough coffee to fuel a small rocket. I'd put my shirt inside out before realizing it in the parking lot and changing in my car. And my hands shook as I wrote the day's objectives on the whiteboard.

"You look like death," Eli said from my doorway during lunch.

"Thanks."

"Didn't you sleep last night?"

"Define sleep."

He walked over to my desk, where I had printouts of budget scenarios and rough drafts of my grant proposal spread out like some kind of deranged treasure map. "Max. Man. You've got to let this go for a few hours."

"I can't. The grant is due Friday and Field Day is in twelve days. Twelve days, Eli. And we only have one hundred dollars."

"Okay," Eli drew the word out, lifting his hands in defense, but that didn't deter me.

"Do you know what you can buy with one hundred dollars? Because I do. I've researched it extensively. You can buy approximately forty pool noodles. Or twelve rolls of duct tape. Or one really nice bullhorn and nothing else."

Eli picked up one of my charts—a Venn diagram comparing cost-to-benefit ratios of different activity options. "This is... impressively neurotic."

"I prefer 'thorough.'"

"You've calculated the cost per minute of student engagement."

"It's a relevant metric!" I protested, rubbing my tired eyes.

He set down the chart and gripped my shoulder. "Here's what you're going to do. You're going to put all this away. You're going to leave school this afternoon at a reasonable hour. And you're going to do something for an hour that doesn't involve spreadsheets."

"But—"

"No buts. Doctor's orders."

"You're not a doctor."

"I play one in the teacher's lounge when people ask me about their weird rashes." He started gathering up my papers. "Your brain needs a break."

I wanted to argue. But he was right. My eyes were as gritty as sandpaper, my thoughts were getting increasingly disjointed, and I was barely holding it together.

The school day was a blur. I hope I made sense when I explained ionic and covalent bonds.

When the final bell rang, I packed up my laptop with the intention of going straight home and taking a nap. But as I walked past the gym, I heard the unmistakable sound of a basketball game in progress.

The doors were propped open. I glanced inside.

Bobby was setting up for a shot, her short hair bouncing as she pivoted. Keith defended aggressively, hands up. On the far end of the court, I spotted Eli and Dante running a fast break.

And Emma.

She stole the ball from Oz with a move so quick I almost missed it.

"HARRISON!" Bobby spotted me and jogged over. "Thank God. We need another player. Keith's friends showed up and now we're uneven."

"I should really—"

"Come on, man!" Keith called. "Unless you're scared Bennett's going to skool you."

Emma looked over, eyebrow raised in challenge.

My exhausted brain made the decision before my rational mind intervened. "I'm not scared of anything."

"Prove it." Emma tossed me the ball.

I caught it reflexively and walked onto the court, glad I wore sneakers with my khaki pants and school polo today.

"Okay, new teams," Bobby announced. "Max, you're with me, Keith, Eli, and Dante. Emma, you've got Oz, Jen, and Thalia."

"This seems unfair," Thalia said. "Height-wise."

"You've got Emma," Bobby countered. "That evens everything out."

We took our positions. I ended up guarding Emma, naturally, because the universe had a sense of humor.

"You look tired," she said as we waited for Bobby to throw the ball in. "Still freaking out about the budget?"

"Is it still freaking out if the panic is completely justified?"

"It is." She smiled, and something in my chest loosened slightly. "But freaking out together tends to work better."

The game started, and for the first time in days, my brain actually quieted down.

There was something meditative about basketball—the rhythm of dribbling, the footwork, the split-second decisions about whether to shoot or pass. It required just enough focus that I couldn't think about anything else.

Emma was good. Better than good. She moved with the kind of fluid confidence that came from years of competitive play, reading the court like it was a language she spoke fluently.

I managed to block her first shot attempt. She grinned and stole the ball back from Eli, passing it to Oz for an easy layup.

"Show off," I muttered.

"You love it."

She wasn't wrong.

The game continued, competitive but friendly. At one point, Emma and I both went up for a rebound at the same time, bodies colliding as we fought for position. Her elbow caught me in the ribs, and I used my height advantage to tip the ball to Dante.

"Foul!" Emma protested.

"That was clean."

"Your definition of clean is very different from mine, Dr. Doom."

"Is this about basketball or something else?" Oz called from down court, waggling his eyebrows.

"BASKETBALL," Emma and I answered too quickly.

Everyone laughed.

Bobby jogged over, apparently tired of being left out. "Wait. Are we interrogating Max? Because I have questions too."

I glanced around at the semicircle of teachers, all watching me with varying degrees of amusement, and that familiar prickle in my chest gathered, part embarrassment, part thrill. Every pair of eyes on me made my stomach tighten, and I couldn't stop sneaking glances toward Emma. She was on the other side of the gym, ostensibly getting water, but the way she kept flicking her gaze toward me told me she knew exactly what was happening.

"Yeah," Eli said, joining the circle. "You're definitely being interrogated. Just go with it. It's easier."

I forced a small, self-deprecating smile, wishing I could disappear and also secretly hoping Emma might come over and rescue me. There was a part of me that loved the teasing and attention, but it also left me exposed in a way that made my chest tighten and my palms itch. I reminded myself to breathe, tried to anchor to the game and the gym around me, and told myself this was fine. It was fine... right?

"Fine," I said. "Yes. Emma and I are... seeing each other. Casually. And very discreetly, so if you all could—"

"OH MY GOD, FINALLY!" Bobby threw her hands up. "Do you know how painful it's been watching you two dance around each other for months?"

"Months?"

"You've had heart eyes since the first faculty meeting," Thalia said. "It was extremely obvious."

"To everyone except you two, apparently," Jen added.

Dante laughed. "Dude, you talk about her constantly. 'Emma was at the school dance.' 'Emma wants to start an Earth Club.' 'Emma took the last danish on the teacher workday.'"

"I don't sound like that."

"You absolutely do," Eli confirmed.

I scrubbed my hand over my face, rubbing the tension out of my eyes. "Great. So everyone knows."

"Pretty much," Bobby said, leaning against the bleachers with a grin. "But don't worry. We're not going to say anything to Kline. Teacher code."

"Teacher code," the others echoed, their voices bouncing around the gym like some kind of sacred oath. My shoulders loosened a little despite myself, though a part of me still bristled at being on display.

"Although," Oz said, scratching the back of his neck and glancing at me with a raised eyebrow, "speaking of Principal Kline and budget cuts... we have an idea."

I tensed, clutching the basketball a little too tightly. "I'm scared."

"Hear me out," Oz said, stepping closer, leaning on the edge of the court. "What if we had a fundraiser?"

I blinked, letting the words sink in. "A fundraiser." My mind immediately jumped to spreadsheets, costs, logistics.

Panic was quick to follow. I'd never run a fundraiser.

"Yeah. Get the community involved," Keith said, bouncing the ball slowly, lost in thought. "Parents open their wallets for that kind of thing."

I rubbed my temple, feeling the late-night fatigue tugging at me. "We only have twelve days," I muttered, more to myself than anyone else.

"So?" Bobby's hands went up, palms open, like he was daring me to say no. "Last year, Marnie organized that bake sale to raise money for fabric for those string bags in a week."

I gave him a skeptical look. "That raised maybe three hundred dollars," I pointed out, letting the tension seep into my tone.

Keith shrugged, a mischievous glint in his eye as he dribbled the basketball. "Okay, so think bigger. What do people pay money for?"

"Entertainment," Emma said, stepping forward with a purposeful stride, her phone already out, fingers hovering over the screen. "People pay for entertainment."

I crossed my arms, leaning on the bleachers, trying to appear calm. "Like what?" I asked, feeling a mixture of dread and curiosity.

"A talent show?"

"Too overdone," Jen said, folding her arms, tapping her foot. "Every school does that."

"A carnival?" Thalia suggested, hands on her hips, tilting her head like she was weighing logistics against chaos.

"Too much setup time," Bobby countered, jabbing a finger in the air for emphasis.

We all fell silent for a moment, the gym humming with the overhead lights and the occasional squeak of sneakers on polished wood. My stomach tightened as my brain ticked through the possibilities, imagining work orders, volunteer lists, and safety concerns.

"What about..." Emma's eyes lit up, and she leaned in, tapping the edge of the bleachers like a kid with a big idea. "What about a teacher competition?"

"Like what?" I asked, blinking, my tone tight but curious. I shifted my weight, bouncing the ball lightly on the court, trying to ground myself.

"I don't know. Something ridiculous," she said, waving her hands animatedly, "something that would make students actually want to buy tickets."

"Teacher Dodgeball Tournament," Dante said, his grin wide as he bounced on his toes.

"Teacher Dance-Off," Jen countered, flinging her hands in the air and striking a pose.

"Teachers versus students in various embarrassing challenges," Oz offered, rolling his shoulders and gesturing dramatically toward the empty court.

I groaned inwardly, but despite the mental chaos, I couldn't help feeling a spark of... maybe excitement. This was insane, but it might work.

"Wait." Eli snapped his fingers. "What if we did a whole event? Like, multiple competitions. Make it a variety show. Sell tickets, sell concessions, maybe get some local businesses to sponsor."

"The Marchfield Teacher Extravaganza," Bobby said, grinning.

The idea hung in the air for a moment, crystallizing.

"That would work," Emma said. "We could have teams. Make it competitive. Sell it as a community event."

"Students would definitely pay to watch teachers make fools of themselves," Keith agreed.

My tired brain was starting to wake up, neurons firing with possibilities. "We'd need events that are funny but not dangerous. Things that require minimal equipment but maximum entertainment value."

"Three-legged race," Thalia said.

"Egg toss," Jen added.

"Pie-eating contest," from Oz.

"Teachers lip-syncing," Bobby suggested, looking delighted by the chaos.

Emma pulled out her phone and started typing notes. "If we sold tickets for ten dollars each, and we got even half the school to come, that's three thousand dollars."

"Plus concessions," I added, my spreadsheet brain automatically calculating. "And if we got local businesses to sponsor..."

"We'd more than pull this off," Emma said, looking up at me.

For the first time in days, the knot of anxiety in my chest loosened.

"We'd need approval from Kline," I said.

"He'll approve it," Bobby said with a nod. "Community engagement, parent involvement, students seeing teachers as real people—he loves that stuff."

"And it would need to be soon," Emma said. "Like next Friday soon. The Friday before Field Day."

“That's insane,” I said, running a hand through my hair. My brain went into overdrive: twelve days to plan an event, get tickets printed, and concessions stocked; hope enough people actually show up to cover costs; and somehow convince every teacher to embarrass themselves publicly without revolt.

Insane didn't even begin to cover it. It was a logistical nightmare, a liability waiting to happen, and out of my control.

"But possible?" Emma's eyes met mine, and I saw the same competitive fire that made her so good at basketball, at teaching, at everything she did.

"Possibly insane," I amended.

"I'm in," Eli said.

"Me too," from Dante.

"Obviously," Bobby added.

One by one, everyone agreed. By the time we'd finished planning the basics—date, time, event ideas—it was nearly six PM, and I'd completely forgotten about my exhaustion.

As the others trickled out, Emma lingered, crouching to adjust her shoe as if it needed tying, waiting until the gym was quiet and we were alone.

"You okay?" she asked.

"Better than I was an hour ago."

"Good." She stood up, shouldering her bag. "For what it's worth? I could see your mind making color-coded spreadsheets and charts? Kind of sexy."

"Really? That's what does it for you? Neurotic planning?"

"What can I say? I have a type." She walked toward the door, then looked back over her shoulder. "Get some sleep, Harrison. We've got a teacher show to plan. And you can't compete if you pass out from exhaustion."

"Is that concern I hear, Bennett?"

"Maybe a little." She smiled. "Don't let it go to your head."

After she left, I stood in the empty gym for a moment, sorting through my feelings. Yes, there was doubt and panic, but also something close to hope.

We had a plan. It was last-minute and possibly doomed to failure.

But it was a plan.

And for the first time since Kline had dropped the budget bomb, I thought we might actually pull this off.

I drove home, cooked some pasta and chicken, and fell into bed before 9 p.m. But before I crashed, I opened my laptop one more time and created a new spreadsheet.

Marchfield Teacher Extravaganza: Budget Projections

I allowed myself a small smile as I started filling in the cells.

Maybe Eli was right. Maybe I was impressively neurotic.

But at least I was a neurotic who knew how to put on a show.

Chapter 14: Max

EMMA SPRAWLED ACROSS my couch, laptop balanced on her knees, hair twisted up in a messy bun that had at least three pens sticking out of it at various angles.

"Read me that sentence again," she said, squinting at her screen. "The one about interdisciplinary collaboration."

I scrolled through my draft. "This grant will facilitate meaningful interdisciplinary collaboration by creating shared learning experiences that bridge the gap between theoretical scientific concepts and practical physical applications."

"Too jargony. Say it like a human."

"I am a human."

"A human who doesn't work for the Department of Education." She looked up, grinning. "Try again. Pretend you're explaining it to your me."

I leaned back in my desk chair, considering. "This grant will help science and PE teachers work together to implement real-world physics into both curriculums. This practical application of science has proven to increase test scores and student engagement, while giving kids a hands-on understanding of concepts that usually feel abstract in the classroom."

"Perfect. Write that."

Emma arrived after school on Thursday, ostensibly to help with the grant application and work on the fundraiser. For two straight evenings, we'd ordered takeout, spread papers across every surface, and somehow managed to be productive.

She'd read parts of my application aloud while pacing my living room, stealing bites of my Kung Pao chicken when she thought I wasn't looking. Then she'd flop onto the couch for a quick break, and I'd spend a few minutes thanking her for all of her help—watching the way she stretched out, the curve of her neck, the small movements of her hands as she reached for her water glass. I couldn't help it; part of my thanks was in how I silently worshiped her presence, memorizing the way she occupied the space, the ease with which she made sitting beside me feel electric.

By ten PM on Friday, papers stacked high around us and half-empty takeout boxes littering the table, I realized I was done. The grant was finished. Maybe it was the adrenaline of the deadline. Maybe it was her.

She stretched and yawned, brushing a stray lock of hair from her face. "I'm getting tired..." she murmured. Her bag was already on the floor, her jacket tossed onto my chair. She was staying over.

"Just a second..." I said, swallowing as I clicked the submit button on the grant and grabbed her hand. "All done."

"Really?" She squealed and threw her arms around my neck.

From his cage in the corner, Darcy ruffled his feathers and let out a piercing whistle.

"MAX IS A SEXY BEAST! AWK!"

Emma snorted. "Did you teach him that?"

"Absolutely not. I think he picked it up from my students. They've been recording TikToks with him."

"Of course, they have." She chuckled, stretching her arms over her head. Her shirt rode up slightly, revealing a strip of skin that immediately commanded all of my attention.

The air between us shifted. Charged.

She caught me staring and bit her lip, a challenge flickering in her eyes.

"See something you like, Harrison?"

"Maybe."

"Maybe?" She leaned closer, her hand settling on my thigh. "That's not very scientific. You should be more precise with your observations."

My laptop slid forgotten to the couch cushions. Papers scattered to the floor. The careful organization we'd maintained all evening dissolved as the space between us disappeared entirely.

She kissed me. Soft at first, then deeper and more insistent. Her hands slipped under my shirt, her touch sending electricity along my spine that had nothing to do with static.

I pulled her onto my lap, and she made a small, surprised sound that turned into a moan as I kissed her again. Her fingers tangled in my hair, tugging hard enough to make me groan against her mouth.

"Bedroom," I managed between kisses.

"Impatient?"

"You have no idea."

I stood up, keeping her wrapped around me. She laughed, the sound vibrating against my throat as I carried her down the hall.

"Show off," she murmured, biting gently at my earlobe.

"You love it."

"Maybe I do."

We made it to the bedroom, and I set her down on the edge of the bed. She looked up at me, violet hair coming loose from its bun, lips swollen from kissing, eyes dark with want, and something in my chest tightened almost painfully.

This wasn't casual anymore. Maybe it never had been.

I knelt between her legs, hands settling on her thighs, and for a moment, I just looked at her. Really looked. The way her chest rose and fell with quickened breaths. The flush that spread down her neck. The way she bit her lower lip, nervous and eager at once.

"You're staring," she whispered.

"Yeah." My voice came out rougher than I intended. "I am."

Her breath hitched, and I saw the exact moment something shifted in her expression, surprise giving way to realization. She saw it, didn't she? Everything I'd been trying not to feel, written across my face.

I should have looked away. Should have made some joke to diffuse the intensity crackling between us. Keep it light, keep it surface-level, keep myself safe. Instead, I traced my thumb along her inner thigh, watching her eyelids flutter, and felt that dangerous tightness in my chest expand until even breathing took effort.

This was supposed to be simple. Fun.

But somewhere between her laugh in the kitchen and the way she'd kissed me in the hallway and now—her looking at me like I was something precious—I'd gone and fallen. Hard.

The panic hit a second later. That old, familiar voice in my head: *Don't. Don't do this. People leave. They always leave.*

And yet here I was, kneeling between her legs, heart pounding, wanting her so badly it terrified me.

"Hey," she said, her hand coming up to cup my jaw. "Where'd you go?"

I blinked, focusing on her face. On the gentleness there. "Nowhere. I'm right here."

But we both knew that was a lie.

"Come here," she said, reaching for me.

I went. Of course, I went. I'd been gone for her from the start, even if I'd only just realized it.

"Max." She reached for me, fingers curling into my belt loops, pulling me close for a hug. "Stop thinking so hard."

"Can't help it. Scientist brain."

"Then let me help." She kissed me slowly, deeply, taking her time. When she pulled back, she was smiling. "Better?"

"Getting there," I smiled back, reaching for the hem of her shirt. She lifted her arms, and I pulled it over her head slowly, letting my knuckles drag against her skin. She wasn't wearing a bra—hadn't been all evening, I realized, and the sight of her breasts made my mouth go dry.

"Your turn," she said, voice breathy but determined.

Her fingers found the buttons of my shirt, working them open one by one. Each brush of her hands against my chest was intentional, like she was learning me. When she pushed the fabric off my shoulders, her palms flattened against my skin, sliding over muscle.

I sank to my knees in front of her, my palms lifting her breasts, fingers rolling her taut rose-colored nipples. She gasped, sitting down on the edge of the bed, and I eased forward to claim her breasts with my lips, sucking her into my mouth.

She arched into me, clutching my hair and pressing her body to mine. Her soft curves, the heat of her skin mesmerized me. She fit against me like she'd been made for my mouth, and I increased the pressure. She moaned, her hips moving restlessly.

"Please," she breathed, and the word reverberated through my entire body.

I stood long enough to shed my jeans, watching as she did the same, wiggling out of hers with an unselfconscious ease that made me smile despite the intensity coiling through me. When we came back together, skin to skin, I had to close my eyes against the sensation.

I mapped the curve of her spine with my hands, the dip of her waist, the way she shivered when I kissed behind her ear. She traced the muscles of my shoulders, my chest, down my stomach, her touch deliberate and curious, making me twitch beneath her fingers.

I settled between her thighs. Her legs wrapped around my waist, pulling me closer, and I had to pause, had to breathe, had to get control of myself because I could lose myself in this completely. I groaned against her mouth, one hand sliding down to grip her hip, the other cradling the back of her head.

Her violet eyes were hazy as she searched my face. Her hand came up to trace my jaw, my cheekbone, smoothing back the hair that had fallen across my forehead. The tenderness of the gesture made my chest ache.

"Please, Max," she whispered again.

I kissed her again, slower this time until her fingers tightened in my hair, and she made a small sound that unraveled something deep inside me.

"You're so beautiful," I whispered, meaning it more than I'd meant anything in a long time.

"You're not so bad yourself, Harrison." Her voice was breathless now, rougher, her pulse racing beneath my lips as I kissed her throat.

"That's all I get? Not so bad?" I nipped gently at the sensitive spot below her ear, felt her shiver.

She pulled me closer, wrapping her legs around my waist, the pressure making us both gasp. Her fingers dug into my shoulders, anchoring herself. "Fishing for compliments?"

"Maybe." I rolled my hips slowly, deliberately, watching her eyes darken and her lips part.

"You're..." She pretended to consider, even as her nails dragged lightly down my back, leaving trails of heat in their wake. "Adequate."

"Adequate?" I shifted my body, kissing my way down between her legs. Her taste was heady as I swirled my tongue around her clit.

"Acceptable," she tried again, but her voice wavered, breaking on the last syllable as I kissed down her neck.

Her words dissolved into a sharp inhale as I slid my hand between her folds, fingers finding the heat of her. She was already wet, ready, and the discovery made something primal surge through me.

"You're killing me here, Bennett." I caught her clit between my teeth, tugged gently. I dipped my finger into her heat.

She laughed, low and warm and barely controlled, vibrating through both our bodies. "Fine. You're gorgeous. Happy?"

"Getting there." I withdrew my finger, easing two into her tightness instead.

"And smart." She pinched my shoulder, hard.

I smiled lazily, working my fingers inside her before finding her clit again. "Keep going."

"And funny. And surprisingly sexy." Her fingers twisted in the sheets, then found my wrist, not to stop me but to guide me, to show me exactly what she needed. The trust in that gesture made my heart stutter in my chest.

"I know," I murmured against her, circling slowly, learning what made her gasp, what made her hips buck against my hand. "I've got you."

"Don't stop," she breathed, and I had no intention of stopping. Not when she looked like this, flushed and wanting, her violet hair spilled across my pillow as if she belonged there. Not when every sound she made went straight through me, unraveling whatever control I'd been clinging to.

Her eyebrows drew together when I found the right rhythm. Her mouth fell open when I added pressure.

"Look at me," I said, and when her eyes met mine, dark and hazy and so open it terrified me, I knew I was done for.

She was hovering on the edge, her body taut with pleasure, trembling beneath my touch. I could feel it in the way her breathing fractured, the way her thighs tensed around my hand, the way she gripped my shoulder hard enough to bruise.

"Harrison, I'm—" She didn't finish the sentence.

And then she went over, eyes wide and locked on mine as her orgasm washed over her. She didn't look away, didn't close her eyes, and I watched every second of it—the way her pupils dilated, the way her mouth opened on a silent cry that became my name, the way her whole body arched and shuddered.

Beautiful didn't cover it. Nothing in my vocabulary covered it.

I shifted onto my side, pulling her against me as aftershocks still rippled through her. Her back pressed to my chest, and I wrapped my arm around her waist, holding her close while her breathing gradually slowed and steadied.

She melted into me, boneless and warm, her fingers tracing idle patterns on my forearm. For a long moment, we breathed together, her heart still racing beneath my palm.

Then, because I couldn't help myself, I pressed a kiss to her shoulder and murmured against her skin, "Surprisingly sexy?"

"I had my doubts about uptight science teachers." Her smile was wicked, challenging, and god, I wanted to kiss it off her face.

"I'm not uptight." I proved my point in a way that made her arch against me with a gasp, her back bowing off the bed, her nails raking down my spine.

"Okay," she breathed, eyes fluttering closed. "Maybe not uptight."

She kissed me again, pulling me back up to her mouth, and we stopped talking entirely. But the silence was full of other sounds—her breathing, my name on her lips, the rustle of sheets, the quiet confession of skin against skin.

"I'm just saying, that's a pretty lukewarm endorsement." I nipped at the curve of her neck; she shivered. "Especially considering what just happened."

She turned in my arms to face me, eyes still hazy but sparkling with amusement. "Fine. Devastatingly sexy. Unfairly hot. Criminally good with your hands." Her palm slid down my chest, lower. "Better?"

"Much." I caught her hand, brought it to my lips. "Though I'm still not convinced you've fully grasped—"

She straddled me, sealing her mouth to mine and cutting off my words. She lowered her body down, taking an inch of me inside her.

I forgot what I was going to say entirely.

We moved together, slowly at first, then faster, finding a rhythm that felt like discovery and homecoming all at once. Every time I found something that made her gasp or arch into me, I filed it away for future reference. Every time she did something that made me lose my train of thought completely, she'd smile against my skin like she'd won a prize.

The tension built between us like a storm gathering strength, pressure mounting. Her nails scraped down my back, and I buried my face in her neck, breathing her in, trying to hold onto some semblance of control.

"Don't hold back," she whispered against my ear, and that was it. That was all it took.

The careful restraint I'd been maintaining shattered. My hips snapped forward harder, faster, and she met me thrust for thrust, her legs tightening around me, pulling me deeper. The sounds she made—broken versions of my name mixed with incoherent pleas—unraveled me completely.

"I'm close," I managed, the words rough and strained.

"Look at me," she whispered, repeating my words. And when my eyes met hers, the intimacy of it nearly undid me.

And when we fell, we fell together. She cried out beneath me as I groaned her name, both of us clinging to each other as if we were the only solid things in a world gone liquid and molten.

For several long moments after, we lay there, tangled together, hearts pounding in sync, trying to remember how to breathe. I traced lazy patterns on her shoulder while she pressed soft kisses to my chest, and neither of us seemed capable of speech yet.

My mind was still reeling, trying to process what had happened—not just the physical intensity of it, but everything underneath. The way she'd looked at me. The way I'd let her see me, really see me, without any of my usual defenses in place.

It terrified me. And yet, lying here with her curled against my side, her hair spilling across my chest, one leg hooked over mine like she had every right to be here—it felt right in a way nothing had in years.

"You okay?" she murmured against my skin, her breath warm.

"Yeah." I pressed my lips to the top of her head, let them linger there. "More than okay."

She tilted her face up to look at me, and there was something searching in her gaze. Like she was trying to read what I wasn't saying. Her fingers traced along my ribs, gentle and unhurried.

"We still need to discuss the fundraiser," Emma said eventually, her voice still rough around the edges.

"Probably."

"But maybe..." She traced lazy circles on my ribs. "Maybe in the morning."

"Yeah." I pressed a kiss to her forehead, breathing her in. "In the morning."

From the kitchen, I heard Darcy's muffled voice: "MAX LOVES EMMA!"

Emma's shoulders shook with silent laughter. "That bird knows too much."

"He's going to be the death of me."

"Or the best wingman you've ever had."

"Obviously."

We stayed like that for a while, the city lights filtering through my bedroom window, the apartment quiet except for the occasional squawk from the kitchen. My fingers combed through her hair, and she hummed contentedly, burrowing closer.

Sleep tugged at the edges of my consciousness, but I fought it, wanting to hold onto this moment a little longer. The weight of her against me. The sound of her breathing evening out. The impossible fact that she was here, in my bed, and planning to stay.

"Max?" Her voice was drowsy, barely above a whisper.

"Yeah?"

"This is nice."

Such simple words. But the way my chest tightened around them, the way something warm and terrifying bloomed behind my ribs—there was nothing simple about it at all.

"Yeah," I managed, pressing a kiss to her forehead. "It is."

Her breathing deepened, and within minutes, she was asleep, trusting and warm in my arms. I lay there in the dark, listening to the city hum beyond the windows, feeling the steady rise and fall of her chest against mine.

I'd spent so long keeping people at arm's length, convinced it was safer this way. Easier. But holding Emma Bennett while she slept, violet hair tickling my chin, her hand curled against my heart, didn't feel easy.

It felt like falling.

And for once, I wasn't trying to catch myself.

Chapter 15: Emma

THE FLUORESCENT LIGHTS in the library flickered as I wedged myself between a book cart and the check-out desk, trying to count heads. I'd expected maybe a dozen teachers to show up for the fundraiser planning meeting—optimistically, fifteen.

But unexpectedly, what I got was closer to forty people crammed between the stacks and perched on sturdy tables. Teachers mingled with the custodial staff, all of them drawn by the rumor that Marchfield Middle was at it again.

Ever since the tricycle basketball games made the local news, especially after Oz's singing proposal went viral on social media, people had learned that when Marchfield planned something, it was worth showing up to see what would unfold. The dozen or so alumni clustering near the biography section had probably been in seventh or eighth grade when both those events happened. Now they were back, eager to see what spectacle the school would produce next.

I should have known better than to underestimate this place's reputation for the memorable and the slightly unhinged.

I'd printed twelve agendas. They were already gone, being passed hand-to-hand through the crowd like contraband. This was either going to be a disaster or the start of something worth doing.

We'd pushed tables together to form a large square in the center of the library, with additional chairs scattered around the perimeter. Bobby was setting up poster paper on easels at the front. Thalia was organizing markers by color, and Eli had somehow procured three boxes of donuts, which were already being decimated by the early arrivals.

Principal Kline stood near the door, greeting people as they came in. When he caught my eye, he gave me a subtle thumbs up.

At least we had administrative approval.

"Okay!" Bobby clapped her hands, calling the room to attention. "Let's get started before all the donuts are gone and people mutiny."

Everyone settled into seats. I recognized most of the teachers—Jen and Thalia sat up front with Dante and Eli. The usual crew had claimed the middle rows: Val with Evan, Audrey with Oz, Rachel with Keith, Bobby and Mel, and my PE buddy, Pat. Even Yona and Han had made it, along with Marnie McQuistion.

But there were also parents I'd met at sports events, a couple of school board members, and—I did a double-take—was that Tommy Ng? He'd graduated high school three years ago and now worked at the community center downtown.

"Thanks, everyone, for coming," Max said, standing up beside me. "As you know, the Field Day and science fair budgets got slashed to basically nothing."

A lot of heads nodded in the group. Someone in the back muttered something about pathetic funding. Jen made a disgusted noise. I caught Audrey shaking her head, and one of the parents—a woman I didn't recognize—put her hand over her heart like the news physically hurt.

I picked up where he left off. "But what you might not know is that Max and I are collaborating to create a new STEM field day. We're combining both events into something bigger."

"And instead of canceling," Max added, "we're hoping to do a fundraiser."

A murmur rippled through the crowd. A few people sat up straighter. I saw Rachel and Keith exchange a look.

"We're thinking of a variety show," I added. "Teachers performing, maybe some alumni. The goal is entertainment that people will actually pay to see."

"How much are we trying to raise?" asked Henry Larkins, the throat singing chorus teacher.

"Ideally around a thousand dollars," Max said. "That would cover equipment rentals, supplies, food, prizes, and give us a small buffer for emergencies."

"When?" asked one of the parents, and I recognized Mrs. Rodriguez, whose daughter was in my PE class.

"Next Friday," I said. "I know that's soon. But Field Day is the following Friday, and we need time to purchase supplies after we raise the money."

"Next Friday?" Yona looked appalled. "That's barely a week away!"

"Which is why we need all hands on deck," Bobby said with a grin. "This is going to be a full community effort. We'll need performers, obviously, but also stage crew, concessions, ticket sales, decorations, programs, publicity..."

"We should split into brainstorming groups," Thalia suggested. "Come up with act ideas, logistics, promotion strategies. Then we can share and vote on the best ideas."

Max looked at me. I nodded. "Perfect. Let's divide into four groups. Count off by fours, please."

The room erupted into chaotic counting. Once people were sorted, we distributed poster paper and markers to each group.

"You have ten minutes," Max announced. "Come up with as many ideas as possible. No idea is too ridiculous, in fact, the more ridiculous, the better. Students will pay to see teachers making fools of themselves."

The room buzzed with conversation as people huddled over their poster paper. Max and I circulated, listening in on discussions, offering suggestions, trying not to laugh at some of the wilder proposals.

At the first table, Oz was sketching something that looked suspiciously like a pie chart. "We need quantifiable entertainment value per minute," he said. "If each act is three to five minutes, and we have a two-hour show—"

"Oz," interrupted Dante. "It's a variety show, not an equation."

"Everything is an equation if you approach it correctly."

The second table had descended into chaos. Eli was demonstrating what appeared to be an interpretive dance about the water cycle while Jen and Audrey argued about whether teachers should lip-sync to current music or throwbacks.

"Throwbacks!" Audrey insisted. "Nobody wants to watch us kill Olivia Rodrigo. But 'Livin' on a Prayer'? That's comedy gold."

"Speak for yourself," Jen said. "I do an excellent Olivia Rodrigo."

"Prove it," Bobby challenged.

Jen stood up and launched into a surprisingly good rendition of *Good 4 U*, complete with the angry pointing choreography. Half the table burst into applause.

"Okay, you're in the show," Bobby declared.

At the third table, Val was in her element as the drama coach. "We need production value," she was saying, gesturing dramatically. "Lighting! Costumes! Choreography! This should be a SPECTACLE!"

"Val, we have a week," one of the parents reminded her gently.

"A week is plenty of time for a spectacle! We did Hamlet in five days once. Granted, it was a disaster and three kids cried, but it was a SPECTACULAR disaster."

The fourth table seemed to be taking a more practical approach. Tommy Ng and several other alumni were listing their various talents—guitar, beatboxing, magic tricks, something called "extreme yo-yo" that I desperately wanted to see.

"What about an alumni showcase?" Tommy suggested. "Show the current students what Marchfield graduates can do!"

"I love that," Pat nodded. "It ties into the school's mission about lifelong learning."

When ten minutes were up, I called everyone back together. "Okay! Time to share. Group one, what have you got?"

Oz stood up, wielding the poster paper like a legal document. "We propose a structured program with clear time markers and measurable objectives. Act categories would include: musical performance, comedy, physical feats, and intellectual demonstrations. Each category would receive equal time allocation to ensure diverse entertainment."

"Translation: we need a mix of different stuff so people don't get bored," Dante added.

"That's what I said," Oz protested.

"Group two?" I prompted before they could continue arguing.

Audrey jumped up. "We've got a killer lineup. Teacher lip-sync battle—throwback edition. Eli doing science experiments but making them dramatic. Bobby and Keith in a three-point shooting competition. And..." he paused for effect, "...teachers versus students in minute-to-win-it challenges."

"Ooh, I like that last one," Max said. "What kind of challenges?"

"Stack cups. Move cookies from forehead to mouth without hands. Stuff like that. Quick, funny, easy to set up."

"Group three?"

Val stood, and I braced myself. "We propose a theatrical journey through the history of Marchfield Middle School! We'll use projections, dramatic lighting, interpretive dance, and a twelve-person vocal ensemble to—"

"Val," Bobby interrupted. "We have one week and approximately seven dollars for decorations."

"...a scaled-down theatrical journey?"

"How scaled down?" I asked cautiously.

"Maybe just the vocal ensemble," Val admitted. "And some simple choreography. And possibly one dramatic monologue about the founding of the school, delivered while wearing a cape."

"We'll workshop it," Max said diplomatically. "Group four?"

Tommy and the alumni presented their ideas, which were impressively concrete. They'd even sketched out a potential running order and calculated how many acts they might be able to have in a two-hour show.

"This is amazing," I said, impressed. "Okay, let's vote. All in favor of including a teacher lip-sync battle?"

Nearly every hand went up.

"Teacher versus student challenges?"

Again, overwhelming approval.

"Alumni showcase?"

More hands.

"Val's theatrical journey?"

About half the hands were raised, with the rest looking uncertain.

"How about a compromise," Mr. Patterson suggested. "Val, what if you directed a group number to open the show? Something energetic that gets everyone excited. Keep it simple but impactful."

Val's eyes lit up. "I could do that. *Don't Stop Believin'!* With the entire staff! And some simple choreography! And maybe a small amount of dry ice!"

"No dry ice," Principal Kline said firmly from the back of the room. "Remember what happened at the winter concert."

"That was one small fire—"

"Val."

"Fine. No dry ice."

We spent the rest of the hour hammering out details. Someone suggested we sell ad space in the program to local businesses. Someone else offered to contact the local newspaper for publicity. Mrs. Rodriguez volunteered to handle concessions and within minutes had recruited a team of parents to make baked goods and popcorn.

The energy in the room was electric. Everyone was talking over each other, throwing out ideas, volunteering for responsibilities. It was less like a meeting and more like a community coming together around a shared purpose.

I caught Max's eye across the table. He was smiling—not his usual careful, measured expression, but a genuine grin as he listened to Eli pitch an increasingly elaborate plan involving Mentos and Diet Coke.

He looked... happy. Settled. Like he'd found his place here.

When had that happened?

Three months ago, Max Harrison had been the uptight new science teacher who color-coded his lesson plans and looked mildly terrified during faculty meetings. Dr. Doom sent passive-aggressive emails and used the phrase "pedagogical best practices" in casual conversation. I used to roll my eyes every time he opened his mouth.

Now I knew what that mouth felt like on mine. What his hands felt like when they weren't clutching a red marker. And somehow, impossibly, we were planning a school fundraiser together like functional adults who enjoyed each other's company.

The weirdest part? It was working.

"Earth to Emma," Thalia said, waving her hand in front of my face.

I blinked. "Sorry, what?"

"I asked if you want to MC the event? You and Max. You're both good with crowds, and it would tie the whole STEM theme together."

"Oh. Um." I looked at Max again. He'd glanced over at the mention of his name, eyebrows raised in question. "Sure. Yeah. We can do that."

"Perfect!" Thalia made a note on her master planning sheet. "Okay, people. Sign-up sheets are going around for specific jobs. We need stage crew, lighting, sound—Henry, can you handle that?"

"On it."

"Decorations team, concessions team, ticket sales, program design, social media promotion—"

"I'll do social media," Krissy, one of the alumni, volunteered. "We can make it viral. TikTok, Instagram, Snapchat—"

"Nothing inappropriate," Principal Kline warned.

"Obviously." Bethany looked offended.

The sign-up sheets made their way around the room. By the time they came back to me, every single slot was filled, with most having multiple volunteers.

"This is incredible," I said, scanning the pages.

"We'll have rehearsal after school on Thursday at five. Plan for about three hours."

"I'll bring pizza," called out Mr. Donetelli, owner of Doughlightful Pies and father to two Marchfield students.

As people started gathering their things, conversations splintered into smaller groups—parents exchanging phone numbers, teachers arguing about song choices, students already filming content for social media.

Max leaned over to me. "That went well."

I looked around the room at the clusters of people still talking, planning, laughing. "I didn't expect this kind of turnout."

"Me neither." He followed my gaze. "It's nice. Everyone coming together like this."

"You're part of it now, you know."

"Part of what?"

"This community. Marchfield."

He was quiet for a moment. When he spoke, his voice was softer. "How did that happen?"

"Gradually, maybe. Or all at once." I bumped his shoulder with mine. "You're stuck with us now, Harrison."

"Could be worse."

"Could be?"

"Fine. Could be much worse." He bumped me back.

"That's the spirit."

Eli, Dante, and Bobby wandered over, still debating the merits of various lip-sync song options.

"I'm telling you, 'Wannabe' is the only correct choice," Bobby insisted.

"Too predictable," Dante countered. "We need something unexpected. Like death metal."

"Nobody wants to see teachers lip-syncing to death metal," Eli said.

"I would pay extra for that," Max interjected.

They all turned to stare at him.

"What? I like Cannibal Corpse."

"Interesting," I said, filing that information away for future reference.

Thalia and Jen joined our circle, followed by Oz and Val, and soon we were all standing in the middle of the library, talking over each other about costume ideas and staging and whether we should sell glow sticks as part of concessions.

This, I thought, looking around at my colleagues, my friends, was what made teaching magical. Not the classroom instruction or the test scores or the budget battles. But this kind of community. People coming together to support their students and each other, turning a crisis into an opportunity, making something out of nothing through sheer determination and slightly chaotic enthusiasm.

Max caught my eye again, and something warm settled in my chest.

Yeah. He definitely belonged here.

And maybe, possibly, what Max and I had wasn't something I wanted to walk away from anymore.

The thought settled in my chest, warm and terrifying in equal measure. When had I become the kind of person who couldn't walk away? I'd always been good at keeping things light, keeping my options open, keeping one foot out the door. Safe. But Max had somehow slipped past all of that.

I wasn't ready to examine that too closely. Not here, not now, maybe not ever.

But that was a thought for later. Right now, we had a variety show to plan and a community to mobilize.

"Alright, people!" Bobby clapped her hands. "Meeting adjourned. We've got five days to pull off the most ambitious fundraiser in Marchfield history."

"No pressure," Eli muttered.

We filed out of the library in a noisy, chaotic group. Max and I walked back to his classroom together.

"How's Darcy? Has he learned any new inappropriate phrases?"

"Oh God. Lynda is going to kill me when she takes him back," he moaned. "Yesterday he told the Mr. Kline 'peer review is bullshit.' Direct quote from me during grading."

I laughed. "At least it's accurate."

We reached his classroom. He unlocked the door, holding it open for me. I stepped inside and he followed, the door clicking shut behind us with a soft finality that made the space feel suddenly smaller, more intimate.

The familiar smell of dry erase markers and that faint chemical tang from the lab supplies hit me. We were still standing close to the door, barely a foot of space between us in the narrow entryway. His hand was on the door behind him, and I was close enough to see the way his breathing had changed—just slightly faster than normal.

"Emma?"

"Yeah?"

"Thanks for dragging me into all this. I know I wasn't enthusiastic about collaboration at first."

"That's an understatement," I said.

He had the grace to look embarrassed. "In my defense, I was—"

"Terrified of me?"

"Something like that." He smiled, and something in my chest did a stupid little flip. "And now I can't imagine working with anyone else."

The warning bell rang, shattering the moment. I had approximately four minutes to get to my own classroom before twenty-eight seventh graders descended.

"I should go," I said, reaching for the door handle. We were standing close enough that the flecks of gold in his eyes were visible. Close enough that it would take almost nothing to close the distance between us.

"Yeah," Max agreed, not moving.

This was stupid. We were at school. Students would be flooding the hallways any second. I had a gym full of pre-teens waiting for me.

But God, I wanted to kiss him. Wanted to slide my hand into his hair and pull him close and forget about bells and schedules and professional boundaries.

"Emma," he whispered, making my stomach flip.

The second bell rang.

I stepped back. "Tonight?" I managed.

"Tonight," he confirmed, his voice rough in a way that promised exactly what tonight would involve.

I opened the door before I could do something reckless.

Yeah.

Definitely not casual anymore.

Chapter 16: Max

EMMA KNOCKED ON MY door at five-thirty, and before she could even say hello, I pulled her inside and kissed her—quick but intense, like I'd been holding my breath all day. The kiss was done, almost as soon as it started, but it left me buzzing, excitement crackling under my skin.

I let the silence stretch, my pulse slowing just enough for my thoughts to line up. Whatever had been buzzing in my head all afternoon was finally real now that she was here. Emma kicked off her shoes while I leaned back against the door, watching her like I was memorizing the moment.

"I've been dying to talk to you about the meeting," I said at last. "Did you see Marnie's face when—"

"—Dante suggested the death metal lip-sync," she cut in, grinning. I stepped aside to let her in, still riding the high of it.

"I thought she was going to spontaneously combust." Emma laughed, following me into the apartment and dropping her bag by the door. "And Val—'a scaled-down theatrical journey,' like that's even possible."

"I heard she asked Kline if she could use pyrotechnics," I said, shaking my head, half awed, half-delighted.

Emma snorted. "Bet that went over well."

From his cage, Darcy let out an enthusiastic squawk. "PRETTY EMMA!"

"Hey, troublemaker," Emma called over to him.

I headed to the kitchen, pulling out two beers from the fridge. "The turnout was insane. I counted forty-three people at one point."

"Forty-five," Emma corrected, accepting the beer I handed her. "You missed the two parents who showed up late with poster boards they'd already decorated."

"The ones with the glitter?"

"So much glitter. I'm pretty sure some of it's still in my hair." She ran her fingers through it, and sure enough, something sparkly came loose.

I laughed, reaching over to brush a piece of glitter from her shoulder. My fingers lingered for a moment before I caught myself and pulled back, taking a sip of my beer.

We settled on the couch, close but not quite touching. My laptop sat open on the coffee table, surrounded by the planning documents we'd been working on all week.

"Tommy Ng was great," I said. "Did you know he teaches guitar lessons now? He offered to pull together an entire alumni band."

"And Mrs. Rodriguez has already recruited twelve parents for concessions. Twelve! We're going to have more baked goods than we know what to do with."

I was quiet for a moment, staring at my beer bottle. The meeting had been overwhelming in the best possible way. All those people showing up, volunteering, committing their time and energy to something Emma and I had started. "I didn't expect people to care this much. About the Field Day, I mean. Or about us pulling this off."

She huffed a quiet laugh. "We didn't volunteer for this, but we work well together. This fundraiser will be successful and so will STEM Field Day. In large part to your spreadsheets."

We. This. The fundraiser. She said it like the partnership was obvious now, like it had always been headed this way. I noticed, though, that she never said *us* when it came to anything outside the work.

What would happen when the field day was over? When we didn't have planning sessions and shared spreadsheets holding us together?

"You say that like spreadsheets are a good thing," I managed.

"They are. I especially like how you used pink and purple columns." She took a drink of her beer, watching me over the rim. "You know what? I think you underestimate your effect on the school."

I shifted. "I'm not exactly Mr. Popular."

"No," she said, setting her beer down on the coffee table. "You're Mr. Shows-Up-and-Follows-Through, which, it turns out, people really respond to."

"They showed up for you, too."

"For the project," she said. "For what we're doing."

There it was again—*we*, safely contained.

I smiled anyway. "Noted."

"So." She leaned back against the couch cushions, angling toward me. "What are you going to do for the show?"

"Me?"

"Yes, you. You and I can't MC the whole thing without performing something; that's not fair to the audience."

"I thought we'd introduce other people's acts and make sure the transitions run smoothly."

"That's part of the job. But you also need to perform." She was grinning now, clearly enjoying my discomfort. "Come on, Harrison. What hidden talents are you hiding?"

"I don't have hidden talents."

"Everyone has hidden talents. What did you do in college? Besides study excessively?"

"I played intramural basketball. That's not a talent, that's just being tall."

"What else?"

I took a long drink of beer, stalling. "I... may have been in a play my first semester."

Emma's eyes went wide. "What?"

"My roommate dragged me to an audition and somehow I made it. I suffered through it and never auditioned again."

"Max Harrison. Science teacher. Former thespian." She was practically bouncing with delight. "This is the best thing I've ever learned about you."

"It's not that impressive."

"It's incredibly impressive! What did you perform?"

"Emma—"

"What. Did. You. Perform?"

I sighed. "It was *Grease*. I played Sonny. It wasn't a big deal."

She blinked at me. "Sonny is on stage a lot," she said. "You don't get through that show without singing and dancing."

"Technically," I said.

"Max."

I shrugged. “Group numbers. Some choreography. I mostly tried not to mess it up.”

Her smile softened, like she was filing the information away. “So you *can* sing. And dance.”

“It was a long time ago, and I wasn’t any good at it.”

"Well, how about doing a lip sync song then."

"Absolutely not."

"Absolutely yes. We'll find you a song. Something fun.”

"Emma, I'm not performing." The thought of standing on stage in front of parents and students and colleagues made my stomach turn. What if I froze? What if everyone saw me fail, and it changed how they looked at me... how *she* looked at me?

"Why not?" She shifted closer, her knee bumping mine. "Scared?"

"Not scared. Just... realistic about my abilities."

"Liar. You're scared." Her eyes were dancing with amusement. "The great Dr. Max Harrison, afraid of a little stage time."

"I'm not afraid—"

"Prove it."

We were close now. I caught the citrusy scent of her shampoo and the spicy scent of her skin.

She was challenging me the way she always did, pushing me out of my comfort zone, making me better. But there was a limit to how vulnerable I could be. I was already too exposed with her, already in too deep.

"What about you?" I asked, trying to redirect. "What are you going to do?"

"I haven't decided yet. Maybe a dance routine with Thalia. Or a comedy bit about PE teacher stereotypes?"

"We should do a song together."

She blinked. "What?"

"If you're going to make me lip-sync, you should do it, too."

“We’re already MCing together. We should do different acts.”

“I’m not doing the song if you aren’t.”

“But...”

I set my beer down next to hers. "So we're agreed. We're both lip-syncing."

"I didn't agree to that."

"You just did. By trying to make me agree to it."

She narrowed her eyes. "You're infuriating."

"You like it."

"I really don't."

"Liar."

She opened her mouth to argue, but I was suddenly very aware of how close we were sitting. Her knee was still pressed against mine. Her hand rested on the couch cushion between us, close enough that I could reach out and touch it if I wanted to.

I wanted to.

"We should..." Emma's voice had gone softer. "We should finalize the running order. For the show."

"Probably."

Neither of us moved.

"And confirm all the volunteers," she continued.

"Right."

"And make sure the program design is ready to send to the printer."

"Important."

Her gaze dropped to my mouth. "Max?"

"Yeah?"

"Are we going to do any work tonight?"

"I don't know. Are we?"

She leaned in, closing the distance between us. "Probably not."

I woke up to the sound of my alarm, momentarily disoriented. Emma was curled against my side, naked, her purple hair spread across my pillow, one slender arm draped over my chest. The room was dark except for the faint glow of the streetlight outside filtering through the curtains.

For a moment, I lay there, memorizing the weight of her against me, the steady rhythm of her breathing, the way her fingers curled loosely against my ribs. This was becoming familiar—*too* familiar. The shape of her in my bed, the scent of her on my sheets, the way my home felt less empty when she was in it.

My alarm buzzed again, and I reached over carefully to silence it, trying not to wake her.

She stirred anyway, making a small sound of protest. "What time is it?"

"Almost five. We fell asleep."

"Mm." She stretched against me, and the movement crashed through my body. "We were supposed to work."

"We were."

"Oops."

I pressed a kiss to the top of her head, breathing in the scent of her. My chest felt tight with something I couldn't quite name.

Or maybe I could name it, I was just afraid to.

Emma shifted, propping herself up on one elbow to look at me. Her hair was mussed, her eyes still soft with sleep, and she looked so perfectly comfortable here that it made my heart ache.

"I should go," she said, but she didn't move.

"Probably."

This was the pattern. She'd get up soon, get dressed, gather her things. She'd kiss me goodbye at the door, maybe make a joke about our lack of self-control. And then she'd leave, and I'd get ready for school alone in my too-silent house.

Four days until the fundraiser. Ten days until STEM Field Day. And then what? Would we still have an excuse to see each other? Would she continue to show up at my door every night with a smile that made me forget why I'd ever thought I needed to keep my distance?

"Max?" Emma's voice pulled me back. "You okay? You got quiet."

"Yeah. Just thinking about the to-do list for today."

It wasn't entirely a lie. I was thinking about today, and the day after that, and all the days stretching out over the summer when I might not have a reason to call her, to text her, to see her looking soft and rumpled in my bed.

"We really do need to finalize that running order," she said, sitting up fully now. "And about a hundred other things."

"Right."

She started gathering her clothes from where they'd ended up scattered on the floor. I watched her dress, committing every detail to memory—the way she had to hop to get her jeans on, the small smile when she found her shirt inside out, the unselfconscious efficiency of someone comfortable in their own skin.

"Want to meet for coffee after school?" she asked, pulling her hair back into a ponytail. "We can actually work this time. I promise."

Stay, I wanted to say: Stay tonight. Stay tomorrow. Stay until I figure out how to tell you that somewhere between spreadsheets and stolen kisses and late-night planning sessions, I stopped being able to imagine doing any of this without you.

"Sure," I said instead.

She leaned down to kiss me, sweet and unhurried. "Thanks for last night. Even if we didn't get anything done."

"Anytime."

The word landed with a dull thud in my head. *Anytime.* As if she'd thanked me for holding a door open, not for an evening I'll replay all day. I should've said something—*I like being with you, I don't want this to just be about work, please don't disappear when this is over.*

Instead, I stood there, smiling like an idiot, as she grabbed her bag and headed for the door. I listened to the sound of her footsteps in the hallway, the front door opening and closing.

From his cage in the living room, Darcy let out a quiet chirp, as if to say, *Max, you're pathetic.*

"I know," I muttered, staring at the ceiling.

I was in trouble. Real, serious, no-going-back trouble.

Because somewhere along the way, this had stopped being casual for me. And I was pretty sure Emma hadn't gotten that memo.

Chapter 17: Max

THE AUDITORIUM SMELLED faintly of stage dust and floor polish when I walked in Thursday afternoon. A few teachers were hovering over the lighting boards and speakers, fiddling with cords and clip-on mics. Emma was already there, pacing with a clipboard like she was conducting an orchestra.

"Everyone's here," she said, handing me the clipboard with the running list of acts.

"Awesome," I muttered, stepping over a bundle of cords.

Jen rushed over. "Here's the program. If you approve it, I'll go make copies."

We settled behind the piano, scanning the program. Val and Evan crouched near the speakers, muttering about feedback and adjusting the volume knobs. Dante paced along the aisle, stopwatch in hand, ready to time each act's entrance and exit. A group of volunteers was on stage taping marks on the floor to make sure everyone hit their spots. Pat had recruited a handful of students to help with the audience participation acts, assigning one to hand out props and a couple more to coach the volunteers on when to jump in.

Thirty-five acts. Teachers were improvising constantly—swapping out music files and helping each other with last-minute costume adjustments. Oz carried a ladder across the stage to fix a hanging spotlight and nearly tripped over a pile of cables. The air buzzed with the low hum of tech, snippets of popular music, and the occasional exasperated instruction: "Watch the timing!" "No, the cue comes after the intro!"

Amid it all, Emma and I huddled over the program.

"I don't see any mistakes. Do you?"

Emma leaned over my shoulder, close enough that I could smell her hair, floral, light, as she traced a line on the program with her index finger. "Is Marnie's name spelled correctly? I think there are two i's in McQuistion."

"Circle it, and I'll check with her," Jen said, handing me a pen.

I marked the spot, and Jen moved off to handle a last-minute question about microphones. Emma and I lingered over the clipboard, scanning the rest of the program.

"So," I said, lowering my voice. "About us lip-syncing..."

A familiar knot grew in my stomach. I didn't want to let her down but the idea of moving my hips and singing along to a song in front of a crowd full of my students made me feel ridiculous. I couldn't shake the image of her watching me, expecting me to actually perform. The thought made my palms clammy and my chest tight. Why does she have to be so good at this? And I'm such a mess? I glanced at her, brushing back a stray lock of hair, and for a second, I wondered if she knew how nervous I was. Or see through my fake confidence?

"Right." She tapped a finger against her chin, overlooking my reluctance. "We need something fun, high-energy... maybe *Love Shack* by the B-52s? It's short, catchy, and people will recognize it instantly."

I hesitated, glancing at the piano. "I don't know... I'm not exactly the dancing type."

Emma raised an eyebrow, smirking. "Max. This isn't just any song. All you need to do is move your hips. Loosen up a little. Come on, let's practice for a second."

Before I argued, she stepped closer, her hand finding my waist. The touch was light, almost teasing, but I felt it like a static shock running up my spine. "Like this," she said, demonstrating a few exaggerated sways, her body brushing against mine.

The chaos around us seemed to fade—the voices, the music, the hammering—all of it dulled to background noise. I tried to follow her rhythm, awkward at first, my hips stiff and uncooperative.

"Relax," she murmured, laughing softly as she guided me. "You're thinking too much."

Her fingers pressed slightly into my side, steadying me, and for a moment I forgot to be self-conscious. The warmth of her palm seeped through my shirt. I caught her eye and she was grinning, genuinely amused, and something in my chest loosened.

"See?" she said. "Easy."

I let out a breath I didn't know I was holding. "Yeah. Easy."

And then a shout echoed from across the stage. "Emma! Max! Could you help with these microphones?"

We both jumped, stepping back. Her hand slipped away and the auditorium rushed back in—loud, bright, chaotic.

"We'll practice the moves later," she said, shooting me a quick, half-apologetic grin before rushing off.

I stood there for a second, still feeling the ghost of her touch on my waist, before shaking myself back into motion.

I ducked under a stray cable and spotted Keith struggling with one of the speakers. "Need a hand?" I asked, crouching down next to him.

"Wouldn't say no," he muttered. "The speaker is tilted wrong, the cord is kinked, and the volume dial has a mind of its own."

Together, we adjusted the angle, untangled the cord, and tested it. A clean note rang out.

"Perfect," he said, giving me a thumbs-up.

I moved down the row, helping a couple of volunteers position chairs for the audience participation acts, showing them where to stand and reminding them of cues. One of the younger teachers looked frazzled trying to get the music queued correctly. I leaned over, pointed at the playlist on the laptop, and walked her through the steps. Her shoulders relaxed, and she nodded gratefully.

Emma caught my eye from across the auditorium and grinned. I waved, then ducked behind the piano to adjust the mic setup. By the time I glanced up again, Jen was folding programs with a few other teachers. I jogged over and took a stack to fold.

Around me, teachers practiced dance movements, laughed at jokes, and juggled books. Normally all of this noise and chaos would make me feel anxious, out of sorts, and I'd want to find a quiet space. But somehow the chaos didn't feel so overwhelming anymore. It felt like... teamwork. Everyone had a place, and we made it work.

Emma sidled up next to me, brushing against my arm as she leaned over to check a note on my clipboard. "You're really good at this," she said.

I shrugged, trying not to let my chest tighten. "I'm just... paying attention. Making sure it all gets done."

She smirked. "And here I thought it was your charming personality."

I laughed, shaking my head, but the grin stayed even as I glanced around. The program, the acts, the fundraiser—it was all coming together. And for the first time in a long time, I was exactly where I was supposed to be.

When my cell rang, I glanced at the screen to see the grant foundation's number, and my chest tightened. I looked up at Emma, who was helping Dante hang a banner across the front of the stage.

I slipped toward the back of the auditorium, weaving through clusters of volunteers. The door to the hallway felt heavier than usual, and I had to push hard to get it open. As it swung shut behind me, the hum of rehearsal faded to a muffled murmur, and the silence of the empty hallway pressed in around me.

My hand shook as I swiped to answer.

"Hello?" I said, trying to keep my voice steady. It came out thinner than I wanted, almost tight.

"Hello, is this Dr. Max Harrison?" a polite, professional voice asked.

"Yes, it is."

"This is Carla Jensen from the Mid-Atlantic STEM in Education Grant Foundation. I'm calling regarding your application."

My stomach flipped. I pressed my back against the cool cinder block wall, needing something solid. "Yes?"

"We've reviewed your submission and would like to invite you to an interview tomorrow at 4:30 PM at our offices in Norfolk, Virginia. We're meeting with the qualified applicants to help make our final decision on the grant."

"Tomorrow?" My voice cracked slightly. I pressed harder against the wall, as if it would hold me up. "I... I see."

"I'm sorry for the last-minute invitation. We hope you can make it."

I ran a hand over my face, my palm catching on the stubble along my jaw. Tomorrow. 4:30. Norfolk was forty-five minutes away—fifty if traffic was bad. And the fundraiser started at six.

My mind raced, doing the math. If the interview lasted an hour—optimistically—I'd be back on the road by 5:30. That would get me here by 6:15, maybe 6:20. Emma would already have the show rolling. The lip-sync wasn't until later in the lineup, and Emma could hold down the MC job without me for a little bit.

On paper, it wasn't a huge gap. I'd slip in during earlier acts, and no one would notice.

But what if the interview ran long? What if there was an accident on the highway? What if—

"Dr. Harrison?" Carla's voice pulled me back.

"I... I'll be there," I said, forcing my voice to sound firm. "Thank you for the call."

"Fantastic. We look forward to meeting you tomorrow at 4:30. I'll text you the location."

The line went dead.

I stood there, staring at the screen, my fingers white-knuckled around the phone. My breath felt shallow, tight in my chest.

This was it. The grant. Everything I'd been working toward. The chance to secure funding that could change things for the school. My students. My programs. I couldn't pass this up.

But the fundraiser.

The door to the auditorium swung open, and a burst of laughter and music spilled into the hallway. I turned to see Emma stepping out, her clipboard tucked under one arm.

"Hey," she said, her expression shifting when she saw my face. "You okay?"

I opened my mouth. The words were right there—I have an interview tomorrow at 4:30. *I might be a little late.*

But then I pictured her face tomorrow night. How she'd glance toward the door every few minutes, checking to see if I'd arrived. Her confidence might falter if she had to cover for me, if she had to explain to Jen or Keith or the volunteers why I wasn't there yet. She'd have enough to manage without worrying about me.

And what if I told her and she tried to talk me out of it? Or worse—what if she said it was fine, but I could see the disappointment in her eyes?

"Yeah," I said, forcing a smile and slipping the phone into my pocket. "Just... a quick parent phone call. Nothing important."

She tilted her head, studying me for a second longer than I was comfortable with. Then she nodded. "Okay. Well, come on. We need you to look at the speaker setup one more time. Val's convinced the left side is too quiet."

I followed her back into the auditorium, the noise and energy washing over me again. Emma moved seamlessly back into the fray, directing volunteers, adjusting cues, laughing with Jen over some inside joke.

I tried to match her energy, helping Keith with the speaker and answering questions. But the whole time, my mind kept drifting back to the phone call. To Norfolk. To 4:30 tomorrow.

I'd be back before my moment onstage. I had to be. It was a compromise, yes, but a necessary one. I wouldn't let the team down. I wouldn't let Emma down.

But as I watched her across the auditorium—laughing, confident, completely in her element—a knot of guilt settled low in my stomach.

I was lying to her. Not directly, maybe, but by omission. And it felt wrong.

Still, I told myself it was the right call. She didn't need this weighing on her, not while the show was happening. She needed to be focused, calm, present.

So I'd carry this alone.

Chapter 17: Emma

BACKSTAGE WAS CONTROLLED chaos.

Val swept past me wearing what appeared to be a cape made entirely of sequins, muttering something about dramatic lighting cues and the transformative power of theatre. Eli was frantically applying more eyeliner for his upcoming Queen lip-sync. Bobby paced back and forth, practicing her choreography as Sporty Spice for 'Wannabe' and nearly taking out a prop table in the process.

And I was about to throw up.

"You okay?" Thalia appeared at my elbow, looking annoyingly calm for someone who'd just finished her interpretive dance about middle school.

"Fine. Great. Totally fine."

"You look like you're going to hyperventilate."

"I'm not going to pass out."

"Your hands are shaking."

I looked down. She was right. "Where's Max?"

"No idea. Haven't seen him since lunch."

My stomach twisted. The show had started forty-five minutes ago, and I'd been covering for him—introducing acts solo, filling dead air with jokes and commentary, pretending like everything was going according to plan. But we were supposed to perform our lip-sync in ten minutes, and my performance partner had vanished.

From the stage, I heard Marnie and Evan wrapping up their stand-up routine about the various disasters that occurred in elective classes. Waves of laughter rolled through the auditorium.

"—and then the kid said, 'But Mrs. McQ, I thought Teen Living meant we could eat whatever we made!'" Marnie's voice boomed through the speakers.

Evan jumped in. "Wait, wait—how much cookie dough are we talking about here?"

"An entire mixing bowl, Evan. I'm talking full-on Cookie Monster level destruction."

"Oh no."

"Oh yes. Chocolate chips smeared all over his face, sitting there looking proud of himself."

Evan turned to the audience. "See, this is why I teach Tech Ed. Nobody tries to eat a bookshelf."

The audience laughed. Marnie waved him off. "So I tell this kid, 'You could get salmonella,' and he just looks at me—totally serious—and says, 'Is that Italian?'"

Evan doubled over laughing. "Is that Italian?"

"I wish I was making this up! We had to call his parents. His dad answered the phone, I said 'cookie dough incident,' and he sighed and said, 'I'll bring the Pepto.'"

"Not even a question!" Evan was wiping his eyes. "Just immediately knew what happened!"

"Apparently this was not the first cookie dough incident in that household."

"How many cookie dough incidents can one child have?"

Marnie shrugged dramatically. "According to his father? This was number four."

The show had been going incredibly well. Karaoke Roulette had opened the night with chaos and glory. Pat had drawn Baby Shark and performed it with such dead-eyed resignation that the entire audience gave him a standing ovation. Oz and Keith got Bohemian Rhapsody and crushed it. The role-swap skit had been inspired madness, and the Dramatic Readings segment was pure gold.

I had introduced every single act myself, standing alone at the microphone and trying to project twice the energy to make up for Max's absence. My face hurt from smiling. My voice was starting to strain. And with each introduction, each transition, the audience's confusion grew.

Where's Dr. Harrison?

I'd made jokes about it at first—light, breezy comments about Max "preparing for his big entrance" or "building the suspense." But as the show wore on and he still didn't appear, the jokes felt hollow.

Principal Kline had pulled me aside to whisper that we'd already exceeded our fundraising goal by almost a thousand dollars.

Everything was going perfectly.

Except that my co-host had disappeared.

I peered around the backstage curtain. The auditorium was packed—parents, students, teachers, community members all crammed into seats, many standing in the back. The energy was electric, the audience loving every moment.

And in approximately eight minutes, Max and I were supposed to walk out there and perform together.

"Still no sign of him?" Bobby appeared at my elbow.

"Nothing."

"Did you try calling?"

"Five times. Straight to voicemail."

"Maybe he's in the bathroom?"

"For an hour?"

Bobby made a face. "Okay, yeah, that would be a medical emergency."

Marnie and Evan were taking their bows now, the audience applauding wildly. I took a breath, smoothed down my shirt, and prepared to go back out there. Again. Alone.

"Emma, wait." Val rushed up, her sequined cape shimmering. "Honey, you've been running this whole show by yourself. Are you okay?"

"I'm fine."

"You look like you're about to either murder someone or burst into tears."

"Can't it be both?"

She squeezed my arm. "He'll show up. Max wouldn't abandon you."

Wouldn't he? The thought arrived sharp and bitter.

I walked back onto the stage. The lights were bright and hot on my face. The audience applauded, but I could see the questions in their expressions. Some people were craning their necks, clearly wondering where Max was.

"Thank you, thank you!" My voice came out bright and energetic despite the exhaustion creeping into my bones. "Wasn't that amazing? Let's give another round of applause for The Comedy Duo!"

More applause. I smiled wider, like everything was normal.

"And now, we have a very special performance from three of our incredible Marchfield alumni, and let me tell you, their talent puts the rest of us to shame. Please welcome to the stage our alumni group: The Knee Highs!"

They ran on stage with their instruments, and I retreated into the wings. My smile disappeared the second I was out of sight. My jaw ached.

Thalia was waiting with a bottle of water. "You're doing great."

"I'm dying."

"You're not dying. You're just carrying an entire variety show on your back with no help from your co-host who apparently fell into a black hole."

I forced myself to take a slow breath. Max wouldn't abandon me. There had to be an explanation. Maybe an emergency. Maybe his car broke down and his phone died and—

I pulled out my phone and tried calling again. Voicemail. I fired off another text: **WHERE ARE YOU??? We're on in 5 minutes! I've been doing this whole thing ALONE.**

No response.

The band was killing it on stage, the audience clapping along. In the wings opposite me, Eli and Dante stretched their calves.

"Maybe you should do the act solo?" Bobby suggested. "You could make it a comedy bit about—"

"It's a lip-sync battle. I can't battle myself."

"Maybe I could step in or Oz?"

"No. We planned this. Max will be here."

But even as I said it, doubt crept in. What if he'd gotten cold feet? What if he'd realized that performing in front of the entire school community was too much?

What if he'd just... left?

My chest tightened. No. Max wouldn't do that. Not after everything. Not after the planning meetings and the late nights and the way he'd looked at me yesterday during rehearsal.

The band took their bows to thunderous applause, but instead of leaving the stage, they launched into an encore—a surprisingly energetic cover of 'Don't Stop Believin''. Half the audience sang along. Parents in the front row swayed with their hands in the air. A group of students started a coordinated clapping rhythm that spread through the auditorium like a wave.

Val appeared at my elbow. "They're running long. Do you want me to cut them off?"

I shook my head. "Let them finish. Everyone's loving it."

And it bought me more time. Time for Max to appear. Time for this nightmare to end.

But the song ended, the band exited to a standing ovation, and Max still wasn't there.

I walked onto the stage again.

"Incredible! Absolutely incredible!" My voice rang out clear and strong, betraying none of the panic coursing through my veins. "Let's hear it one more time for our amazing alumni!"

The audience obliged with enthusiastic applause.

"You know, folks, I have to say—tonight has been magical. Every single act has brought their A-game, and you all have been the most wonderful, supportive audience."

I paused, scanning the crowd. Smiling faces. Happy families. Students bouncing in their seats with excitement.

All of them trusting me to keep this show running smoothly.

"Up next, we have the moment I know you've all been waiting for—our Lip Sync Battle extravaganza!"

I gestured dramatically, trying to channel every ounce of energy I had left. "We've got three incredible groups who are about to battle it out for the title of Marchfield's Lip Sync Champion. First up, our very own interpretation of Queen's 'We Are the Champions'. And let me tell you, this performance is going to be legendary!"

The stage crew was already wheeling out the setup—a makeshift throne and what appeared to be a fog machine that had definitely not been authorized.

"Then we'll have a performance of 'Wannabe' that involves sequins and possibly pyrotechnics, so buckle up!"

The audience laughed and applauded.

"And then—" I paused, my smile frozen on my face, "—Dr. Harrison and I will close out the battle with our own performance of 'Love Shack'. Assuming Dr. Harrison decides to grace us with his presence."

I said it lightly, like a joke, but I could hear the edge in my own voice.

"Please welcome to the stage our first performance! Get ready to vote."

Eli and Dante burst onto the stage to massive cheers, and I retreated once more to the wings.

Val was already cueing the stage crew for our transition. She was setting up two microphones and the props we'd carefully selected. Everything was ready.

Except for Max.

Eli launched into the most over-the-top lip-sync performance I'd ever witnessed, complete with air guitar and enough attitude to power a small city. The audience lost their minds.

I paced behind the curtain, phone clutched in my hand, willing it to buzz. Nothing.

"Emma, you need to make a decision," Val said, all business despite the sequined cape. "If Max doesn't show in the next few minutes, we need a backup plan. Can you do your act solo? Can we swap the order? Can we—"

"He'll be here."

"But if he's not—"

"He'll be here, Val."

She looked at me for a long moment. I saw something shift in her expression—pity, maybe, or concern. "Okay. I trust you. But have a backup plan in your head just in case."

Eli and Dante finished their performance with a dramatic drop to their knees, arms spread wide, soaking in the applause. The audience gave them a standing ovation. They took their bows and exited to the wings on the opposite side.

Which meant I had to go back out there and introduce our act.

Our act.

Max's and mine.

Except Max wasn't here.

I closed my eyes, trying to calm the panic rising in my throat. I could do the lip-sync solo. Make it a comedy bit about being stood up. The audience would laugh. It would be fine.

Except it wouldn't be fine because Max was supposed to be here, and his absence felt like a weight in my chest.

"One minute!" Val called.

My phone buzzed. Finally.

I looked down at the screen, expecting an explanation, an apology, directions to wherever he'd gotten lost.

Max: Running late. Start without me. Be there soon.

I stared at the words. Read them again.

Running late.

To the show he'd spent hours planning. The show that began more than an hour ago. The show where he was supposed to be my co-host, standing beside me for every introduction, every transition, every moment. The show I'd been carrying entirely by myself while he was... what? Running late?

The phone was slippery in my hand. The letters blurred and refocused. Running late. Start without me.

I had already started without him. I'd been starting without him for the past hour and a half.

"Thirty seconds!" Val hissed.

The air in the backstage area felt thick, suffocating. Around me, people were moving—Bobby adjusting her costume, Thalia stretching, Val checking her clipboard—but they all seemed far away, like I was watching them through water.

Where was he? What could possibly be more important than this? Than the four hundred people in that auditorium, than the fundraiser we'd built together, than all the teachers who'd trusted us, than standing beside me while I introduced act after act, alone, pretending like everything was fine—

I shoved those thoughts away, but it left a cold, hard knot in my chest.

"Emma?" Bobby's voice cut through the fog. She was looking at my face, then at my phone. "What did he say?"

I handed her the phone wordlessly. She read the message, and her expression shifted from concern to anger.

"Running late?" She looked up at me, incredulous. "He's missed almost the entire show! Where the hell is he?"

"It doesn't matter." My voice sounded strange—distant, hollow, like it was coming from someone else's mouth. "He's not here now. That's what matters."

"Emma—"

"Fifteen seconds!" Val called, her voice sharp.

I straightened my shoulders. The cold knot in my chest spread outward, numbing everything as it went. Good. Numb was better than whatever this other feeling was that made me want to scream or cry or both.

"I'll do the act. Keep things moving," I said, proud of how steady my voice sounded. "That's what we do, right? The show must go on."

Thalia grabbed my arm. "You don't have to do this. We can skip the act, move on to—"

"No." The word came out harder than I intended. "Everyone's here for the fundraiser. Supporting Field Day. I'm not going to let them down."

Even if Max just did.

I didn't say that last part out loud, but I saw it in their faces that they heard it anyway.

I walked toward the stage entrance, my legs moving on autopilot. Behind me, I heard Thalia whisper something urgent to Bobby, felt their worried gazes on my back.

But I kept walking.

The wings were dark, but beyond them, the stage lights blazed white-hot. I heard the audience—rustling programs, a smattering of conversations before the expectant hush.

I stopped before the curtain, my hand gripping the heavy fabric. My heart hammered in my throat, behind my eyes, in my fingertips.

I closed my eyes and took one more breath. When I opened them, the cold numbness was back, solid and reliable.

Time to figure out what I was made of.

I stepped onto the stage.

The lights hit me like a physical force—hot and white and overwhelming. For a second, I couldn't see anything beyond them. Just a dark mass of people, all watching me.

Alone.

The applause started, but there was a questioning quality to it. People were looking around, wondering where Max was. Heads turned, murmurs began.

I grabbed the microphone. The metal was cool against my palm, solid. Real.

"Good evening, everyone!" My voice came out bright, energetic, like I wasn't dying inside. Years of teaching had taught me how to fake enthusiasm. "Wow, weren't Eli and Dante absolutely spectacular?"

The audience applauded enthusiastically. I smiled wider.

"So, I have a confession to make." I kept my voice light, playful, even though my chest felt like someone was standing on it. "My co-host—the wonderful Dr. Max Harrison—seems to be running a little late this evening."

Some nervous laughter from the crowd. A few people glanced at their watches. Keep going. Keep smiling.

"Which means you've been stuck with me all night. And I know what you're thinking. You're tired of me." I laughed, making it sound like a joke, like this was all part of the plan. "Dr. Harrison is apparently a firm believer in fashionably late entrances. Very dramatic. Very theatrical. We love that for him."

More laughter, but I could hear the uncertainty beneath it. Where is he? Is everything okay?

"So here's what's going to happen," I said, my voice steadying even as my heart cracked a little more. "I'm going to perform this lip-sync. By myself. And it's probably going to be a disaster, and I'm definitely going to mess up the dance moves that were choreographed for two people, but you know what? We're all going to laugh together, and we're going to have fun."

"Hit it!" I called to the sound booth, and the opening notes of *Love Shack* filled the auditorium.

And I danced.

Chapter 18: Max

THE GRANT INTERVIEW had gone well. Better than well—it had gone perfectly.

Carla Jensen and the two other board members had asked thoughtful questions about my STEM curriculum proposals. They'd nodded enthusiastically when I'd explained our plans for hands-on learning stations. They'd actually laughed at my joke about making science accessible "even to students who think mitochondria is a pasta dish."

"Dr. Harrison," Carla had said as we wrapped up, "I have to say, your application was impressive on paper, but hearing you talk about your vision—it's clear you're the kind of educator we want to support."

My chest had swelled with something that felt dangerously close to hope.

"We'll be making our final decision next week," she'd continued, "but I want you to know you're a very strong candidate. One of our top three, actually."

Top three. Out of hundreds of applicants.

I'd thanked them, shaken hands all around, and walked out of the Norfolk office building at 5:37 PM feeling like I was floating.

The fundraiser started at six. I'd be about half an hour late, but I'd make it in plenty of time for our lip-sync act. Emma would understand. She had to understand. This was the grant—the thing that would change everything for my entire career.

I'd texted her as I jogged to my car: **Running late. Start without me. Be there soon.**

I'd hit send, slid into the driver's seat, and pulled out of the parking garage at 5:40 PM.

I hit traffic at 5:58.

Not slow traffic. Not heavy traffic. Complete. Dead. Stop.

I sat there, engine idling, staring at an endless sea of brake lights stretching as far as I could see down I-64. Cars packed bumper to bumper. Nobody moving. Not even inching forward.

My GPS cheerfully informed me: "Heavy traffic on your route. Estimated arrival time: 7:43 PM."

7:43.

The show started at six. Our lip sync was scheduled for around 7:15. I was going to miss it. I was going to miss everything.

I grabbed my phone to call Emma, to explain, to tell her about the interview and the traffic and—

No signal.

I stared at the screen. One bar. No, wait—no bars. The signal flickered in and out, teasing me with brief moments of connectivity before disappearing again.

I tried calling anyway. The call failed immediately.

Tried again. Failed.

I opened my messages, noticing that my message hadn't been sent either.

Stared at the screen, willing it to connect.

Sending...

Sending...

Sending...

The message just sat there, mocking me with its refusal to go through.

Around me, other drivers were getting out of their cars, standing on the highway, trying to see what was causing the backup. In the distance, I heard sirens.

I checked the time. 6:04 PM. The show had started. Emma was emceeing the show, looking for me, wondering where I was.

I tried the message again. Still sending.

A man in the car next to me had his window down. "Accident up ahead!" he called over. "Sounds like a bad one. We're gonna be here a while."

I was going to miss the entire show.

I tried calling Emma again. Nothing. I tried texting. The message wouldn't send.

6:11 PM.

She'd be introducing the first acts now. Alone. Wondering where the hell I was. Covering for me with jokes and that bright smile she used when she was trying to hold everything together.

I slammed my hand against the steering wheel.

This was my fault. All of it. I should have told her about the interview. Should have been honest from the start instead of convincing myself I could attend the interview and make it back in time for the show. Should have trusted her enough to understand that this grant mattered.

But I hadn't told her. Because some part of me had known she'd be hurt that I'd even considered missing any part of the show. Because I'd been a coward, taking the interview slot without discussing it with her, hoping I'd make it work without anyone having to know.

And now I was sitting in traffic, unable to reach her, while she carried our show alone.

The message finally sent at 6:57 PM.

Running late. Start without me. Be there soon.

I stared at the words on the screen. They looked pathetic. Inadequate. Like I was blowing off some casual coffee date instead of abandoning her.

But it was all I could send. The signal was too weak for a call, too spotty for anything longer.

I tried typing more: **I'm in Norfolk. Had an interview. Traffic is completely stopped. I'm so sorry—**

The message failed to send.

Tried again. Failed.

The cars in front of me hadn't moved an inch. My GPS now said: "Estimated arrival time: 8:02 PM."

8:02. The show would be over by then. I imagined her standing on that stage alone, making jokes about me being late, covering for my absence with that determined brightness she used when she was worried. I imagined the audience wondering where I was. The other teachers whispering. Principal Kline looking concerned.

I imagined Emma realizing I wasn't coming.

My throat tightened.

The grant interview had been important. It was important. But sitting here in standstill traffic, cut off from Emma, unable to explain or apologize or even hear her voice, I couldn't remember why I'd thought I could do this without telling her.

Why had I believed I would make it back in time?

Why did I think any of this would be okay?

At 6:45 PM, I managed to send another text: **I'm so sorry, Emma. I'll explain everything. You are incredible.**

I had no idea if she'd get it. Had no idea if my first message had reached her before she walked on stage or if she'd been blindsided.

The thought made me feel sick.

Cars started moving at 6:47 PM. A slow crawl forward, past the accident scene where emergency vehicles lined the shoulder, past the twisted metal and shattered glass that had brought an entire highway to a standstill.

I drove in silence, my phone sitting uselessly in the cup holder, still showing no signal.

By the time I reached the school parking lot, it was 8:09 PM.

I could see people streaming out of the auditorium. Parents with their kids, teachers still in costume, students laughing and taking selfies. The show was over. I'd missed all of it.

I parked and sat there for a moment, gripping the steering wheel, trying to figure out what to say when I saw Emma.

I had a grant interview in Norfolk.

I thought I'd make it back in time.

I got stuck in traffic and couldn't reach you.

All true. All completely insufficient.

I'd left her alone. That was the bottom line. I'd made a choice—consciously, deliberately—to prioritize something else over being there with her. And then, when that choice had blown up in my face, I'd been unable to even explain myself.

I grabbed my phone. Full signal now, of course. Now that it was too late.

Three missed calls from Emma. Two voicemails I was too afraid to listen to.

And a text from Eli: **Dude. Where are you? Emma's doing the whole show solo. She's killing it but she looks like she's dying inside.**

The timestamp: 7:15 PM.

Right around when she would have been performing our lip-sync. Alone.

I got out of the car and walked into the auditorium on shaking legs.

Through the open doors, I could see the lobby emptying out. Bobby talked animatedly with some parents. Val directed the cleanup crew, still wearing her sequined cape. Dante helped students carry props back to the storage room.

And there, in the far corner near the stage entrance, was Emma.

She was talking to Principal Kline, smiling and nodding, but even from here I saw the exhaustion in her shoulders, the way she held herself like she might shatter if she relaxed even slightly.

I started toward her.

Bobby saw me first and waved goodbye to the parents. Her expression went from cordial to furious in half a second. She whispered something sharp to Val, who turned and spotted me.

Val's face was harder to read. Disappointment, maybe, mixed with something that looked like pity.

By the time I reached the stage entrance, a small crowd had gathered. Bobby, Val, Thalia, Dante, Eli. All of them looking at me as if I'd kicked a puppy.

"You have some nerve showing up now," Bobby said, her voice low and dangerous.

"I know. I'm sorry. I got stuck—"

"We know. Traffic. We got your extremely helpful text." She crossed her arms. "Emma did the entire show by herself. Every introduction. Every transition. Your lip-sync act. Everything."

"I need to talk to her."

"Maybe give her a minute," Eli suggested. "She's pretty—"

"No, I should talk to her now." I pushed past them, my heart hammering.

Principal Kline gestured enthusiastically about something, still talking, but Emma's eyes had found mine over his shoulder.

For a moment, we just looked at each other.

I couldn't read her expression. Was she angry or hurt or relieved to see me? All three at once?

"Ah, Dr. Harrison!" Principal Kline turned, beaming. "There you are! We were wondering where you'd gotten to. Emma's been telling me what a tremendous success the evening was. Over twenty-five hundred dollars raised! Absolutely remarkable!"

"That's great," I managed. "Emma, can we—"

Kline continued, oblivious to the tension, "I'm so impressed with the results that we're going to allow you to each have your own separate extra-curricular. No more sharing! You've both earned it."

Emma's face remained perfectly blank. "That's wonderful news."

"Indeed! Well, I'll let you two celebrate. Excellent work tonight. Truly excellent." He patted both our shoulders and bustled off.

The auditorium had mostly cleared out now. Just our colleagues were left, trying very hard to not look like they were watching us.

Emma looked at me. Really looked at me. And my first stupid thought was *oh good, she's not crying.* As if that meant anything.

I saw it all there—the exhaustion, the hurt, the barely contained fury. The kind that doesn't explode, just burns everything down quietly.

"Emma, I'm so sorry. I got stuck in traffic and I couldn't—"

"Where were you?"

Her voice was quiet. Calm.

My stomach dropped. Calm meant she'd already gone through the screaming in her head. Calm meant I was too late.

"Norfolk. I had an interview and—"

"An interview," she said flatly. "On the night of our fundraiser, the one we spent hours planning. The one where you were supposed to be my co-host."

I opened my mouth, already scrambling, already trying to reorder the night in my head into something that didn't make me the villain.

"It was important. The foundation could only do today, and I thought I'd make it back in time, but—"

"Are you leaving? Taking a job somewhere else?" She laughed, but there was no humor in it. "And you... didn't tell me?"

The word *leaving* hit harder than it should have. I hadn't thought that far ahead. I hadn't thought at all—just one step ahead of the next, convincing myself I thought everything would work if I moved fast enough.

"No. Not a job. It was for the grant, and I didn't think I'd be this late. I thought maybe twenty minutes, and you're so great at introducing the acts anyway, so—"

Even as I said it, I heard how bad it sounded. How much it sounded like I'd already decided she'd pick up the slack like she always did.

"So you thought it would be fine to leave me alone?" Her voice cracked a bit. "To let me stand up there by myself, introducing act after act, making jokes about where you were, pretending like everything was okay when I had no idea you were okay?"

The image slammed into me. Emma smiling under the lights, scanning the wings, checking her phone between acts. I hadn't let myself picture that before. I hadn't wanted to.

"Emma—"

"I did our lip-sync solo, Max. Do you understand that?" She swallowed. "I stood on that stage in front of six hundred people and performed the act that we planned together. By myself. Because my partner doesn't value this school or me."

Something inside me twisted painfully.

"No, no, no, Emma, I tried to call you," I said desperately. "I tried to text. There was no signal and—"

"You should have told me." She stepped closer, and I saw her hands shaking now. That somehow made it worse. "You should have told me you had an interview. That you might be late. That I might have to do this alone. You should have given me the choice to prepare for that instead of blindsiding me."

She was right.

God, she was right. And the worst part was that I'd known it the moment I accepted the interview and still told myself it would be fine.

"I'm sorry," I said. "I'm so sorry. I should have told you. I —I didn't want you to worry, and I really thought I could make it back on time, and—"

"You didn't want me to worry." Her laugh was sharp, bitter. "Well, guess what? I was beyond worried, Max. I called you five times. Five."

Five. I pictured my phone lighting up in my pocket while I sat there nodding at the interviewer, telling myself I'd check it in a minute.

"I thought maybe you'd been in an accident. Maybe you were in the hospital. Maybe something terrible had happened." Her voice rose. "But no. You were fine. You were just at an interview you never bothered to mention, making a choice about what matters more to you."

The words hit like a physical blow. Because some part of me—the part I didn't want to look at—knew how it looked. Knew what choice it resembled.

"That's not—Emma, that's not what happened. I would never—"

"Wouldn't you?" She cut me off. "Because from where I'm standing, that's exactly what happened. You chose the grant interview over our show. Over me. And you know what the worst part is?" She shook her head. "You didn't even respect me enough to tell me the truth."

I wanted to say I'd been scared. That I didn't want to disappoint her if the interview went badly. That I was trying to build something *for us*. But every version of that sounded like a justification, not an apology.

"I didn't mean for it to happen like this—"

"But it did happen like this." Her eyes were bright with unshed tears, but her voice stayed steady. "You made a choice, Max. You agreed to go to that interview, and you didn't tell me. That wasn't an accident or bad luck. That was you deciding I didn't need to know."

"I thought I was going to make it back in time—"

"Stop." She raised a hand. "Stop. Because every word out of your mouth right now is just another excuse for why you thought it was okay to lie to me."

The word *lie* landed and stayed. I didn't have a defense for it. Only the sick realization that she was right.

"I wanted to be here," I said, quieter. "I tried to be here."

"But you weren't." She wrapped her arms around herself, suddenly smaller. "I'm going home because I'm exhausted, and I can't do this right now."

Panic flared, hot and useless.

"Please. Can we talk about this? Let me explain—"

"You explained already." She picked up her bag from a nearby chair. "Congratulations on the interview, by the way. I hope you get the grant. I really do."

That hurt more than if she had yelled.

She walked past me toward the exit, Jen and Thalia flanking her like a wall.

I didn't move. I couldn't. If I did, the whole thing might become real.

"Emma, wait—"

She stopped at the door but didn't turn around.

"I love you," I said.

The words were out before I understood them, before I decided whether they were true or just fear wearing the shape of truth. They sounded desperate even to me.

She stood there for a long moment, her hand on the door handle. I held my breath, waiting for anything. A look back. A word. A crack.

Then, quietly: "I can't do this right now, Max."

And she left.

I stood alone in the empty lobby, the echoes of the fundraiser still ringing faintly in my ears, and finally understood what I'd done.

I'd broken something that might not let me fix it.

Chapter 19: Emma

I DIDN'T REMEMBER THE drive home.

One minute I was walking out of the auditorium, Jen and Thalia flanking me like bodyguards, and the next I was sitting on my couch in my apartment above Share Your Buds, still wearing my fundraiser clothes, staring at nothing.

"Tea," Thalia announced, heading to my kitchen. "You need tea."

"I need something stronger than tea," I muttered.

"Coming right up," Jen said, pulling a jar of THC gummies from the cabinet.

I heard footsteps on the stairs that led up from the flower shop, and then Aunt Stella appeared in my doorway, her gray hair pulled back in its usual messy bun.

"I had to leave the fundraiser early to get Kendra Hault's wedding flowers done. She's marrying Tony Ridicchio. I think he was in your graduating class..." she petered, taking in the scene: me on the couch looking like I'd been hit by a truck, Jen handing out gummies, Thalia aggressively making tea. "What happened?"

"Max happened," Jen said darkly.

Stella's expression shifted from concern to something harder. She came in, closed the door behind her, and sat down next to me on the couch. She didn't say anything. Just put her arm around my shoulders and waited.

That's when I started crying.

Not pretty crying. Ugly, messy, hiccupping sobs that came from somewhere deep in my chest. The kind of crying I'd been holding back all night while I smiled and performed and pretended everything was fine.

Stella just held me. Didn't tell me it was okay or that everything would work out. Just let me cry until I couldn't anymore.

Thalia appeared with tea. Jen waved the gummies at me. I took both.

"Tell me," Stella said.

So I did. How I introduced every act alone, making jokes to cover Max's absence. How I did our lip-sync battle solo while six hundred people watched. How his text messages explained nothing. And how the confrontation in the lobby came afterward.

"He had a grant interview," I finished, my voice raw. "In Norfolk. On the night of our fundraiser. And he never told me."

Saying it out loud made it sound worse, not better. More deliberate. Less like a mistake.

"Why?" Jen's voice went sharp. "He knew the show was the same night."

"Apparently, he thought he could do both and just be a little late. It was like the show was an inconvenience to be managed, and I'd fill the space until he arrived."

"And he didn't think to mention this to you?" Thalia looked incredulous.

"Nope. Just left me to figure it out when he didn't show up." I took a long drink of tea, letting it burn my mouth. "And the worst part is, when he got there and tried to explain, all I could think was... of course."

Of course, this was how it went. Of course, I was the one standing alone under the lights, smiling through it. Of course, he'd found a way to choose something else without ever saying it out loud. It felt like he was already closing the door on me, on Marchfield.

"He chose something else over me," I said, "Why wouldn't he?"

Stella's arm tightened around my shoulders where we were already curled together on the couch, her thigh warm against mine. The living room was too quiet, the lamps turned low.

"Emma—"

"No, it's true." The words came out bitter. "It happens. It's fine. I'm used to it."

"That's not fair," Jen said from the armchair across from us. She leaned forward, elbows on her knees, like she was trying not to push too hard. "Max isn't—"

"Isn't what? Isn't like everyone else who's ever let me down?" I laughed, but it came out broken, sharp in the stillness of the room. "Because from where I'm sitting, he's exactly like them."

Thalia, standing near the window with her arms folded, exchanged a quick look with Jen as if deciding whether to intervene or let the moment play out.

Stella didn't look away. She watched me with those too-knowing eyes, her hold steady, grounding.

"Your parents," she said. Not a question.

I closed my eyes. "Can we not—"

"When's the last time you talked about them?"

"I don't need to talk about them. They're in prison. End of story."

"Is it?" Stella shifted to face me more fully. "Because I'm looking at you right now, and all I'm seeing is that fourteen-year-old girl who showed up on my doorstep convinced she was too much trouble for anyone to handle."

My throat tightened. "Stella—"

"Your parents made choices, Emma. Terrible choices. They chose drugs over you. They chose themselves over you. And you've spent the last twenty years trying to prove you're not like them by being the most optimistic, never-let-anyone-down person you could possibly be."

"What's wrong with that?"

"Nothing," Stella said. "Except when it means you can't forgive anyone else for being human. For making mistakes."

I pulled away from her, the couch suddenly too close. It hurt more than I expected, Stella's words landing like a quiet accusation I hadn't braced for.

"This wasn't a mistake. Max made a choice. He chose that interview over our show. Over me."

I'd replayed it too many times to believe otherwise. His trip to Norfolk. His silence. Those weren't accidents. Those were decisions.

"Did he?" Thalia asked. "Or did he make a bad choice about timing and then get screwed by circumstances?"

The room seemed to tilt, just slightly. I shook my head, too quickly.

"He knew about this interview and he didn't tell me." My voice rose. "That's the part you keep glossing over. He let me think we were doing the show together, and the whole time he was planning to show up late. He didn't even give me the chance to prepare."

"You're right," Jen said. "That was wrong. He should have told you."

"Thank you."

"But—" Thalia held up a hand when I started to protest, "—I have to ask. If he had told you, what would you have said?"

I opened my mouth. Closed it.

"Would you have told him to skip the interview?" Jen pressed. "Would you have been okay with him being late?"

"I don't know. Maybe."

"Or would you have told him the fundraiser was more important?" Thalia cut in. "Would you have made him feel like he had to choose between supporting you and getting the grant?"

"That's not fair."

"Isn't it?" Stella's voice was gentle but firm. "Emma, sweetheart, you have a pattern. When people let you down, you write them off. Your parents let you down in the worst possible way, and you've been protecting yourself ever since by never really trusting anyone."

“That’s not true. I trust people,” I said quickly, almost too loudly.

But even as I said it, a part of me knew they were right. I wanted to trust. I *did.* But trusting hadn’t stopped my parents from walking away. It hadn’t stopped Max from standing in Norfolk while I was under those lights. I wanted to believe in people, but every time I let my guard down, I felt the sting of being left behind all over again.

I bristled, hating that my own thoughts were giving Stella’s words weight. I didn’t need someone to point out my patterns. I saw them plain as day. But admitting it out loud? That felt like surrender.

Thalia tilted her head. “You always show up for everyone, Em. You’re the reliable one. The one who never lets anyone down. But remember when Han missed the Tricycle Basketball game at the last minute? You’ve never trusted him to co-lead since.”

“Yeah, I remember. I had to scramble the whole lineup. Everyone looked at me to fix it. And Han didn’t even apologize properly.”

“His mom was sick. He had to take her to the hospital, Em. That’s not his fault.”

“Like being stuck in traffic,” Jen pointed out. "Not because he didn’t care. Not because you weren’t important to him. It was out of his hands.”

It hadn’t felt that way when I was up there alone, covering for him, pretending everything was fine.

I shook my head. "He wasn't even sorry, not really. He made excuses."

"Or he was scared," Thalia said. "And trying to explain. And you shut him down before he could."

"Because there's nothing to explain! He chose—"

"He chose both," Stella interrupted. "He tried to do both things. And yes, he should have told you. That was wrong. But Emma, love, sometimes people make mistakes. They mess up. And if you can't forgive that, then you're never going to let anyone close enough to love you."

I wanted to argue, to tell her that love didn't erase humiliation and abandonment. But even as I opened my mouth, I remembered his words—the ones he blurted out, raw and desperate.

I love you.

Jen leaned forward, voice soft. "He told you he loved you, Em. That has to count for something. He wasn't trying to hurt you intentionally."

A flare of irritation raced through me. Three words didn't make it better. It didn't undo the waiting. The panic.

Thalia's hand touched mine. "Even if it was clumsy or late, he tried. You can't pretend he doesn't care at all."

I shook my head, torn. Part of me wanted to believe them, to let that tiny fact soften the edge. But the rest of me couldn't get past the choice, the absence, the crushing proof that even love didn't stop him from leaving me standing there.

I felt tears burning behind my eyes again. My chest tightened, hot and heavy, like it was trying to push the air out before I could even catch it. My hands curled into fists in my lap, nails pressing into my palms.

I swallowed hard, tasting the gummy's effects sweep over me, relaxing some of my tension away.

Stella said softly, "Max made a mistake. A big one. But from what you've told me about him, he's not your parents."

"He should have told me."

"Yes. He should have. And he knows that now." Jen sat down on my other side. "But, Emma, are you mad because he missed the show? Or are you mad because him missing the show confirmed what you've always believed about yourself? That you're not worth staying for?"

I wanted to argue. Wanted to tell her she was wrong.

But the words stuck in my throat.

Because she wasn't wrong. When Max hadn't shown up, when I'd read that text, my first thought hadn't been anger. It had been: Of course. Of course, he's not here. Why did I think he would be different?

Just like when my parents had promised to come to my eighth-grade graduation and never showed up. Just like when they'd promised they were getting clean and I'd come home to find them wasted again.

"Max isn't like your parents," Stella said softly. "And if you can't see the difference—if you can't let him make a mistake without it confirming every fear you have about not being worthy of love, then you're going to lose something real because of something that happened when you were fourteen."

I wrapped my arms around myself. "I don't know how to do this. I don't know how to trust that people will stay when they've proven they won't."

"Max came back," Thalia corrected. "He made a bad decision, but he came back."

"He lied to me."

"He didn't tell you something he should have told you," Stella said. "That's not the same as lying. And it's definitely not the same as choosing drugs over you, stealing from you, or any of the other things your parents did."

I knew they were right. Somewhere in the rational part of my brain, I knew Max wasn't my parents. That missing one event because of traffic wasn't the same as years of broken promises and abandonment.

"What do I do?" I asked finally, my voice small.

"You decide what you want," Stella said. "Do you want to protect yourself and push Max away? Or do you want to risk getting hurt and give him a chance to make this right?"

"What if he hurts me again?"

"He will," Stella said simply. "Not on purpose. But Em, he's only human."

I thought about Max in the lobby tonight. The desperation in his voice when he'd tried to explain. The way he'd said I love you like it was being ripped out of him.

And then I thought about him choosing the interview. Not telling me. Letting me stand there alone.

"I don't know if I can trust him," I admitted.

"That's fair," Jen said. "He broke your trust. It's going to take time to rebuild that. But, Emma—" she waited until I looked at her, "—you have to decide if you'll give him that chance."

"Why?"

"Because otherwise, you're proving your parents right." Stella sighed. "You're confirming that you're not worth fighting for by not letting anyone fight for you."

The words landed like a punch.

Thalia's hand found mine. "You are worth fighting for, Em. But you have to believe that before anyone else can prove it to you."

Maybe they were right. Maybe I was so busy protecting myself from being abandoned that I couldn't see when someone was trying to stay.

Maybe I should give Max a second chance.

But I didn't know. I didn't know anything except that I was exhausted and hurt and so, so tired of being the one who always held everything together.

"Can I just be mad for tonight?" I asked, even as the THC smoothed those stressful emotions away. "Can I sit here and be angry and hurt without having to figure out what I should do about it?"

Stella kissed the top of my head. "Of course, love."

"But tomorrow," Thalia added, "you're going to have to make some decisions."

I nodded, not trusting my voice.

We sat there for a moment in comfortable silence. The edible kicked in, softening the edges. The hurt was still there, but it was more distant. Manageable.

"You know what we should do?" Jen said suddenly. "We should order pizza. Like, an obscene amount of pizza."

"It's almost nine o'clock," Thalia pointed out.

"Pie in Your Eye is open until ten."

"She's not wrong," I admitted. "And I am kind of hungry."

"See?" Jen was already pulling out her phone. "Crisis pizza. It's a thing."

"Is it a thing?" Stella asked with a laugh.

"It is now." Jen squinted at her phone screen. "Okay, we're getting one pepperoni, one veggie, one cheese—"

Stella considered this. "Might as well get four, one for each of us."

A giggle bubbled up in my chest. It felt wrong—laughing when my heart was broken—but also kind of nice. Like maybe I didn't have to be tragic and devastated.

"Can we get French fries?"

The three of them stared at me. "Pizza and fries?"

"I want something salty."

Thalia raised her hand. "I vote for breadsticks."

"Yes, breadsticks," Stella agreed. "They're kind of salty."

Jen nodded but added both breadsticks and fries to the order.

"Can we get some ranch dressing?" Thalia asked.

"Okay," Jen nodded.

Stella frowned at them. "Wait, are you seriously going to dip pizza in ranch? That's barbaric."

"I'm not barbaric," Thalia said, mock-offended. "It's a delicacy."

"Pepperoni with ranch is cursed," Stella declared.

"Deliciously cursed," I said, laughing despite myself.

"Can we just finish the order, please?" Jen muttered, pretending to be irritated, but her eyes were smiling.

I sank deeper into the couch, letting their bickering wash over me. Tomorrow, I'd have to figure out what to do about Max. About whether I could forgive him. About whether I even wanted to try.

But tonight, I had my people. And pizza. And enough THC in my system to make everything feel a little bit less impossible.

"Extra garlic sauce," I called out.

"See, this is why I love you," Stella said. "You have your priorities straight."

I threw a couch pillow at her. She threw it back. Within seconds, all four of us were in a full-blown pillow fight, laughing like teenagers, the edibles making everything funnier than it had any right to be.

By the time the pizza arrived, we were sprawled across my living room floor, surrounded by scattered pillows.

"I'm too high to answer the door," I announced.

"I'll get it," Thalia said, pulling herself up. "But only because I'm the most sober."

"You told me ten minutes ago that my ceiling fan was judging you," Jen pointed out.

"It was! Did you see the way it was spinning? Very judgmental."

I dissolved into giggles again.

The pizza was perfect. The company was perfect. I'd figure out the rest later.

And for tonight, that was enough.

Chapter 20: Max

BARREL WAS STILL HUMMING with activity when Eli and Dante dragged me in. The low thrum of music, laughter, and clinking glasses hit me before I even got through the door, and for a moment I just wanted to turn around and go home. Wallow. Sit in silence. Let the night stretch on without pretending anything was okay.

But they wouldn't let me. Eli's grip on my arm was firm, relentless, and Dante was right behind us, prodding me forward.

"Come on," Eli said, voice sharp but teasing. "Sulking is for losers."

I opened my mouth to protest, but the words got caught somewhere between guilt and exhaustion. They insisted that I couldn't stay wrapped up in my own misery, and part of me wanted to resent them for it, but another part of me couldn't help but follow.

"You have to say something eventually," Dante said once we were settled at a table with beers. "Just sitting there looking tragic isn't helping."

"I ruined everything."

"There it is." Eli, sprawled in the seat across from me, raised his own beer in mock salute. "The Max Harrison specialty. 'I ruined everything and therefore I should just accept my fate as a lonely hermit who dies alone surrounded by color-coded socks.'"

"I'm serious."

"So am I." Eli leaned forward, elbows on his knees. "You screwed up. Big time. But you're sitting here acting like it's proof you don't deserve happiness."

I swallowed hard, rubbing at my face in frustration. I wanted to tell him I knew I screwed up, but the words stuck in my throat. "I missed the entire show."

"Because you were stuck in traffic after a grant interview," Dante said. "Not because you were at a bar or you forgot. Not because you didn't care."

I couldn't meet their eyes. "I didn't tell her about the interview."

Eli leaned back, his face blank. "Worst decision ever."

"Yeah, that was stupid," Dante said, tossing his hands in the air. I felt my cheeks heat up at his cheerful bluntness. "What were you thinking?"

I closed my eyes for a second, pressing my palms to my face. What had I been thinking? I knew it was a huge mistake. I knew she'd been hurt. And now, I felt small, completely exposed, and utterly responsible for it all.

I set my beer down on the table. "I thought I would make it back in time. The interview was at 4:30. The show started at six. It's a forty-five-minute drive. I'd be a little late, but—"

"But you didn't account for traffic," Eli finished. "Or for the possibility that the interview might run long. Or for any of the thousand things that could go wrong."

I sighed, pressing my palms to my thighs, trying to push down the tight knot in my chest. "I should've told her."

"Yeah." Dante's voice was gentle now. "Why didn't you?"

I ran my hands through my hair. "Because I knew she'd be upset. I knew she'd think I was choosing the grant over the show. Over her."

"Were you?"

"No! I wasn't choosing. I was trying to do both. The grant is important to me. It could change everything for my students, for my career. But the show mattered too."

"You thought you could have it all without having to compromise or be disappointed," Eli said. "Noble, but also impossible."

I slumped back in my seat. Outside the bar's windows, I could see the lights of Marchfield. Somewhere out there, Emma was upset or angry. Probably both.

Because of me.

"I told her I loved her," I said.

Eli snorted. "Yeah, we were there. Did you mean it?"

I closed my eyes. "I've never said it to anyone before. And the first time I do, it's while she couldn't even look at me."

"Okay, that's rough," Eli admitted. "But, Max, you know she was hurt—"

"I ruined it." I opened my eyes and looked at them both. "Her background. Her parents. A lot of people have chosen other things over her."

"You weren't—"

"Emma's parents went to prison when she was in middle school." My voice came out flat. “They were addicts. They chose drugs over her, over and over, until they got arrested and she had to go live with her aunt. And tonight, I reinforced her fear that I won’t stay."

Dante and Eli exchanged a look.

"So what are you going to do?" Dante asked.

“I don’t know.” The words came out quieter than I meant them to. I stared at my hands, at the faint dent my thumbs pressed into my palms.

Eli rolled his eyes. “Are you going to prove her right by giving up? By walking away?”

“I don’t deserve her.” I said it quietly, my shoulders curled inward as my heart throbbed with the dull certainty that I’d managed to ruin the best thing I’d ever had.

Eli threw up his hands. "Max, man, I love you, but this whole 'I don't deserve good things' routine is getting old."

"It's not a routine. It's reality. Emma deserves someone who shows up for her. Who puts her first. Who doesn't—"

"Who doesn't make mistakes?" Dante cut in. "Who doesn't have their own life and career and obligations?"

"That person doesn't exist." Eli’s voice was quiet but firm. "Emma doesn't need someone perfect. She needs someone who shows up even after they screw up. Someone who fights for her instead of running away when things get hard."

“You don’t get it. It’s not human nature to stay. Real life isn’t a fairy tale. People leave when it’s hard. I grew up bouncing from one home to the next. I’ve seen it a thousand times; caregivers, friends, foster families, everyone moves on.”

Dante and Eli shared a look.

“Hey, man, your childhood sucked. And I’m sorry,” Dante said. “You spent your childhood getting moved from family to family, and you internalized that you weren't worth keeping."

"That's not—" I stopped. Took a breath. "Maybe."

"Definitely," Eli said. "You've told us about it. The Hendersons. The Parkers. The Kowalskis who kept you for two years and then gave you back when their bio kid came home. All of them were assholes."

Just hearing the names made something twist in my chest. "What's your point?"

"My point is that those families made choices that weren't about you," Eli said. "Their limitations, their circumstances, their choices affected you."

"Every time I got moved, I'd hope that the next family would keep me," I said quietly. "I tried so hard to be perfect—" My voice cracked. "But it never worked out for longer than a year or so."

"And when they didn't keep you, you decided you weren't good enough," Dante finished. "And you've been operating under that assumption ever since."

I didn't answer. Couldn't answer.

"Max." Eli leaned forward, elbows on his knees. "The Kowalskis didn't send you back because you weren't worth keeping. They sent you back because their son needed them more. That's not the same thing."

"It felt the same."

"I know. But it wasn't." He held my gaze. "And Emma's hurt because you made a mistake, but that doesn't mean she's going to give up on you."

"She already did. She walked away."

"She walked away from a conversation," Dante corrected. "Not from you. There's a difference."

"How do you know?"

"If she didn't care about you, she wouldn't be upset. But according to Jen, who has been texting me, Emma's devastated. Which means this matters to her. You matter to her."

I wanted to believe that. Wanted to believe that Emma needed time.

But the fourteen-year-old version of me, who'd watched Mrs. Kowalski pack my bags while crying and apologizing—that kid knew better. Knew that caring wasn't enough. That love didn't mean someone would choose you.

"What if I can't fix this?" I asked.

"Then at least you tried," Eli said. "At least you showed up and fought for her instead of just accepting that you don't deserve her and walking away."

"But I don't—"

"Stop." Dante's voice was sharp. "Stop saying you don't deserve her. Because you know what? Maybe you don't. Maybe none of us deserve the people we love. But that doesn't mean we give up."

"That's not what I'm doing."

"Isn't it?" Eli challenged. "Because from where I'm sitting, you're already halfway out the door. You've already decided that Emma's going to leave, so you might as well save yourself the pain and leave first."

The words hit too close to home.

"I'm not—" I stopped. Took a breath. "I don't want to leave."

"Then don't," Dante said. "Stay. Fight. Show Emma that you're different. That you're not perfect, but you still care."

"What if she doesn't forgive me?"

"What if she does?" Eli countered. "Max, you can't control whether Emma forgives you. All you can control is whether you show up and give her the chance."

I sat there, turning that over in my mind. My deeply ingrained instinct was to protect myself, to assume Emma was done with me and start building walls before she could hurt me more.

That's what I'd done my whole life. As soon as I sensed a family was getting tired of me, I'd start pulling away. Making it easier for them to let me go. Proving I didn't need them before they could prove they didn't need me.

It had kept me safe but also lonely.

"I love her," I said.

"We know," they said in unison.

"No, I mean—" I struggled to find the words. "I've never loved anyone before. Not like this. Every other relationship, every other person, I could walk away because I never really let them in. And Emma, she got in." My voice caught. "But I hurt her. I proved that I'm exactly what she was afraid of."

"You're human," Eli corrected. "You made a bad choice. You should have told her about the interview. But, Max, making one bad choice doesn't erase everything else. It doesn't mean you're going to choose your career over her every time. It doesn't mean you don't love her."

"She doesn't know that."

"So tell her." Dante stood up, started pacing. "Stop sitting here wallowing in your foster kid trauma and go tell her. Explain about the grant. Apologize for not being honest. And then show her that you're not going anywhere."

I looked at both of them—my friends, the first real friends I'd ever had. They'd refused to let me keep them at arm's length, pushed past my walls, and decided I was worth the effort.

Maybe they were right. Maybe I owed it to Emma—and to myself—to at least try.

"And if she says no?"

"Then you respect that," Eli said. "But at least you'll know you tried. That you didn't just run away when things got hard."

We sat there for a while longer, not saying much. Eventually Dante left, and Eli offered me his spare room, but I declined. I needed to go home. To sit with my mistakes and figure out what I was going to do.

I wasn't the child who had been moved from family to family anymore. I wanted to be the person Emma made me believe I could be. Someone who belonged. Someone who stayed.

Someone worth fighting for.

And that meant fighting for her, too.

Chapter 21: Emma

SUNDAY MORNING HIT me like a hangover, though I hadn't touched a drop. I woke up on my couch, still wearing Saturday's wrinkled jeans and a faded t-shirt that smelled faintly of tomato sauce, with a crick in my neck that sent sharp protests down my spine every time I moved. Sunlight poured through my apartment windows in thick golden bars, offensively bright and cheerful, dust motes dancing in the beams like they were celebrating something I'd missed.

Jen and Thalia had slept over at my house on Friday night, so Saturday had begun with laughter that echoed off my kitchen walls and half-formed plans that never quite solidified: a lazy morning that melted into an afternoon of naps on opposite ends of my sectional and streaming shows we'd all seen before, which quietly slid into the purple dusk without any of us noticing the hours pass.

By the time they finally drifted down the stairs with promises to text later, I was more centered. Even lighter somehow, as if the sharpest edges of my troubles had been sanded down just enough so that I wouldn't cut myself on them.

I had no memory of turning off the lights or making the conscious decision to abandon my bed for the couch. Now I was left with the archaeological evidence of the weekend: crumbs embedded in couch cushions, grease-stained pizza boxes balanced on the coffee table, and hair that felt like a wild-bird's nest when I touched it. I needed to get up, to reclaim what remained of my weekend before it slipped through my fingers like water.

My phone sat on the coffee table where I'd abandoned it last night, screen dark and silent. Three new text messages glowed when I picked it up, notifications I'd somehow slept through.

I reached for it, then stopped, my hand hovering in midair.

What if one of them was from Max? If he'd reached out? Even a simple "how are you" or "thinking of you" would crack something open in my chest and break the fragile armor I'd been trying to build around my heart. Already I could feel my pulse quickening, rehearsing what I'd say, what I wouldn't say, how carefully I'd craft each word to sound casual when I was anything but.

But what if his name wasn't there? That would be worse, somehow. It would feel like a quiet confirmation settling into my bones—that this was really happening, that he was moving on, finding it easier than I was.

I grabbed the phone before I could talk myself out of it.

One was from Stella: **Can you help me deliver flowers at 4?**

One from Bobby: **How are you feeling today? Want to get brunch with the gang?**

One from Principal Kline: **Excellent work on the fundraiser! Please see me first thing Monday morning.**

I told myself I was relieved that there was nothing from Max. I had asked for space, after all, and he was giving it to me. That was the point.

So why did the disappointment sit so heavy in my chest, like a stone I'd swallowed?

I'd chosen this distance, but still some small, irritating, irrational part of me kept waiting for him to push back, to fight for us the way I couldn't seem to even fight for myself. I didn't want apologies or explanations. Just a sign. Something that meant he cared.

I stared at the screen a moment longer before setting the phone down and dragging myself to the shower. I let the hot water beat against my shoulders until the bathroom was thick with steam, the mirror fogged over. When I emerged, wrapped in my ratty purple bathrobe with its fraying belt, I felt almost human.

But my apartment was too quiet. Below me, Stella moved around in the flower shop, preparing for the wedding she had scheduled for 5 p.m.—the Thompson-Rodriguez ceremony, with centerpieces of white peonies and dusty rose garden roses.

I needed coffee. Real coffee, not the stale grounds I kept in my cupboard for emergencies.

Twenty minutes later, I was dressed in black leggings and an oversized navy sweatshirt, heading down Main Street toward The Percolator, my hair still damp and leaving wet spots on my shoulders.

I loved Sunday mornings in Marchfield—most people were at church or sleeping off their Saturday nights. The streets belonged to the small society of the restless and the early risers. It was peaceful. Quiet. And it asked very little of me.

Spring lingered in the air, cool enough to raise goosebumps on my bare arms. The trees that lined Main Street were budding in that almost golden-green color that only lasted a few days, that perfect in-between moment when you could still see the architecture of bare branches through the haze of new leaves. A breeze carried the smell of rich earth and wet pavement, mixing with the faint sweetness of the cherry trees.

I was half a block from the coffee shop when I saw him.

Max climbed out of his practical gray Nissan and walked across the street toward the shop with that purposeful stride I'd recognize anywhere. He wore dark jeans and a forest-green henley, his dark hair messy, standing up in the back as if he'd run his hands through it several times. Even from this distance, I could read the tension in his shoulders.

Every instinct screamed at me to turn around. But my feet kept moving forward. I watched through the large front windows as he ordered from the counter, his shoulders broad but somehow weary. The barista—Megan—laughed at something he said, and an unexpected stab of jealousy raced through me.

He accepted two cups of coffee, turned toward the door, and our eyes met through the glass.

For a second that stretched like taffy, neither of us moved. Then his expression shifted—surprise, hope, fear, all flashing across his face in rapid succession.

The door chimed. He stepped onto the sidewalk.

I turned and ran.

"Emma, wait—"

I broke into a jog, my sneakers slapping against the pavement, my heart hammering so hard I thought it might crack my ribs. I heard him call my name again, his voice raw with emotion.

I'd almost convinced myself yesterday that I could forgive him. But seeing him in person—solid and real—the hurt came rushing back so fast it nearly knocked the wind out of me. Physical. Visceral. Like being plunged into ice water.

His footsteps pounded behind me, rapid and determined.

I turned onto Oak Street and ducked into the small park, that pocket of green with a playground. Maybe I could cut through here, lose him—

"Emma."

I stopped. Turned. Max stood at the park entrance, breathing hard, still holding both cups of coffee. A lock of hair had fallen across his forehead.

We stared at each other across twenty feet of grass that might as well have been miles.

"I'm sorry," he said, his voice rough and unsteady. "I didn't mean to chase after you. I just—when I saw you, I thought maybe—" He stopped. Took a breath that seemed to hurt. "I'm making this worse."

He was. But he also looked like he hadn't slept in days—dark circles under his eyes, a hollowness in his cheeks. Some traitorous part of my heart wanted to close the distance between us.

I stayed where I was, feet planted in the dew-wet grass.

"Max, I—" My voice came out steadier than I felt. "I'm not ready to talk to you."

Something in his expression crumpled. "Okay, yeah, I understand." He looked down at the coffee cups, seemed to notice them for the first time. "It's just—I bought you this coffee. I was going to leave it with Stella."

He walked to a nearby bench and set one cup down carefully. "I really am sorry, Emma. For all of it."

Then he left, shoulders hunched, free hand shoved deep in his pocket. I waited until he was out of sight before walking over to the bench on unsteady legs.

The cup was still warm in my hands. I peeled back the tab and looked inside.

Dark roast, oat milk, one sugar. Exactly right.

Of course. Max remembered everything. The way I took my coffee, my favorite songs, the fact that I couldn't sleep if there was any light in the room. He noticed things, cataloged them, held onto them like they mattered.

I sat down and took a sip. It was perfect, still hot enough to warm me from the inside out.

I hated that it was perfect.

I hated that he'd known, even after everything, exactly how to make me feel cared for. I hated that a simple cup of coffee could make my throat tighten and my eyes sting. I hated that I was sitting alone on a park bench on a Sunday morning, drinking coffee meant as a peace offering, while the person who'd brought it walked away because I'd told him to.

But mostly, I hated that I didn't know what I wanted anymore. Space or closeness. Distance or reconciliation. To hold onto the hurt or to let it go.

I took another sip and watched a robin hop across the grass. The sun climbed higher, warming the air, and somewhere in the distance, church bells began to ring.

Chapter 22: Max

I TURNED AWAY FROM Emma and headed back toward my car, feeling something crack open in my chest. It was the kind of break that doesn't heal cleanly, that left jagged edges to catch on everything.

The morning air was colder now, biting through my henley. My hands were shaking—from adrenaline, from the crash after that brief, desperate surge of hope when I'd first seen her through the coffee shop window. For one perfect, stupid second, I'd thought maybe she'd smile.

Only two days since Friday night, but it felt like a lifetime.

I tossed my full cup of coffee in the trash outside The Percolator, the dark liquid splashing against the plastic liner.

"You okay, Max?"

Megan stood in the doorway, arms crossed against the morning chill, her expression carefully neutral. She'd seen the whole thing through the window.

"Yeah," I lied, the word scraping out like gravel. "I'm fine."

Her eyebrows raised. "That was Emma, wasn't it?"

I nodded, not trusting my voice.

"She ran away from you pretty fast."

The words hit like a punch to the sternum. "She has good instincts," I said with bitterness that surprised even me.

"No." Megan's expression softened. "I don't think so. She looked like she wanted to stay. Before she ran, I mean. The way she was looking at you..."

I shook my head, cutting her off before she could give me any hope to hold on to. "Doesn't matter what she wanted. What matters is that she ran." I forced my feet to move toward my car. "Thanks for the coffee."

"Max?"

I stopped but didn't turn around.

"Give her time," Megan said. "Sometimes people run because they're scared of how much they still feel."

I didn't respond. What could I say? That two days felt like an eternity already? That time wouldn't erase the look on her face at the fundraiser when everything fell apart?

I walked to my car and sat there, hands on the steering wheel, staring at the empty street ahead. Somewhere down the block, a dog barked. Life continued, indifferent to the fact that mine felt like it was ending.

I started the car and drove. I passed the hardware store. Passed the library. Passed the park where I'd apologized for things I couldn't take back.

God, I'd taken it for granted—All of it. The easy comfort of her hand in mine. The way she'd lean into me when we walked. The soft sound of her laugh.

I thought we had time. That I could keep my past compartmentalized, protect her from the messy complications. But that just made me a selfish, short-sighted idiot.

My phone buzzed. For a second, hope flared bright and desperate. Maybe it was her—

I pulled over behind the post office and grabbed the phone with trembling hands.

Eli: Brunch at Egglectic in 20. You coming?

The disappointment was physical, a weight dropping through my chest.

Me: Can't. Sorry.

I pressed the heels of my hands against my eyes until I saw stars. The darkness behind my eyelids was a relief from the bright, cheerful Sunday morning.

I should go home. Do something productive. But as I put the car back in drive, I caught sight of Share Your Buds at the end of the street, Stella's flower shop with its cheerful green awning.

Before I could talk myself out of it, I pulled into a parking space and got out.

The door chimed when I pushed it open. The shop smelled overwhelmingly of roses and lilies mixed with potting soil and green stems. Stella looked up from her arrangement, surprise flickering across her face.

"Max," she said, setting down her shears. "What are you doing here?"

The question hung in the air with everything she wasn't saying.

"I don't know what to do," I said, the honesty surprising me. "I thought maybe... you might have some insight, or—" I trailed off, realizing how desperate I sounded.

"She needs time," Stella sighed, sympathy in her voice but also firmness.

"I get that. I do." I shoved my hands in my pockets to stop them from shaking. "Is she okay?"

It was a selfish question. I had no right to ask. I couldn't stop myself.

Stella hesitated, and that hesitation told me everything I needed to know.

"She's hurt and confused," she said, choosing her words carefully. "But she's strong. She'll figure it out."

The finality of it—she'll figure it out, not "you'll figure it out together"—made my throat tight.

I turned to leave, hand already on the door handle, when Stella's voice stopped me.

"Max?"

I looked back over my shoulder.

Her voice was gentler now. "Don't give up on her."

I didn't know what to say to that, so I nodded and left, the bell chiming cheerfully as if I hadn't just had my heart handed back to me in pieces.

Back in my car, I gripped the steering wheel so hard my knuckles went white. I tried to breathe—slow, measured breaths—but the air was thin, insufficient.

I drove home on autopilot. Before I even got the key in the lock, Darcy's loud squawking sounded from inside. I'd left early this morning, too anxious about potentially running into Emma to remember to uncover his cage. Great. Add that to the list of things I'd screwed up this weekend.

The door swung open and Darcy started shouting from his corner cage in the living room. "HELLO! HELLO!"

I headed straight for his cage to remove the cover. His brilliant red feathers were slightly ruffled, and he had that indignant look parrots seemed to get when you've disrupted their routine. He gripped the bars with his gray claws and bobbed his head up and down, yellow eyes fixed on me with laser focus.

"I know, I know," I muttered. "I'm the worst."

"BAD BOY!" he squawked in agreement, then immediately followed it with "PRETTY BIRD!"

I couldn't help but smile, just a little. Darcy would cycle through every phrase he knew until he found one that got a reaction.

I opened the cage door, and he waddled out onto my extended arm, his claws gripping tight as I carried him to his feeding station by the window. He climbed onto his perch and waited, watching me expectantly as I filled his bowl with pellet mix and fresh fruits and vegetables.

"GRAPE!" he announced, spotting the container of sliced grapes.

"Yeah, yeah, hold on."

I added grapes to his bowl along with apple slices and bell peppers. Emma had researched parrot nutrition and shown me articles about the importance of a varied diet.

I'd teased her about extending her obsessive tendencies to a bird I was only babysitting.

She'd said someone had to look out for Darcy, since I clearly thought "a handful of seeds and some crackers" constituted a balanced diet.

I'd kissed her to shut her up. She'd kissed me back, the research forgotten.

That felt like a lifetime ago.

Darcy dove into the grapes enthusiastically, making happy little chirping sounds between bites. Then he looked up at me, head cocked to one side. "EMMA?"

The words hit me like a physical blow.

"She's not here, Darcy."

"EMMA! PRETTY EMMA! KISS KISS!"

"She's not coming." My voice came out rougher than I intended.

Darcy tilted his head the other way, studying me with unsettling intelligence. "MAX SAD?"

I stared at the parrot. Sometimes I forgot how perceptive he was, how much he picked up on emotions and tones of voice.

"Yeah," I said. "Max is sad."

"POOR MAX." He made a kissing sound, then added, "WANT CRACKER?"

Despite everything, I almost laughed. Leave it to a parrot to offer carbs as emotional support.

At least someone in this house wasn't disappointed in me.

I made myself eat a sandwich—turkey and cheese on bread that tasted like cardboard. The sandwich sat heavy and uncomfortable in my stomach, but at least it was something.

Darcy finished his food and flew over to land on the back of the couch, his wings making that distinctive whooshing sound. He preened for a moment, then waddled closer to where I was sitting.

"What?" I asked him.

"WHATCHA DOING? WHATCHA DOING?" he said, mimicking Emma, and the way she always talked to Darcy that when she came over.

My chest tightened. "Nothing. Just sitting here."

"SILLY BOY!" Darcy announced, then started whistling.

I tried to work on lesson plans for the week, pulling out my laptop. We were supposed to start balancing chemical equations tomorrow. But the words on the screen blurred together, swimming in and out of focus.

Darcy hopped onto the coffee table and walked toward my laptop, his head bobbing with each step.

"Darcy, come on. Don't—"

He stepped directly onto the keyboard with one foot, hitting random keys and making clicking sounds.

"You're not helping."

He lifted his other foot and placed it on the space bar, looking at me like he knew exactly what he was doing. "GOOD BOY!"

"You're really not."

I moved him gently to the side and he climbed onto my shoulder instead, nuzzling against my cheek and making soft clicking sounds. Despite everything, I smiled again. Darcy and I had come a long way in the last few weeks. I hadn't needed a Band-Aid in days.

I closed the laptop. There was no way I was getting work done with a parrot on my shoulder and my brain replaying this morning's disaster on an endless loop.

Darcy nibbled at my ear affectionately, then said in Emma's voice, "LOVE YOU!"

The words stabbed through me. If only Emma had said those three words back to me on Friday. Forgiven me for being a stupid ass.

Tears threatened to spill down my cheeks, and I brushed them away.

I should go to the gym, to work off this restless energy. But Darcy was settled on my shoulder, preening my hair like I was a fellow parrot who needed grooming, and moving seemed impossible. Besides, getting up, securing Darcy back in his cage, changing clothes, driving to the gym—it was all too much. It required energy I simply didn't have.

Instead, I stayed on my couch, one hand occasionally reaching up to scratch Darcy's head when he demanded it, staring at the ceiling and watching the afternoon light move across the white paint. The house settled around me with small creaks and groans.

Darcy made soft muttering sounds, the kind of contented noises he made when he was relaxed. Occasionally, he'd say something—"GOOD MAX" or "SILLY BIRD" or "WANT GRAPE?"—but mostly he sat there, a warm weight on my shoulder.

My phone buzzed again. Darcy's head swiveled toward the sound. "PHONE! PHONE! ANSWER PHONE!"

I didn't want to look. But some masochistic part of me reached for it anyway.

Mr. Kline: Excellent work on the fundraiser! Please see me first thing Monday morning.

I didn't deserve any recognition. I hadn't been there—not when it mattered, not when Emma needed me. Emma had handled every crisis, smoothed over every problem, made it look effortless even though I knew how much stress she'd been under.

Emma deserved all the praise, all the recognition, all the credit.

I set the phone face down on the coffee table.

"MAX SAD," Darcy said, nuzzling against my neck. "POOR MAX."

"Yeah, bird. Poor Max."

"GOOD BOY, MAX. GOOD BOY." He made kissing sounds, then added in Emma's voice, "IT'S OKAY. IT'S OKAY."

I closed my eyes, feeling the weight of the bird on my shoulder, hearing Emma's voice coming from Darcy's beak, and tried not to let it break me completely.

I pulled up my photos app. I scrolled back until I found it.

A picture of Emma and me on the couch, surrounded by laptops, flyers, and printed spreadsheets. Darcy was sitting on her head, the bird's red feathers contrasting with Emma's purple hair. We were both laughing, Emma's eyes crinkled at the corners, her smile genuine and unguarded. Darcy's wings were slightly spread, caught mid-movement.

"PRETTY EMMA!" Darcy said, seeing the photo. "KISS KISS?"

Two days. It had only been two days since everything fell apart.

I looked at that picture—at the evidence of what we'd had just two days ago, what I'd destroyed in the span of one awful night—and felt something crack in my chest all over again.

I should delete it. Looking at it made everything worse. But I couldn't make myself do it. Because deleting was like admitting it was really over.

Two days. How was I supposed to get through the rest of this Sunday? Let alone tomorrow, and the day after that, and all the days stretching out into an uncertain future?

The afternoon light continued its slow march across the ceiling. Somewhere in the neighborhood, a lawnmower started up. Life went on, indifferent and relentless, while I sat on my couch with my parrot and tried to remember how to breathe around the crushing weight of regret.

Darcy finished his almond and climbed back onto my shoulder, settling in with soft churring sounds. He nibbled at my ear gently, then said in a softer voice, "LOVE YOU, MAX. LOVE YOU."

I reached up to stroke his bright red feathers and tried to focus on that—the simple, uncomplicated comfort of a bird who loved me unconditionally, who didn't care about my mistakes or my secrets or the ways I'd failed.

I closed my eyes, Darcy's weight warm on my shoulder, and tried to figure out how to get through.

Until Emma was ready to talk.

If she ever was.

If I hadn't broken us too badly to repair.

"IT'S OKAY," Darcy said in Emma's voice. "IT'S OKAY, MAX."

But it wasn't okay. And I didn't know if it ever would be again.

Chapter 23: Emma

MONDAY MORNING ARRIVED with a sense of dread that permeated my whole body. I arrived at school earlier than usual so I could slip into my classroom without running into anyone. Without having to smile or make small talk or rehash Friday night's fundraiser.

I knew I needed to see Principal Kline. The text he'd sent was still on my phone, but I couldn't face the debrief and follow-up conversations about what went well. It was standard procedure. Expected. I should have gone to his office first thing.

Instead, I was hiding behind my desk, clicking through emails and refreshing my inbox like something urgent might materialize and give me an excuse to stay exactly where I was.

An email arrived. A message from Tyler's mom asking about Field Day logistics and her volunteer station at the Tug of War and Center-of-Gravity Station. I stared at the words without reading them. My chest felt tight. Not anxiety. Something heavier. Guilt, maybe. Or doom. I closed my computer, promising myself I'd come back to the email when I knew how to respond.

The phone on the wall by my office door rang, and I slowly made my way over to it. "Hello, this is Emma."

"Emma?" the administrative assistant's patient voice followed. "Principal Kline would like to see you in his office—now, please."

My stomach dropped. Max would probably be there and I'd have to pretend as if nothing had happened. I didn't know if I could do it

"Emma? Are you there?"

"Oh, yes," I answered too quickly. "I'll be right down."

I walked through the quiet hallway, past the pictures of field day and the trophies. Each step echoed too loudly, the cheerful photos and gleaming metal mocking the knot of dread settling deeper in my stomach.

I was waved back to Principal Kline's office as soon as I entered the hive of the administration wing. Low voices drifted around me as I threaded between cubicles and desks acutely aware of every glance. The door to his office loomed at the end of the corridor, and I hesitated before lifting my hand and knocking.

"Come on in," Principal Kline said brightly.

His office smelled faintly of peppermint and printer toner, with an undertone of whatever cleaning spray the custodial staff used after hours. Sunlight slanted through the half-closed blinds, striping the plaques on the wall—*Excellence in Leadership, Ten Years of Service*. The clock above his filing cabinet ticked audibly. Kline looked genuinely pleased, perched behind his desk with his hands folded.

Max sat in the chair opposite him, angled away, as if even the furniture had chosen sides. He looked put together and calm in his khaki pants and school polo—handsome, I noted against her will. I took in the broad set of his shoulders, the careful way his hands rested on his knees, his expression neutral and unreadable. I stopped myself there. What he looked like didn't matter anymore.

I lowered myself into the remaining chair, the seat stiff, unforgiving. Folding my hands in my lap and fixing my gaze on the edge of Kline's desk, I braced myself for whatever came next.

"I wanted to thank you again," he said, beaming at us both. "The fundraiser was a huge success. Best turnout we've had in years. Parents loved it. PTA loved it. I loved it."

Relief loosened something in my shoulders I didn't know was knotted. I should have felt vindicated. I mostly felt tired.

"And," Kline continued, shuffling papers on his desk with the satisfied efficiency of a man who thought he was solving problems, "since things went so well, I thought I should circle back to your extracurriculars. I know you made... adjustments this year. But now we have enough money for you both to have what you originally wanted."

He spread a paper on his desk, tapping it with one cheerful finger. "Separate activities. Emma, Field Day can go on as usual, and Max, I hope there is enough time for a science fair."

The immediate, reflexive, relief hit first like muscle memory. Field Day was mine again. My activities, my whistle, my neat rotation of events. No negotiations. No additional complications. No having to check in, coordinate, wonder if someone else's idea might actually be better than mine.

The thought sat in my chest like a stone I couldn't cough up.

"Oh," I said because silence would be strange, but I couldn't quite manage enthusiasm. "Okay."

Kline nodded, satisfied, already moving on. "I know there isn't much time to shift gears, but I want you both to know I'm here to support you anyway I can." His smile was big. "I think this will be the best for everyone involved."

I smiled too, because that's what you do when the principal tells you everyone will be happy.

I left the office in a daze. My legs carried me forward without instruction, retracing the same path past bulletin boards and glassed-in offices, while my thoughts lagged behind, stuck on what had been said. The door clicked shut behind me, and the air in the hallway was cooler somehow. My smile was gone now, my body feeling hollow and unsettled.

Max stepped up beside me; neither of us said anything as we walked shoulder to shoulder past bulletin boards layered with bright construction paper and classroom doors shouting growth-mindset slogans in capital letters.

A bell rang, and the sounds of the school swelled around us. Students poured in—lockers slamming, sneakers squeaking against linoleum, voices colliding and separating in a restless tide.

"Well, I guess..." Max began, his voice tentative, like he was testing how much space he was allowed.

"Yeah," I said too quickly. I told myself to keep my distance. I'd asked for space, fought for it, and even though he's apologized, I needed to rebuild my walls before we could be friends. Before I could smile at him again and laugh. "Good luck with your science fair."

He slowed. "Emma—"

"Max, I have to go." I didn't look at him. "We have students waiting."

"Okay, but—"

I turned and walked away before he could finish, before whatever he was about to say could settle between us and take root. I gathered my emotions tightly, folding them inward, holding myself together by sheer will, so I wouldn't cry here, in the middle of the hallway, surrounded by middle schoolers.

The gym was alive when I arrived, echoing in a way that made every sound twice as loud. Kids darted in and out of the locker rooms, their energy ricocheting off the cinder-block walls and the high ceiling with its exposed ductwork. The air smelled like rubber, sweat, and that powdery stuff they put on the floors. Brianna spotted me and waved both arms like she was directing traffic, nearly smacking the kid beside her.

"Ms. Emma! Is it Field Day yet?"

"It's Friday," I said, "We're doing the PACER test today."

Brianna groaned theatrically, throwing her whole body into it. "Ugh. I hate the PACER test."

"That's why you timeout so fast," Tyler added, leaning in with a grin sharp enough to cut paper. "You give up before you start."

"I do not," Brianna insisted. "I just don't like running."

I watched them bicker, the way kids do—loud, affectionate, unselfconscious, completely unaware that I was lost in my own thoughts. Their voices rose and overlapped, full of urgency over things that would matter intensely for about five minutes. I envied the simplicity of it, remembering a time when Max and I bickered over everything.

Their laughter pulled me back to the role I was supposed to be playing. Tyler grabbed two foam balls from the equipment cart and pretended to juggle while Brianna tried to knock them out of his hands.

I glanced down at my clipboard. Two pages were attached: a roster of students and my plain black and white lesson plan.

A sense of loss hit me. There was no pristine schedule with color-coded tabs.

Last year, Field Day had been mine alone—predictable, but successful in all the ways that could be measured. It had been stressful, yes, but clean in its own way. Every decision, every problem, every upset parent or confused volunteer had come back to me, and I'd handled it.

This year was different. Despite the compromises, the responsibility had been shared, the weight spread between two people instead of one. But trusting Max had come with a price. And disappointment settled in quietly, dulling my enthusiasm, turning something I once cared about into a task I was simply going to endure.

By every reasonable standard, going back to the chopping block should be considered a success. It was easier. The administration was pleased. The event would be a success.

I should feel grateful.

I should be happy. I was happy.

Weren't those the same thing?

"Ms. Bennett," Tyler said, snapping me back. "I can't wait to drop my egg at Field Day. I have a foolproof system."

I hesitated. Just a beat too long. Long enough that Tyler's expression shifted from hopeful to uncertain.

"We'll see," I said, and the words tasted like retreat. "There might be some changes."

Brianna's eyes narrowed. "But why?"

"It's all very complicated right now."

Tyler squinted at me, skeptical in that way that eleven-year-olds are when adults start hedging. "Is Field Day going to be cancelled?"

I smiled at that, small and real. "No. Field Day's still on—I'm finalizing a couple of things."

Tyler looked like he was about to push when the bell rang, cutting through the gym like a knife. Kids scattered into motion, finding their morning spot and sitting. A group of girls laughed too loudly and someone's phone buzzed in a backpack they weren't supposed to have in the gym.

I started my routine—taking attendance, going over the instructions for the day—and soon fell into the familiar rhythm of it all while Pat set out cones for the PACER test. My body moved on autopilot, voice steady, clipboard balanced against my arm. The kids knew what to do. I knew what to do. It all worked because it always had.

And that was the problem.

Standing there, watching the students move easily through the space, hearing the low buzz of conversation, I felt something shift inside me. Last year, this competence had felt like pride. Now it was like insulation—like I'd built walls so high around my little kingdom that nothing new could get in. Nothing challenging. Nothing unexpected.

I hadn't been pushing myself forward. I'd been standing still, calling it stability.

The realization settled over me like dust. When had I stopped wanting more? When had good enough become my ceiling instead of my floor? I'd spent so long protecting what I'd built here—my reputation, my territory, my control—that I'd forgotten how to reach for something just out of grasp. To take risks.

Pat led the kids through their warm-ups, their laughter echoing off the gym walls, their energy infectious. I watched them stretch and joke and challenge each other, and the truth I'd been dodging since Friday crystallized into something I couldn't ignore anymore.

I didn't want Field Day the old way. I wanted the challenge, mess, and excitement of trying something new. Old Field Day didn't fit the version of myself I was becoming—the one who'd stayed up late reworking stations, who'd felt that spark of possibility when Max suggested adding center of gravity to tug of war, who'd enjoyed the planning instead of just doing it.

I wanted to collaborate. I wanted to celebrate how physical education could be part of something bigger, something that showed kids that movement, science, and learning were all connected. That taking risks was worth it.

But wanting it and admitting I wanted it were two different things.

Because admitting it meant I'd have to do something about it, and that terrified me.

Chapter 24: Max

MONDAY AFTERNOON DRAGGED. The minutes stretched like taffy, each one sticky and slow. I sat at my desk staring at the science fair planning spreadsheet on my laptop screen. The rows and columns should have been satisfying but instead looked like empty placeholders.

I needed to talk to the kids. Get them excited. That was the whole point—student engagement, hands-on learning, giving them something to look forward to that lived outside worksheets and textbooks. The science fair was a chance for them to feel capable and in control, to cheer for one another, to apply their knowledge to something real.

If my enthusiasm faded, they would feel it. And I wasn't willing to let my guilt and heartache be the thing that flattened their anticipation. The science fair wasn't about me. It was about the kids, about creating a program that mattered to them.

The bell rang for dismissal, and I stepped into the hallway, catching the tide of bodies flowing toward lockers and buses. Kids jostled past, backpacks slung over one shoulder, conversations overlapping into white noise.

I spotted Sophia first, walking with Dominic.

"Hey, Sophia," I called, waving her over. "Got a second?"

She veered toward me, Dominic trailing behind.

"What's up, Dr. H?" Sophia asked, hitching her backpack higher.

"The science fair," I said, trying for enthusiasm, "is back on and coming up in a few weeks. How do you feel about entering?"

Sophia's face went carefully blank, the way kids' faces do when they're about to disappoint an adult they actually like. "Um. Maybe? I haven't really thought about it since it got cancelled."

"You should," I pressed, because I was desperate and also because I believed it. "You could do something with physics. Build a catapult, test projectile motion, that kind of thing."

"That sounds cool," Sophia said, in the tone of someone who did not think it sounded cool.

Dominic bounced on his toes. "Are we still doing science events? During Field Day"

My stomach dropped. "Well, Field Day isn't—we're talking about science fair right now."

"But Field Day is way more fun," Dominic said, grinning like he'd delivered an irrefutable truth. "Ms. Bennett said there might be changes. Do you know what the changes are?"

"I don't—" I started, but Sophia cut me off.

"Aren't you guys working together anymore?" she asked, and there was something sharp in her voice. Not accusatory, just... aware. Kids always knew more than you thought they did.

"We're still working together," I said, though the words felt slippery. Technically true. Professionally accurate. Completely beside the point.

"Good," Sophia said. "Last year's Field Day was boring. This year sounds way better. More activities and fun stuff."

Dominic nodded enthusiastically. "Yeah, and Ms. Bennett is so good at making it fun, so together you're like—" He gestured with both hands, trying to illustrate synergy and only succeeding in nearly dropping his binder. "You're like a super team."

"Thanks," I managed. "But seriously, science fair—"

"I'll think about it," Sophia said, edging away. "I gotta catch my bus."

"Me too!" Dominic said, and they disappeared into the stream of kids, leaving me standing there in the hallway like driftwood.

I tried three more times.

Three more kids, three more versions of the same conversation.

Each one ended with them asking about STEM Field Day and Emma. Not one of them was interested in doing the science fair. Nobody cared about catapults or baking soda volcanoes or any of the things I thought would matter.

By the time the hallway emptied, I was standing alone near the water fountain, listening to the hum of the vending machine in the teacher's lounge down the hall while guilt and realization washed over me in waves.

I couldn't bury my feelings anymore. Couldn't pretend this was something I could logic my way out of or fix with the right words.

My problem wasn't about the science fair or reaching kids through hands-on learning. It wasn't just about collaboration or sharing a budget or proving I could work well with others.

It was about Emma.

It was about the way my pulse kicked up when she smiled at one of my ideas instead of shooting it down. How I'd started timing my arrivals to the teacher's cafeteria to match her lunch period. How I caught myself scanning hallways hoping for a glimpse of her and manufacturing reasons to walk past the gym.

I'd been calling it teamwork. Building bridges. Professional growth.

But standing here in the empty hallway, I couldn't lie to myself anymore.

This was about missing the fundraiser. About the look on her face when I hadn't shown up. The way her expression had shuttered, like she'd been expecting it all along. I'd let her down in the exact way she'd been braced for since the beginning, proving every cautious instinct she'd had about me right.

I'd done that. I'd hurt her.

And that scared me more than I wanted to admit because I had no idea if she'd ever let me close again, or if I'd already used up my one chance and blown it.

I pulled out my phone, thumb hovering over her contact. Then I shoved it back in my pocket. This wasn't a text conversation. This was a walk-down-the-hall-and-knock-on-her-door conversation.

My classroom felt too small on the way back. I grabbed my keys. Darcy squawked from his perch protest, ruffling his scarlet feathers.

"DARCY GO!"

"Yes, buddy, you're coming with me." Emma would be less likely to turn Darcy away. "We're going on a field trip."

He settled onto my shoulder, his claws gripping the fabric of my shirt as I headed toward the gym. My heart hammered against my ribs, each step echoing too loud in the empty corridor. What was I going to say? How did you tell someone you'd been an idiot without sounding like an idiot?

"MAX IS A DUMMY!" Darcy chirped near my ear, as if reading my mind.

"Not helping," I muttered.

The gym was quiet when I got there, but there was light under her office door.

I knocked. Two quick raps that sounded braver than I felt.

"Come in," she called.

I opened the door. She looked up from her desk, surprise flickering across her face before she smoothed it into something neutral. Professional. I recognized it as the same mask I'd been wearing all day. Then her eyes landed on Darcy, and her expression shifted.

“EMMA!” Darcy did a little head-bobbing dance. “KISS KISS!”

She smiled.

"Hey," I said.

"Hey." She tilted her head slightly, studying the bird. "You brought backup?"

"Moral support," I said. Darcy bobbed his head and flew to her shoulder.

“KISS KISS!” he demanded and Emma stroked him and kissed his neck.

The silence stretched. I cleared my throat.

"I need to talk to you," I said. "But first, I need to apologize. Again. I know I said it before, but I need you to hear it. I'm sorry I let you down. I'm sorry I wasn't at the fundraiser when I said I would be. And I'm sorry I didn't communicate with you when things went sideways."

She started to speak, but I held up a hand.

"Let me finish. Please." I took a breath. "I've never had anyone in my life that I needed to keep in the loop this way. I've always handled things on my own, made decisions solo. But that's not fair to you. I won't forget that again. You deserve to be included, to know what's going on. I promise I'll do better."

Her expression softened slightly, concern flickering across her face.

"I can't promise that life won't throw curveballs," I continued. "But I can promise that I won't disappear on you again. I'll communicate. You deserve that. You deserve someone who shows up."

She was quiet for a moment, her fingers still on Darcy’s feathers.

"Thank you," she said, her voice soft. She nodded slowly, weighing my words, wondering whether to trust them.

The fact that she was even considering it—that she hadn't shut me down immediately—was more than I deserved.

"And we should also talk about Field Day."

She nodded slowly. "Okay."

My pulse kicked up again. This was it—the moment where I either fixed what I'd broken or made it worse. Where I found out if she'd give me another shot or if I'd burned that bridge completely.

"I don't want to do it separately," I said, the words coming out in a rush. "I know Kline said we could go back to the old way, and I know that's what we originally wanted, but I don't—" I stopped, trying to find the right words. "I don't want that anymore."

Her expression shifted, something cautious and hopeful breaking through. "You don't?"

"No." I stepped further into the room, letting the door swing shut behind me. Darcy shifted on her shoulder, his tail feathers brushing her neck. "And the kids don't want it either. I tried to get them excited about the science fair today, and all they wanted to talk about was STEM Field Day. About what we did together. About how it was going to be better."

"Really?" she asked.

"Really," I said. "And the point is—they're right. STEM Field Day is better."

She sat down in her chair, jostling Darcy who hopped onto her desk. "That's a lot of self-awareness for a Monday afternoon."

There it was—that dry humor I'd been craving since Friday. The tension in my shoulders eased just a fraction.

"I've had a rough day," I said, and she laughed, the sound hitting me square in the chest.

Her laugh was quiet, a little hesitant, but real. And after everything, it felt like forgiveness I hadn't earned but desperately wanted.

Darcy whistled. "MAX AND EMMA!"

Emma's eyebrows shot up, her cheeks flushed as she looked from the macaw to me.

"Did you teach him that?" she asked, amused.

"Absolutely not," I said, though I couldn't help grinning. "But I'm not complaining about his editorial commentary."

She shook her head, still smiling, and reached out to scratch Darcy under his beak. The bird leaned into her touch, humming contentedly.

The moment stretched between us—lighter, but still weighted with everything unsaid. She looked up at me, her expression serious, more searching.

"So what are you saying about Field Day?" she asked.

"I'm saying I want to work together again," I said. "Officially. Not just because Kline is making us, but because I want to. Because I think we make a good team. Because—" I hesitated, then pushed forward. "Because I don't want to do this without you."

She was quiet for a long moment, her fingers drumming lightly on the desk.

"Max," she said carefully, "we need to be clear about what we're doing here. Field Day is one thing. But we've been more than colleagues. We crossed that line. Multiple times. We can't pretend we didn't."

"Emma—"

"I'm not saying it was a mistake," she interrupted, her voice steady but her eyes uncertain. "But I can't pretend it didn't happen."

I stepped closer to her desk, my heart hammering. "You're right. And I'm not going to stand here and hide the fact that I'm in love with you."

Her eyes widened, her breath catching.

"I love you, Emma," I said, the words steady even as my pulse raced. "I love the way you fight for what you believe in. I love how fiercely you protect your space and your students. I love that you're stubborn and brilliant and that you don't make anything easy—because nothing worth having should be easy."

I held her gaze, letting her see everything I'd been trying to keep buried. "And I love that every time we've touched, every time we've been together, it brought me closer to you. And the way you look at me when you think I'm not paying attention, it destroys me and fills me with hope at the same time. All of it means something, Emma. All of it matters."

Her breath caught slightly, and I saw her fingers tighten on the edge of her desk.

"I'm not asking you to trust me," I said, my voice dropping lower. "I know I have to earn that back. But I am asking you to believe that when I say I don't want to do this without you, I'm not just talking about Field Day."

I took another step closer, close enough that I could see the flutter of her pulse at her throat. "I'm talking about everything. The planning sessions that run too late. The coffee runs. The moments when you let your guard down and I get to see who you really are. I want all of it, Emma. And I'm willing to wait however long it takes for you to want it too."

She stared up at me, her lips parted, and for a moment, neither of us moved.

Had I miscalculated everything? Pushed too hard, said too much, laid myself bare when she didn't want to hear it?

When her eyes filled with tears, I panicked.

Shit. Shit. What was wrong with me? I'd dumped my entire heart at her feet when she was still trying to decide if she could trust me. This was exactly the kind of emotional ambush that made people run, and Emma Bennett already had one foot out the door. I should've eased into it. Should've waited. Had I torpedoed any chance I had left?

I opened my mouth to backtrack, to apologize, to take it all back even though I knew it would be impossible to unsay.

But then she met my eyes.

"Max," she whispered, her voice breaking slightly. "I—"

"You don't have to say it back," I said, even though the hope in my chest was almost painful. "I just needed you to know. I needed you to understand that this isn't casual for me. That you're not—"

"I know," she interrupted. She stood up, closing the distance between us until she was close enough that I could see the gold flecks in her violet eyes. "And that terrifies me."

My heart hammered. "Emma—"

"I want to believe that you mean it. That you'll stay. That this—" she gestured between us, "—is worth the risk." She took a shaky breath.

The knot in my chest loosened just enough to breathe.

"Then let me prove it to you," I said, meaning every word. "Every single day."

Her breath hitched, and she bit her lower lip, eyes searching mine like she was looking for any trace of doubt or hesitation. Whatever she found there must have been enough, because she nodded.

"Okay," she whispered.

A tear slipped down her cheek, and without thinking, I reached up and brushed it away with my thumb. She didn't pull back. Instead, she leaned into my touch, just barely, her eyes closing for the briefest moment.

When she opened them again, there was something raw and hopeful in her expression that made my chest ache.

She took a small step back, creating space between us, and I let my hand drop even though everything in me wanted to keep touching her.

"But I need to know we can do this—work together, trust each other—without sex clouding it. And I need to prove to myself that I can finish what we started without getting distracted..." She gestured vaguely between us, color rising in her cheeks.

I felt the loss of her immediately, but I understood. "Okay."

"Until Field Day is over, we keep this professional during school hours. We focus on the work, on the kids, on making this the best event we can. No... complications."

I wanted to argue. To close the distance between us and kiss her until she forgot every careful boundary she was trying to draw. To tell her that a week was an eternity after I'd finally said out loud what I had been feeling.

But I would give her what she needed. And if she needed proof that I respected her boundaries and put her needs before my own, then I would give it to her.

"I can do that."

Darcy strutted between us, planting himself directly on top of the clipboard, demanding pets.

Emma laughed and obliged, scratching under his beak. "He's very insistent."

"He knows what he wants," I said, watching her. "Can't fault him for that."

She met my eyes over Darcy's bright red feathers, understanding flickering in her expression. A faint blush colored her cheeks, but she didn't look away.

"Four days," she said softly.

"Four days," I confirmed.

She smiled and gently moved Darcy aside to flip open her clipboard. "So. The obstacle course. I was thinking we could incorporate more of the water cycle elements..."

And just like that, we were partners again. Planning. Collaborating. Building something together.

But this time, I knew exactly what we were building toward.

And I was patient enough to wait.

Chapter 25: Emma

THE PLANNING SESSION on Tuesday felt like slipping into a well-worn groove—familiar, comfortable, but somehow better than before.

Max showed up at my office door at 3:45 with two coffees and Darcy perched on his shoulder, looking absurdly pleased with himself.

"I brought reinforcements," he announced, holding up the cups.

"Which? The coffee or the bird?" I asked, taking the cup he offered.

"Both. Darcy's moral support. The coffee's a bribe."

"Smart man." I took a sip—perfect, just the way I liked it. The fact that he'd remembered still made my chest tighten in a way that had nothing to do with caffeine.

Darcy hopped onto my desk, investigating my pile of colored markers with intense interest. He selected a red one and began rolling it across the surface like it was the most fascinating thing he'd ever encountered.

"He's got excellent taste," I observed. "Red's a good choice."

"He's very discerning," Max said seriously, settling into the chair across from me. "Only the finest Crayola for Darcy."

I snorted, and just like that, we fell into the easy back-and-forth that came naturally when we weren't overthinking things.

"Okay," I said, pulling out my notes. "I've been mapping out the stations. We've got the obstacle course, the relay, the egg drop, weather stations—"

"The egg drop is going to be chaos." Max grinned.

"Controlled chaos," I corrected. "There's a difference."

"Is there though? Because I'm picturing raw egg everywhere and twelve-year-olds screaming."

"That's why we're doing it on the grass. And why we ordered extra paper towels."

"You mean I bought extra paper towels. With my own money. Because someone—" he pointed at me with his coffee cup, "—said the budget was 'tight.'"

"The budget was tight. It was fiscally responsible."

"You mean cheap."

"I'll pay you back out of our new budget."

Darcy squawked loudly, as if weighing in on the debate.

"See?" Max said. "Even Darcy agrees with me."

"Darcy also thinks shiny objects are food. His judgment is suspect."

He laughed, and the sound settled something warm in my chest. This was what I'd missed. The way he made everything feel lighter without making it feel less important.

We worked through the station logistics, debating equipment needs and timing. Darcy provided commentary by occasionally squawking "FIELD DAY!" at random intervals, which Max claimed was very helpful input.

"He's basically our third co-chair at this point," Max said.

"Does he get a vote?"

"He has the deciding vote."

I was laughing when someone knocked on my office door.

"Come in," I called, still smiling.

The door opened, and Ms. Peterson walked in, looking significantly more rested than the last time I'd seen her. Her color was back, her eyes bright.

"Ms. Peterson!" Max stood immediately. "You're back. How's your father?"

"Much better, thank you." She smiled warmly at both of us, then her eyes landed on Darcy. "And there's my darling boy."

Darcy's head swiveled toward her voice, and he let out an excited shriek. "HELLO BEAUTIFUL!"

He launched himself off the desk in a flutter of red feathers, landing on her outstretched arm with clear delight. He bobbed his head enthusiastically, dancing from foot to foot, then nuzzled against her cheek with obvious affection. Lynda responded by gently preening her hair, making soft cooing sounds.

"GOOD BOY! GOOD BOY!" he announced, then whistled a complicated tune that made Ms. Peterson smile even wider.

"I've missed you too, sweetheart," she cooed. "Were you good for Dr. Harrison?"

"We had a transition period," Max said. "But he kept me company and caused minimal destruction."

"MINIMAL!" Darcy squawked proudly.

Ms. Peterson beamed. "I can't thank you enough for watching him. It meant so much knowing he was in good hands." She glanced between us, seeming to notice the coffee cups and scattered papers for the first time. "Oh, I'm interrupting. I can—"

"No, no, it's fine," I said quickly. "We were just planning Field Day."

"Together?" Her eyebrows rose with obvious approval. "Well, that's wonderful. I heard through the grapevine there was some... tension."

"We worked it out," Max said, and when his eyes met mine, there was something in them that made my heart skip.

"I'm so glad." Ms. Peterson adjusted Darcy on her arm. "Well, I won't keep you. I wanted to collect this one and let you know I'm back."

"I'll bring his things to the library."

"Wonderful."

"It's good to have you back," I said, meaning it.

She smiled. "It's good to be back. You two have a lovely afternoon."

She left, Darcy chattering happily on her shoulder, and the door clicked shut behind them.

The office felt heavier without the bird's presence.

"Well," Max said after a moment. "There goes our comic relief."

"And your roommate."

"Yeah." He ran a hand through his hair. "My house is going to feel weird without him screaming my name at six in the morning."

"You could get your own bird."

"No, no. I think pet ownership isn't for me." He was smiling, but it didn't quite reach his eyes.

I understood. Darcy had been a menace, but then he'd become more—a companion, a conversation starter, an excuse to show up at my office with a bird on his shoulder to break the ice. His house would feel emptier without the bird. And the thought that he might be lonely made my chest ache a little.

"We should probably finish this," I said, gesturing to the papers spread across my desk.

"Right. Yeah." He pulled his chair closer. "Though I have to say, our meetings were more entertaining with Darcy screaming random phrases."

"You mean more chaotic."

"Chaotic, entertaining—same thing."

"They are absolutely not the same thing."

"Agree to disagree."

And we were off again, falling back into the rhythm. But I was more aware of him now—the way his shoulder was close enough to brush mine when he leaned over to point at something on my diagram, the way he absently tapped his pen against his knee, the small smile that played at the corner of his mouth when I shot down one of his ideas.

The warmth radiated from where our arms nearly touched. My pulse kicked up when he laughed at something I said, like my body was keeping score of every moment he found me funny.

This was dangerous territory. This hyperawareness, this cataloging of details I had no business noticing. We'd agreed to keep things professional until Friday. But the way my stomach flipped when he smiled at me was anything but collegial.

I told him I needed distance, but instead, I was noticing the exact shade of brown in his eyes and wondering what it would feel like if he reached over and took my hand.

"Emma?"

I blinked, realizing he'd asked me something. "Sorry, what?"

"I asked if you wanted to run through the volunteer assignments." He was watching me with an expression I couldn't quite read. "You okay?"

"Yeah. Just... thinking."

"About?"

About you.

About the way your hands move when you're explaining something you're passionate about.

About us.

About how badly I want to close the distance between us right now and forget every careful boundary I drew.

About kissing you and holding you close to me.

My heart was hammering so loud I was sure he could hear it. Heat crept up my neck, and I had to look away, taking a deep breath to steady myself.

"About whether we have enough hula hoops," I said, my voice not quite steady.

He didn't look convinced, but he let it slide. "I counted. We're good on hula hoops."

"You're sure?"

"Emma. We have seventeen hula hoops for a station that needs eight. We're good."

"But what if—"

"What if nothing? We're prepared. It's going to be great." He leaned back in his chair, studying me. "You know what I think?"

"What?"

"I think you're looking for problems because you're nervous about it actually working."

I opened my mouth to argue, then closed it. He wasn't wrong.

"Maybe," I admitted.

"It's going to work," he said. "We're going to pull this off, and it's going to be amazing, and the kids are going to love it. You know why?"

"Why?"

"Because we're doing it together. And we're really good together, Emma."

We were good together. In planning, in teaching, in this easy rhythm we'd found. But it was more than that, wasn't it? We were good at the quiet moments too. At the laughter, the stolen glances, and the way he made me feel like I could take risks without losing myself....

Oh my God.

The realization hit me so hard I had to grip the edge of my desk.

I was in love with Dr. Max Harrison.

My breath stopped in my chest like I'd been punched. The pen slipped from my fingers, clattering against the desk. Heat flooded my face, then drained away just as quickly, leaving me cold and shaky. My hands trembled as I gripped the edge of the desk, knuckles going white.

I was in love with Max.

"Emma?" His voice was concerned now. "Seriously, are you okay? You look—"

"I'm fine," I managed, my voice coming out steadier than I felt. "Just... realized we forgot to order the medals."

It was a lie. We'd ordered the medals a week ago. But I needed something, anything, to say that wasn't 'I realized I'm in love with you and I have no idea what to do with that information.'

"We ordered them last Tuesday," Max said. "Remember? You made me call three different companies to compare prices."

"Right. Yes. Of course." I shuffled papers aimlessly. "I knew that."

His expression shifted from concern to something more speculative. Like he could see right through me, straight to the panic thrumming under my skin.

"Three more days," he said.

I looked up. "What?"

"Field Day. Three more days, and then..." He trailed off, leaving the rest unsaid.

Three days didn't seem long enough for me to figure all of this out. Not long enough to untangle what I was feeling from what I was afraid of. Not long enough to decide if I was brave enough to risk everything I'd spent years protecting. Not long enough to prepare for the conversation we'd have to have. The one where I'd either let him in completely or watch him walk away.

And yet, it was an eternity, too. Three more days of sitting this close to him without being able to reach out. Three more days of pretending my heart didn't skip every time he smiled at me. Three more days of carrying this secret that I'd already fallen, already lost the battle.

Friday couldn't come fast enough.

And I was terrified of what would happen when it did.

Chapter 26: Max

THURSDAY AFTERNOON brought the kind of spring day that made you feel light and energetic. The warm sun, light breeze, blue sky were the perfect conditions for setting up what was either going to be the best Field Day Marchfield Middle School had ever seen or a spectacular disaster.

I was betting on the former.

"Okay, people!" Emma stood in the middle of the field, looking every bit like the general commanding her troops. "We've got two hours before sunset, so let's make them count. The obstacle course goes here—" she gestured to the far end of the field, "—relay stations here, and the egg drop zone is over by the water hookup for easy cleanup."

"You mean the eggs that will definitely shatter and traumatize the children?" Jen called out, already unloading cones from a cart.

"It's character building!" Emma shot back, and several teachers laughed.

I caught her eye across the field, and she smiled.

My chest tightened in response, breath catching as the instinct to jog over and kiss her flared hot and immediate. Instead, I rolled my shoulders, a useless attempt to bleed the tension out of my body. I hated the discipline of it and the way I had to choose restraint when every nerve ending screamed for impulse.

Tomorrow, I reminded myself. She'd asked for time, and I would give it to her, even if it felt like holding my breath underwater. But after field day, all bets were off. Twenty-four hours. One thousand four hundred and forty minutes. I counted them down like a promise.

"Max!" Bobby jogged over. "Where do you want the weather station supplies?"

"Near the north goal," I said, checking my own notes. "We'll set up the anemometers and the hygrometers, keep them away from the high-traffic areas."

"Got it." She paused. "This is going to be awesome! All the kids are stoked about it."

"Yeah?"

"Yeah. Some of them have been asking if they could help set up." She grinned. "I told them absolutely not, this is teacher manual labor only, but the fact that they wanted to? That's huge."

Something warm settled in my chest. "It is pretty cool, isn't it?"

"It's very cool. You and Bennett make a good team."

Before I could respond to that loaded statement, she was off again, hauling a table toward the goal.

The next hour passed in a blur of activity. Talia and Dante worked on marking the relay lanes with chalk while Eli helped me assemble the PVC pipe framework for the obstacle course. Emma moved between stations like a conductor, adjusting, correcting, making sure everything was where it needed to be.

"Emma!" I called, struggling with a particularly stubborn connector. "Can you hold this while I—"

She was there before I finished the sentence, hands steady on the pipe while I tightened the joint.

"Thanks," I said.

"Teamwork," she replied, her voice softer than it needed to be.

There was something in her voice that snapped my attention to her, and my eyes jerked up to meet hers. Our fingers brushed as she let go, and the contact sent a sharp awareness up my arm. I saw her breath hitch—just a fraction—before she turned away, retreating to her clipboard, her checklist, the careful shelter of logistics. But the pause lingered, hanging between us like a question neither of us was ready to ask, let alone answer.

Time slowed.

Eighty-six thousand four hundred seconds until I could touch her. Until I could do more than catalog the way her throat moved when she swallowed, the way her fingers tightened on that pen like it was the only thing keeping her tethered. I wanted to close the distance between us, to trace the line of her jaw, to feel the heat of her skin under my palms instead of just imagining it. But the rules were clear, and I'd already pushed too far. So I stayed where I was, counting down seconds like a prisoner marking days on a cell wall.

My phone buzzed in my pocket, shattering my thoughts.

"Hold that thought," I said, pulling it out.

It was an unknown number. I almost declined, before remembering I'd been waiting to hear back about—

My stomach dropped.

The grant.

"I need to take this," I said, stepping away from the noise. "Two seconds."

Emma nodded, but I caught the flicker of concern in her expression as I walked toward the bleachers.

"Hello?"

"Dr. Harrison?" A woman's voice, professional and crisp. "This is Carla Jenson from the grant committee."

"Ms. Jenson, yes. Hello." My heart was hammering.

"I'm calling with good news. The committee was very impressed with your initial presentation, and we'd like to invite you back for a second-round interview."

"That's—that's fantastic. Thank you."

"Would you be available tomorrow afternoon at two o'clock? I know it's short notice, but we're hoping to make final decisions by early next week."

Tomorrow.

Friday.

Field Day.

"I—" My mind raced. "Actually, Ms. Jenson, I have a prior commitment tomorrow. It's the STEM Field Day event I spoke to you about at the last interview. It runs from twelve to three."

There was a pause. "I see. Unfortunately, Friday is the only day we have available slots for second interviews. The following week we'll be in final deliberations."

I looked back at the field. At Emma directing Jen on cone placement. At Eli and Pat hauling water balloons. At the obstacle course taking shape, the stations being marked out, all of it coming together exactly like we'd planned.

"Ms. Jenson, I understand this is unconventional, but would the committee be interested in attending the event? It's the practical application of everything I discussed in my presentation—hands-on, real world STEM education, student engagement, and interdisciplinary collaboration. You'd be able to see the model in action."

Another pause, longer this time.

"That's... an interesting proposition, Dr. Harrison."

"I know it's not standard," I said, "but this event is exactly what the grant would support. Real students, real learning, real results. And I can't miss it. I've made a commitment to my colleague and to our students."

"Let me consult with the committee," she said. "Can I call you back within the hour?

"Absolutely. Thank you for considering it."

I hung up, my hand shaking as the full weight of my decision hit me. What if they see my invitation as presumptuous? Overstepping? What if showing them the work before it is fully documented made me look unprepared, desperate even, and cost me the grant entirely?

But I couldn't leave. Not tomorrow. Not with the community event less than twenty-four hours away. Emma had shouldered too much already and carried the load while I ran off during the fundraiser. And I wasn't doing it again. Not when she'd shown up for this project and me without hesitation.

Emma stood in the center of a crowd of teachers, answering questions and thanking them. She said something to Talia, then walked over, her expression carefully neutral.

"Everything okay?" she asked.

"That was the grant committee."

Her face went carefully blank. "Oh."

"They want me to come back for a second interview. Tomorrow at two."

I watched her process that. Saw the exact moment the walls started going back up, the careful distance sliding into place.

"Tomorrow," she repeated. "Field Day."

"Yeah."

"Well." She straightened her shoulders. "That's great, Max. I'll ask Bobby if she can step up—"

"Emma."

"No, really. This is a huge opportunity. We can handle Field Day. You should—"

"I'm not going."

She stopped. "What?"

"I told them I couldn't make it. That I had a prior commitment." I stepped closer, needing her to hear this. "I told them about STEM Field Day. Asked if they wanted to come see it instead and see the practical application of everything I'd proposed."

She stared at me. "You did what?"

"I'm not missing Field Day, Emma. I made a commitment. To you, to the kids, to this. And I'm not backing out. Not for a grant, not for anything."

"Max, that's insane. This is your goal. Your future. You can't just—"

"Yes, I can." I held her gaze. "I told you I'd prove it to you. That I'd show up. This is me showing up."

Her eyes were wide, something fierce and fragile warring in her expression. "But if they say no—"

"Then they say no. But I'm not walking away from this. From us." I gestured to the field, to everything we'd built. "This matters. You matter. And I'm not going anywhere."

For a long moment, she looked at me. Then she nodded, once, sharp and certain.

"Okay," she said. "Okay."

My phone rang again.

"Dr. Harrison?" Ms. Jenkins sounded almost amused. "The committee discussed your proposal. We're intrigued. We'll send a team to observe your STEM Field Day event tomorrow afternoon, and we can conduct the interview on-site afterward if that works for you."

Relief flooded through me. "That works perfectly. Thank you so much."

"We'll see you tomorrow, Dr. Harrison. This should be interesting."

I hung up and looked at Emma. She was fighting a smile, her teeth catching her bottom lip.

"They're coming?" she asked.

"They're coming." I slipped my phone back into my pocket, pulse still hammering.

"To Field Day."

"To Field Day."

"So now we have to be perfect." She crossed her arms, but her eyes were bright.

"We were always going to be perfect," I said, taking a step closer. "We're a good team, remember?"

"MAX!" Eli shouted from the obstacle course. "This thing is falling apart!"

"EMMA!" Jen waved frantically. "The chalk paint isn't working on this grass!"

Emma looked at me, one eyebrow raised. "Still think we're perfect?"

I grinned despite everything. "Perfectly crazy."

She shook her head, but she was smiling as she turned away, already moving toward Jen with purpose in her stride.

Chapter 27: MAX

11:00 AM

I stood at the edge of the field watching volunteers explore their stations. Emma directed traffic near the registration tent, clipboard in one hand, the other pointing toward the far corner where Eli was testing the obstacle course.

We'd turned this space into something that belonged in a science fair and a carnival at once.

At the twenty-yard dash, four parent volunteers set up stopwatches, measuring tape, and calculators. Kids would race, calculate their speed, then race again to test if longer strides made them faster.

Near the long jump pit, Mr. Kline positioned force plates in the sand while his daughter Talia arranged measuring tapes in a fan pattern. Jump, measure the force and distance, adjust your angle, jump again.

Eli waved from the obstacle course as he tested the balance beam. Signs were posted every few feet: "Predict which position is most stable. Test it. Were you right?"

To my left, Dante and Jen filled water balloons at the launcher station. Kids would calculate trajectory angles, fire, and see where the balloon landed, adjust, and try again.

A few parents tested the bean bag toss, throwing at targets marked five feet, ten feet, and fifteen feet. Beneath each target sat a basket of worksheets where kids would calculate the arc angle needed for each distance, make their prediction, then throw and adjust. The farther the target, the higher the arc required and the more force behind the throw.

The friction station sat nearby with its ramps, toy cars, and different surface materials—sandpaper, wax paper, carpet, bare wood. Kids would race identical cars down each surface, time them, then rank the materials by coefficient of friction without ever realizing they were doing it.

And at the far end of the field—I couldn't help smiling—the empty space we'd reserved for the fire truck. By 11:45, it would be parked there, ladder extended, firefighters ready to drop eggs wrapped in cardboard and hope. Kids would calculate impact force before they ever picked up the tape, predict which designs would distribute energy best, then watch physics prove them right or wrong. The rebuild was the other half of the lesson—figuring out why the egg cracked, where the structure failed, how to engineer it better the second time.

Emma appeared at my side and handed me a coffee. "The egg drop supplies are organized by age group: built-in scaffolding."

"You thought of everything."

"We thought of everything." She gestured toward the registration tent where snacks and prize ribbons were laid out on tables. "Ribbons for most improved velocity, best hypothesis, most creative egg capsule design, highest accuracy on the bean bag toss calculations. Participation certificates for everyone."

"Awards for the science, not just the athletic performance," I said.

"Exactly. A kid who can't run fast can still win for calculating their improvement rate. A kid who drops their egg can still win for the best engineering analysis of why it failed." She smiled. "Everyone gets to be good at something today."

"What time does the committee arrive?"

"Soon." I wrapped both hands around the coffee cup, my brow furrowing as I looked at my watch.

"Max?" Emma leaned in slightly. "What's wrong?"

"What if they hate it?"

"They won't."

"What if they don't see the potential? What if—"

"Max." She stepped closer, her voice dropping. "Look at this place. Look at what we built. This is what you told them it would be—community science in action. They're going to see that."

I wanted to believe her. God, I wanted to believe her.

"Besides," she added, a smile playing at the corner of her mouth, "it's too late to panic now. They're already coming."

"That's supposed to make me feel better?"

"A little bit." She bumped my shoulder with hers, a brief contact that sent awareness shooting through me despite everything else I should have been focusing on. "We've got this. Trust me."

I did. I trusted her completely.

AT 11:18, A DARK SEDAN pulled into the parking lot.

Three people emerged, and I recognized Ms. Jenkins from my first interview. She was in her late fifties, her silver hair pulled back. She carried a leather portfolio that cost more than my monthly salary. The two people with her were younger, serious, and already scanning the field with evaluative eyes.

"Show time," Emma murmured beside me.

We met them halfway across the field. My palms were sweating.

"Ms. Jenkins." I extended my hand. "Thank you so much for coming."

"Dr Harrison. Thanks for the invitation." Her handshake was firm, professional. "And this must be your project coordinator?"

"Emma Bennett." She stepped forward smoothly, shaking hands with all three of them. "We're so glad you could join us today."

"This is Dr. Michael Okafor and Sarah Patel," Ms. Jenkins said, gesturing to her colleagues. "They're part of our evaluation team."

"Welcome to Marchfield Middle," I said, trying to sound confident. "The students are eating an early lunch but will be outside at noon. If you want to see the setup first, understand how we've integrated the STEM components with traditional field day activities, I can take you around."

"That would be helpful," Ms. Jenkins said.

We walked them through the stations. At each one, I explained the science while Emma highlighted the community partnerships—the teachers who'd helped design activities, the parent volunteers we'd trained, the high school students who'd be acting as junior coaches.

"The velocity station is my favorite," Emma said as we approached the timing setup. "Kids run the twenty-yard dash, and then they calculate their own speed. Most of them don't realize they're doing physics. They just think they're racing."

"Education disguised as play," Dr. Okafor said, making a note.

"Exactly," I said. "That's the whole point of this project—making science accessible, exciting, part of their everyday experience instead of something that only happens in a classroom."

Ms. Jenkins paused at the long jump pit, studying the force calculation worksheets we'd prepared. "And all of these materials—you developed them yourself?"

"Emma and I did most of the work," I said. "But the science teachers helped align everything to the state standards so teachers can actually use these activities as an extension of their curriculum."

"Smart," Sarah Patel said, still writing.

At 11:50, teachers began arriving with their classes. Kids in sneakers and bright t-shirts, everyone chattering with excitement as the field filled with noise and color and energy.

Ms. Jenkins stepped back, observing. "Where would you like us during the event?"

"Wherever you'd like," Emma said. "Feel free to dive in, participate, talk to the students."

Ms. Jenkins nodded slowly. "We'll circulate, then."

They moved toward the perimeter, and Emma touched my elbow briefly.

"Breathe," she said quietly.

"I'm breathing."

"You're vibrating."

She wasn't wrong. Every nerve in my body felt like a live wire.

Then Jen appeared with a bullhorn, and there was no more time to worry.

"Welcome to Marchfield's first annual STEM Field Day!" Jen's voice boomed across the field. "We've got eight stations, each one combining a physical challenge with a science activity. At the end, everyone who completes at least five stations gets a ribbon and a certificate. Most importantly—have fun and learn something cool!"

The kids scattered like marbles, racing toward different stations. Within seconds, the field was controlled chaos.

I found myself at the velocity station, helping a group of sixth-graders set up the timing equipment.

"Okay," I said, crouching down beside a boy named Marcus. "You're going to run from this line to that cone—that's twenty yards. Your friend here will time you with this stopwatch. Then we'll do some math to figure out how fast you ran. Make sense?"

"I'm going to be so fast," Marcus announced.

"Then let's find out exactly how fast."

He took off like a shot when his friend hit the timer. 4.2 seconds.

"Okay, Marcus. Twenty yards in 4.2 seconds. Now we need to convert yards to meters first—do you know how many meters are in a yard?"

He squinted at the conversion chart. "Point nine one four?"

"Correct. So twenty yards times 0.914..."

"Is 18.28 meters!" His friend shouted, calculator in hand.

"Perfect. Now divide that by 4.2 seconds..."

Marcus's eyes went wide as he punched numbers into his own calculator. "4.35 meters per second?"

"Now convert that to miles per hour using this formula," I said, pointing to the worksheet.

A moment later: "I ran 9.7 miles per hour!" Marcus looked stunned. "That's almost ten miles an hour!"

"You're basically a car in a parking lot," his friend added.

They high-fived so hard, my ears rang

I glanced up and found Ms. Jenkins watching from twenty feet away, her pen moving across her notepad.

My heart hammered.

Then I saw Emma across the field at the long jump station, crouched beside a tiny girl with pigtails, showing her how to measure her jump distance with a tape measure. The girl said something that made Emma laugh—head thrown back, genuine delight—and something in my chest went tight.

She was magnificent. Completely in her element, moving between kids and parents and volunteers like she'd been doing this her whole life. Making everyone feel welcome, explaining concepts without talking down, turning learning into joy.

This whole thing—the event, the success of it, the way the community had shown up—that was Emma's doing as much as mine. More, maybe.

She caught me looking and smiled, and for a second the noise and chaos faded to nothing.

Then a kid tugged on my sleeve. "Can I run again? I want to go faster this time."

"Absolutely," I said. "What's your strategy?"

By 1:30, I'd lost count of how many kids had cycled through the velocity station. My throat was hoarse, and my shirt was covered in grass stains. I'd never been happier.

The grant committee continued circulating. I'd caught glimpses of them—Ms. Jenkins talking to a parent volunteer, Dr. Okafor watching the obstacle course with interest, Sarah Patel crouched beside a kid who was carefully graphing her jump distances.

At 2:15, I was helping at the water balloon trajectory station (a huge hit, if messier than anticipated) when Ms. Jenkins approached.

"Dr. Harrison, do you have a moment?"

My stomach plummeted. "Of course."

She gestured away from the noise, toward the quieter edge of the field. I followed, very aware that Emma had stopped what she was doing to watch.

"We were planning to conduct a formal interview after the event," Ms. Jenkins said. "Standard procedure—ask about sustainability plans, long-term vision, community partnerships."

"Right," I said. My mouth had gone dry. "I have materials in my classroom—"

"That won't be necessary."

I blinked. "I'm sorry?"

"We've seen what we needed to see." She glanced back at the field, where kids were still running and jumping and calculating, where parents were cheering and volunteers were managing chaos with impressive efficiency. "A proposal tells us what you hope to accomplish. An interview tells us what you plan to do. But this?" She gestured at the organized chaos behind us. "This was eye-opening."

"Ms. Jenkins—"

"You've built something real here. These kids aren't just using science equipment. They're falling in love with science itself. That's what we're looking for."

Hope flared so bright in my chest I could barely breathe. "Does that mean—"

"We'll make our final decision within the week, but I can tell you that your project is very favorably positioned." She smiled, the first real warmth I'd seen from her. "You and Ms. Bennett have done excellent work."

"She's incredible," I said, before I could think better of it. "This whole event—the organization, the community buy-in, getting everyone here—that's all Emma."

"Then you're lucky to have her," Ms. Jenkins said. "Good partnerships are rare in this work."

After she left, I stood frozen for a moment, trying to process what had happened.

No interview.

Favorably positioned.

Excellent work.

The words kept replaying in my head, gaining weight each time. Favorably positioned. That was grant committee talk for yes—or as close to yes as they could say before the official decision. They'd already made up their minds and just needed the paperwork to catch up.

We'd done it. Against all every odd, every setback, every moment I'd been convinced this project would collapse under its own ambition—we'd actually done it.

Emma appeared at my shoulder. "Max? What did she say?"

I turned to her, and whatever she saw in my face made her eyes go wide.

"They don't need the interview," I said, a grin breaking across my face.

“Is that good?”

"It means they're not looking for reasons to say no." I couldn't stop grinning. "Emma, I think it's really good."

Her face lit up, and before I thought better of it, I pulled her into a hug. Not the side hug colleagues share when something went right, but a real hug. Her hands pressed against my back, and I heard her breath catch, and we stood there holding on tighter than we should have.

She pulled back first, cheeks flushed. "We should... there are still kids around."

"Right. Yeah." I cleared my throat, stepping back and looking down at my watch. "Sixty-eight thousand seconds."

Her eyes met mine, and the look that passed between us said everything we couldn't.

"Sixty-eight thousand seconds," she repeated.

Then she turned and headed back toward the chaos, and I watched her go, my heart hammering in my chest.

Soon.

Chapter 28: Emma

THE MOMENT MAX UNLOCKED the front door, and we stepped inside, I noticed the missing commentary on our arrival.

"Weird, right?" Max said, following my gaze. "I keep expecting Darcy to yell at me for being late."

He set his keys in the bowl by the door, that small domestic gesture somehow more intimate than it should have been. "Lynda sent me a video of Darcy eating grapes on her shoulder. He looked smug."

"He always looks smug."

"Fair point." Max moved toward the kitchen, rolling his shoulders like he was trying to shake off the day's tension. "I'm starving. Please tell me you're hungry."

"Starving," I confirmed, following him. "What are we celebrating with?"

"Well, I have pasta, I have vegetables and a bottle of wine."

"Pasta sounds perfect. How do you feel about gummies, Max?"

"Like THC? I don't have a problem with it."

I pulled a small jar out of my bag. "I feel like wine will put me to sleep after today's amount of crazy. Want one?"

We both ate gummies while he pulled ingredients from the refrigerator, and I claimed a seat at the kitchen island, the same spot I'd sat in weeks ago when we'd been planning Field Day and fooling around.

"I feel like my ears are ringing," Max said, filling a pot with water. "It's so quiet."

"Darcy—"

"No, I mean—" He gestured vaguely. "Today was wild. Three hours of nonstop noise and kids and people needing things. And now it's just... the two of us."

I understood what he meant. The silence felt louder somehow, more present. Without the buffer of work and volunteers and grant committees.

"I kind of like it," I said.

He looked at me across the kitchen, something warm and careful in his expression. "Yeah. Me too."

The way he said it made my pulse skip. Not the words themselves, but the weight behind them. The intimacy of standing in his kitchen, sharing the quiet, admitting we both wanted this stillness together.

While the water boiled, Max moved around the kitchen with ease. He chopped vegetables without checking his phone. He stirred sauce without looking at his watch. He was in the moment with me. His movements were unhurried, almost languid, like he was savoring the simplicity of this. Of us, alone together, nothing between us but marinara sauce and fading daylight.

I watched his hands as he worked, the same hands that had tightened bolts and steadied equipment and hugged me so carefully this afternoon. Strong hands. Capable hands. Hands I wanted on me.

The thought sent heat rushing through me.

What had he said earlier?

Sixty-something thousand seconds.

The number had been echoing in my head all evening, counting down like a timer I felt in my bones. And it made my blood sing with anticipation. Every hour that passed brought us closer. Every minute meant one less barrier between wanting and having.

I shifted on the barstool, crossing my legs, trying to steady myself.

Max glanced over, caught me watching him, and something flickered in his eyes before he looked away. His jaw tightened almost imperceptibly.

He felt it too. This current running between us.

"To Marchfield Middle." Max raised his glass of water with a hand that wasn't quite steady.

"To physics disguised as play," I added, raising mine. My voice came out lower than I intended.

"To eggs that didn't survive the drop."

"To Ms. Jenkins not needing an interview."

We clinked water glasses, and the sound rang clear in the quiet house.

"I knew today would be a success," I said, needing to say something, anything, to fill the charged silence.

"You did?" He set his glass down but didn't step away from the counter. Didn't put more distance between us.

"Well, mostly I knew."

"Thank you, Emma, for giving me another chance." His voice was rough around the edges, genuine.

I smiled, warmth blooming in my chest. "We designed the event together. I couldn't have done it without you."

He held my gaze a beat too long. I saw his throat work as he swallowed. Saw the way his knuckles whitened against the counter edge.

Then he turned back to the stove, stirring the sauce with unnecessary focus, his shoulders tight with restraint.

The tension in the room shifted, thickened like humidity before a storm.

I gripped my water glass tighter, the cool condensation slick against my palm. My heart hammered against my ribs. The kitchen suddenly seemed smaller, the air between us dense with everything we weren't saying, weren't doing.

Not yet.

"So," I said, trying for lightness. "What happens now? With the grant?"

"Paperwork. So much paperwork." He added pasta to the boiling water. "I should find out next week. Then fund disbursement, final budget approval, maybe another site visit to confirm everything's proceeding according to plan."

"Sounds thrilling."

"It's riveting stuff. You'll love it." He shot me a grin, then his expression shifted to something more thoughtful. "I've been thinking, I want to expand the program. Not just Marchfield Middle. The elementary school, the high school. Make this a district-wide initiative."

My heart did something complicated. "You mean... stay here? Long-term?"

"Yeah." He met my eyes. "I know I said before that I might move if I got the grant, find a bigger district or a university position. But that was before—" He stopped, stirred the sauce. "This community showed up today, Emma. They believe in this. And I want to be here to see it through. All of it."

Before what? I wanted to ask. Before us? Before you fell in love with me?

But I knew the answer in the way he was looking at me.

He leaned against the counter beside me, close enough that I could feel the warmth of him. "We'll figure it out. Together. That's what we do, right?"

"Is it?"

"I think so." His voice dropped lower. "I've been figuring it out for weeks now. I've just been waiting for you."

My heart hammered and a soft ringing began in my ears. I opened my mouth to tell him. To say the words.

"Max—"

"Pasta's going to overcook," he said abruptly, pushing off the counter and returning to the stove. But his hands shook slightly as he drained the pot, and I knew he felt the pull between us.

Sixty-something thousand seconds.

How many was that now? Fifty? Forty?

Not enough. Still not enough.

We ate on his small patio, looking out over the backyard. The evening air was soft and warm, carrying the scent of freshly cut grass and wisteria blooming somewhere in his neighbor's yard. The sun had dropped below the roofline, leaving the sky streaked with pink and orange. Birds called to each other in the trees, settling in for the night, their songs winding down to sleepy chirps.

The pasta was perfect. Butter, garlic, fresh basil, and parmesan tasted better than anything I'd eaten in weeks.

I was happy. Deeply, simply happy.

"This is delicious," I said.

"It's butter and garlic and desperation."

"The best kind of cooking."

He laughed, and god, I loved that sound. Loved the way his whole face changed when he was relaxed like this—the tension leaving his jaw, the lines around his eyes deepening with genuine amusement instead of stress. He looked younger somehow, lighter, like he'd set down a weight he'd been carrying for months.

"Tell me something," he said, refilling both our water glasses.

"Anything."

"When did you stop hating me?" His eyes found mine, curiosity and something else lingering there—vulnerability, maybe. Like my answer actually mattered.

I twirled pasta around my fork, my heart picking up speed. "Honestly? It was that day last year when you demanded to use the field twenty minutes before class started. You were so determined, so completely convinced that what you were doing was important enough to break protocol for."

He laughed, the sound warm in the evening air. "You could have fooled me. We got in a screaming match about the gym for the science fair not long after that."

"You wanted to set up equipment three days before the fair."

"It was the only time that worked for the setup!"

"Max, you tried to move the basketball hoops."

"In my defense, I thought those hoops were on wheels."

I shook my head, grinning despite myself. "You were impossible."

He raised an eyebrow. "Past tense?"

"Are. You are impossible." I laughed, feeling the THC making me bold. "But that day with the field... when you finally explained what you were trying to do, why it mattered. I saw it. The passion. The vision. You weren't being difficult. You actually cared."

"And that made you stop hating me?"

"Not stop, exactly. More like... complicated the hate." I met his eyes. "It's hard to hate someone when you can see they're trying to make things better. Even if their timing is terrible, and they have no respect for scheduling protocols."

"I respected your protocols," he protested.

"You absolutely did not."

"I respected them in theory."

"That's not how protocols work, Max."

Max was quiet for a long moment, just looking at me. The air between us was charged, heavy, and I wished he would lean forward and kiss me.

"What about you?" I asked, needing to fill the silence. "When did you stop seeing me as the enemy?"

"I never saw you as the enemy." He smiled. "Adversary, maybe. Obstacle, definitely. But never enemy."

"That's just semantics."

"Important semantics." He leaned back in his chair, eyes never leaving mine. "You want to know when it changed? Really changed?"

I nodded.

"Remember when we were at Barrel, and you were explaining velocity to Eli? You made it sound so simple and exciting that he got it. His whole face lit up." Max's voice dropped lower. "And I thought, 'I want to watch her make things make sense for the rest of my life.'"

My breath caught. The rest of my life.

"That's when I knew I was in trouble," he continued. "Because it wasn't about the project anymore. It wasn't about proving something or building something. It was just about being near you. Hearing you laugh. Watching you solve problems. I wanted all of it."

I couldn't speak. Couldn't do anything but feel the weight of those words settling around us.

"Emma—" He started to reach across the table, then stopped himself, hand falling back to his wine glass. "God, I want to touch you."

"I know." My voice came out barely above a whisper. "I know. Me too."

The silence stretched between us, taut with longing.

"I'm in love with you," he whispered and the words landed like a physical thing, solid and real in my heart.

"I know my timing is terrible," he continued, speaking faster now like he had to get it all out. "But I can feel myself getting high and I want you to know, I've been counting down every single second, to this moment, Emma, because I'm in love with you, and I can't pretend I'm not."

I couldn't breathe. Couldn't think. Could only feel the way my heart was trying to break out of my chest.

"Max—"

"You don't have to say anything," he said quickly. "I just needed you to know. I needed you to know that for me this—It's not casual. It's not temporary. It's—"

"I love you too," I interrupted.

He stopped mid-sentence. Stared at me.

"I love you too," I repeated, and saying it out loud felt like jumping off something high and trusting there'd be ground beneath me. "I didn't realize until this week, but, Max, I'm completely in love with you."

The smile that broke across his face was the most beautiful thing I'd ever seen.

"Yeah?"

"Yeah."

He stood up, moved around the table, pulled me to my feet. We stood there in his backyard, inches apart, both of us grinning like idiots.

"Can I kiss you?" he asked, his voice rough.

"Yes," I breathed. "God, yes."

Chapter 29: Max

I'D IMAGINED THIS LATE at night when sleep wouldn't come, my hand wrapped around my cock, her name caught between my teeth. I'd imagined it in the shower, in my car, during meetings where I should have been paying attention to anything else.

I'd been holding myself back all week—every interaction measured, every word chosen with care, every accidental brush of hands sending a jolt up my spine that I had to pretend meant nothing. I counted down hours, minutes, seconds. Waiting. Trying to be professional. Trying to be good.

But none of that prepared me for the real thing: the weight of her body against mine, the actual taste of her mouth, the small, desperate sounds she made—things no amount of imagining could have ever gotten right.

My hands reached for her before I'd made the conscious decision to move. Restraint had wound me so tight that now, with her permission granted, I unraveled.

Her mouth opened under mine, our tongues tangling together. My palm found her waist, fingers spreading across her ribs, and every shred of self-control I'd clung to burned away like paper.

I forced myself to slow down, to pull back just enough to breathe. My hand came up to cup her face, thumb brushing her cheekbone the way I'd wanted to a thousand times before. Her skin was warm, impossibly soft. Her eyes were dark and wanting, pupils blown wide.

"Tell me this is okay," I said, voice rough. I needed to hear it. Needed her to say it even though every line of her body was already answering yes.

"Don't stop." Her fingers tightened in my shirt. "Don't you *dare* stop."

The world narrowed to the taste of her lips, harder this time. The small sound she made in the back of her throat that went straight through me. The way she pressed closer like she'd been starving for this too, like the careful distance had been killing her the same way they'd been killing me.

Her fingers tangled in my hair, tugging, and I groaned against her mouth. I pulled her flush against me as I backed her against the patio table, heard dishes rattle and clatter, didn't care. My hands slid down to her hips, gripping, and she gasped.

But then she pushed at my chest.

I froze instantly, releasing her, stepping back, my heart hammering. "I'm sorry, I—"

"Inside." She was breathless, flushed, her lips swollen from kissing. "I'm not putting on a show for your neighbors."

Relief crashed through me, followed immediately by a fresh wave of want so intense it made my knees weak. She grabbed my hand and pulled me toward the door, and I followed, helpless, already reaching for her again.

"Inside," she gasped against my mouth. "Max, we should—"

"Yeah. Inside. Good idea."

We stumbled through the patio door in a tangle of hands and mouths and barely controlled desperation. I kicked the door shut behind us, pressed her against it, kissed her like I was trying to memorize the taste of her.

Her hands fumbled with my belt, but I lifted her and felt her legs wrap around my waist. Without releasing her mouth, I carried her to the kitchen island, sliding her onto the granite counter.

Breaking the kiss, I stepped back to peel her shirt up.

She lifted her arms up over her head, and I was struck by her beauty and strength. Her arms curved up, fingers gracefully arched, her creamy breasts lifted high in her violet lace bra. The delicate fabric contrasted with the lean muscle definition in her shoulders and abs—she was built like a dancer, controlled power under soft skin.

I removed her sneakers, tickling her feet lightly and making her giggle—the sound bright and unexpected, cutting through the heavy desire in the air. Her stretchy pants followed, topping the pile on the floor.

Her toned thighs flexed as she shifted on the counter. A small constellation of freckles dotted her collarbone and the swell of her breasts. Her stomach was flat, defined, with those subtle lines of muscle that came from actual strength, not just aesthetic. The matching violet panties sat low on her hips, and I could see the slight curve of her hipbones, the taut lines of her obliques.

She was stunning. Real. Strong.

"You're staring," she said, breathless, a smile playing at her lips.

"Can't help it." My voice came out rough. "You're incredible."

Stepping into her embrace, her hands tangled in my hair as I kissed her throat, the scent of her skin sending my senses wild. My palms cupped her breasts, pinching her nipples beneath the thin fabric. She arched into my touch with a sharp intake of breath, her head falling back against the cabinet.

"God, yes," she breathed, and the sound of her voice—wanting, needy—nearly undid me.

I reached behind her to unclasp her bra, fumbling slightly in my haste. The violet lace fell away, and I took a moment to look at her, flushed and bare before me, her chest rising and falling rapidly. Then my mouth was on her, tongue circling one nipple while my hand worked the other, and she made this broken sound that shot straight through me.

We were both gasping for breath when I returned to her mouth, swallowing her moans and drawing out more with my tongue.

Her legs tightened around my waist, pulling me closer, and I could feel the heat of her even through my jeans. My free hand slid down her stomach, tracing those defined lines of muscle, feeling them jump and tighten under my touch. I hooked my fingers in the waistband of her panties.

"Tell me what you want," I murmured against her skin.

"You." Her voice was ragged. "All of you. Now."

I lifted my head to look at her. Lips parted, eyes dark with desire, purple hair falling wild around her shoulders. Beautiful.

"Not yet," I said, dropping to my knees. "I've been waiting too long for this. I'm not rushing it."

She lifted her hips, and I stripped the panties down her long legs. I kissed my way slowly up her thighs, spreading her legs wide. She leaned back, angling herself up for me, bracing her hands on the counter behind her.

The sight of her like this—open, wanting, trembling with anticipation—made my mouth water. I pressed a kiss to her inner thigh, then another, closer, her muscles tensing beneath my lips.

"Please," she whispered, and the desperation in that single word nearly broke me.

I took my time, teasing her with my breath, my lips ghosting over sensitive skin until she was squirming, one hand leaving the counter to tangle in my hair again, trying to guide me where she needed me.

When I finally tasted her, we both groaned. She was already so wet, so ready, and I lost myself in it—in the taste of her, the sounds she made, the way her thighs trembled against my shoulders. My tongue worked in slow, deliberate strokes at first, reveling with her every gasp, her hips bucking against my mouth.

"Oh god," she moaned, her fingers tightening in my hair almost painfully. "Just like that. Don't stop."

I had no intention of stopping. I'd spent too many nights imagining this, and now that I had her here, coming apart under my mouth, I wanted to memorize every reaction, every sound, every shudder.

She arched up, crying out, and I felt her coming apart. Her legs tightened around my head, and her head lolled back.

"Max," she cried as she came, her body shaking, her pleasure rolling over her in waves I could feel against my tongue.

I worked her through it, gentling my touch as the aftershocks subsided, pressing soft kisses to her thighs as she trembled and gasped for breath. When I finally pulled back and stood, her eyes were glazed, her chest heaving.

"That was—" she started but couldn't seem to finish the sentence.

My clothes joined hers on the floor as I stripped quickly, urgently, unable to take my eyes off her sprawled on the counter, flushed and satisfied and still wanting more. I could see it in the way she watched me undress, her gaze dropping down my body and lingering.

"Come here," she said, reaching for me, and I went willingly.

She wrapped her legs around me again as I stepped between her thighs, and the feeling of skin on skin, nothing between us now, made us both freeze for a moment. Her hands came up to frame my face, pulling me down into a kiss—slower this time, deeper, telling me she loved me without words.

"I need you," she whispered against my lips. "I need you inside me."

I reached between us, positioning myself. "Look at me," I said roughly. "I want to see you."

Her eyes locked on mine, dark and open and trusting, and I pushed inside slowly, watching her face as I filled her. Her mouth fell open, her breath catching, and god—she felt incredible. Perfect. Like she was made for me.

Thrusting into her, I knew I wouldn't last long—pent-up desire had me already wound too tight. The reality of her was so much better than any fantasy. The way she gripped me, hot and tight, the sounds she made with each thrust, the way her nails dug into my shoulders.

"You feel so good," I groaned against her neck, trying to slow down, to make this last. "So fucking good."

"Harder," she gasped, her hips rising to meet mine. "Don't hold back. I want all of you."

That was all the permission I needed. I gripped her hips, pulling her to the edge of the counter, and drove into her with a desperate intensity I'd been holding back. I braced a palm on the cool counters myself while I circled her with my other thumb.

She was all heat—her body, her breath, the way she wrapped around me.

"Yes, god, yes," she moaned, and I could feel her tightening around me already, could feel another orgasm building in the way her body tensed.

"Come for me again," I said, my voice ragged. "I want to feel you come on my cock."

I circled her with my thumb. Her breath hitched, her whole body going taut beneath me.

"Max—I'm—oh god—"

I could feel it building in her, the way her inner walls fluttered around me, the way her thighs trembled against my hips. She was close, so close, and I was right there with her, barely hanging on. The pressure at the base of my spine was overwhelming, my rhythm getting erratic as I chased both our releases.

"That's it," I groaned, watching her face—the way her brow furrowed in concentration, the way her lips parted, the flush spreading down her neck to her chest. "Let go for me, baby. I've got you."

Her fingers dug into my back hard enough to leave marks, and I relished the bite of pain mixing with pleasure. She made desperate little sounds with each thrust, getting higher, more urgent, and I could tell she was right on the edge.

I pressed harder with my thumb, angling my hips to get even deeper inside her.

She gasped, and I felt the exact moment she broke.

Her back arched, her head falling back as she cried out, and the feeling of her clenching around me, pulsing, sent me over the edge.

I buried myself deep as I came, her name torn from my throat, pleasure crashing through me so intensely my vision went white. Every muscle in my body tensed, then released in waves that seemed to go on forever. I could feel myself pulsing inside her, could feel her still contracting around me in diminishing rhythms that prolonged both our pleasure until we were both overstimulated and shaking.

We stayed locked together, both trembling, both gasping for air, as the waves slowly subsided. My forehead dropped to her shoulder, my arms barely able to hold me up. Her legs were still wrapped around me, looser now, her heels resting against the backs of my thighs. I could feel our hearts hammering against one another, racing in tandem, gradually slowing.

Her fingers gentled my hair, stroking now instead of gripping, and the tenderness of it made my chest ache in a way that had nothing to do with exertion. I pressed a kiss to her collarbone, tasting the salt of her sweat, feeling the rapid flutter of her pulse beneath my lips.

"I love you," she breathed, her voice wrecked and wonderful.

I lifted my head to look at her. Her hair was a mess, her lips swollen, her eyes soft and satisfied. She'd never looked more beautiful.

"I love you, too," I managed, still trying to remember how to form coherent thoughts. "That was—"

"Amazing?" she finished, a smile playing at the corners of her mouth.

"Understatement of the fucking century."

I laughed, and a second later, she joined me, the sound bright and unguarded in the quiet kitchen. The tension that had been coiled between us for days had broken, leaving joy in its place.

I carefully pulled out of her, both of us wincing slightly at the sensitivity, and she immediately tugged me back into her arms. We stayed like that for a long moment, her legs still loosely wrapped around my waist, my hands wrapped around her back, breathing together.

"Your kitchen counter," she said eventually, glancing around with mock seriousness. "We just had sex on your kitchen counter."

"I'll disinfect it later," I offered, grinning.

She swatted my shoulder, but she was laughing again. "You're terrible."

"You weren't complaining two minutes ago."

"Two minutes ago, I wasn't thinking clearly." Her fingers traced idle patterns on my chest, her touch soft and exploratory now that the urgency had passed. "You scrambled my brain."

"Good." I caught her hand and brought it to my lips, kissing her knuckles. "Fair is fair. You've been scrambling mine for weeks."

Her expression softened, something vulnerable flickering across her face. "Really?"

"Really. I thought I was going insane. Every time you walked into a room, every time you smiled at me, every goddamn time you existed near me—" I shook my head. "I've never wanted anyone like this."

She pulled me down into a kiss, slower and sweeter than before, and I could feel her smiling against my lips.

"Shower?" she murmured when we finally broke apart.

I took her hand, led her through the house, to the bathroom. I turned on the water and waited for it to heat up. The domesticity of it struck me—this simple act of caring for her, of sharing this space. Emma was in my house, heading toward my shower, planning to stay.

"What?" she asked, catching my expression.

"Nothing. Just—you're here."

"I'm here." She stepped closer, ran her hands up my chest. "Where else would I be?"

"I don't know. I keep thinking I'm going to wake up and this will all be some elaborate dream."

"If this is a dream," she said, pulling me toward the shower, "don't wake up yet."

We took our time, learning each other, washing away the stress of the day and the last vestiges of restraint we'd been clinging to. My hands mapped the curves of her body with soap-slicked palms—the dip of her waist, the muscles of her back, the soft weight of her breasts. She did the same, her touch reverent and exploratory, tracing the lines of my shoulders, my arms, running her fingers through my hair as she worked shampoo into a lather.

Steam filled the bathroom, fogging the mirrors. Emma's hair was slicked back, the purple looking black as the water streamed over it, droplets catching on her eyelashes, running down the elegant column of her throat. She'd never looked more beautiful.

"I love you," I said, because I could now. Because we were past the point of pretending.

"I love you too." She smiled against my mouth.

"Those words on your lips feel like a dream." I kissed her forehead, her nose, and her mouth.

"It's not a dream."

"But I wouldn't mind hearing them again."

"I love you," she repeated, punctuating each word with a kiss. "I love you, I love you, I love you."

We eventually made it to the bedroom, clean and warm and thoroughly exhausted. I pulled back the covers, and Emma slid in beside me, her body fitting perfectly against mine.

"Come here," I said, pulling her close. One arm slid behind her neck, the other draped over her waist. Our legs tangled together naturally.

I buried my face in her damp hair, breathing in the scent of my shampoo mixed with something distinctly her. Her fingers laced with mine as they rested against her stomach, her body relaxing, melting into me.

"This okay?" I murmured against her neck.

"Perfect," she whispered. "Don't let go."

"Never."

"Are you sure this isn't adrenaline? The excitement of the grant, the relief of today being over."

I pulled back enough to look at her. "Emma, I've been in love with you since before the grant was even submitted. This isn't adrenaline. This is just... you. Us."

She was quiet for a moment. "Okay."

"Okay?"

"Okay, I believe you." She pressed a kiss to my chest, right over my heart. "Because I feel it too. It scares the hell out of me how much I feel it."

"Good scared or bad scared?"

"Good scared. The kind that means it matters."

I tightened my arms around her. "It matters. You matter. This matters."

She didn't answer, just burrowed closer, and within minutes, her breathing had evened out into sleep. The soft, steady rhythm of it against my chest, her body completely slack and trusting in my arms, made my throat tight with love.

I lay there in the dark, this incredible woman in my arms, and let myself feel the full weight of it. The project we'd been killing ourselves over for months coming together. The grant that could change everything for me. Emma—brilliant, beautiful Emma—choosing me, loving me back.

It felt too good, almost. Like the universe had miscalculated somewhere and given me more than my fair share of happiness. I tightened my hold on her, as if I could anchor this moment, keep it from slipping away. Her hair tickled my chin. I could feel her heartbeat, slow and steady, against my forearm. The warmth of her skin, the gentle rise and fall of her breathing.

I pressed a kiss to her shoulder, careful not to wake her, and closed my eyes.

I must have fallen asleep eventually because I woke to moonlight streaming through the window and Emma's hand trailing down my chest. My eyes fluttered open to find her propped up on one elbow, watching me in the silver light. Her hair was wild, her hair falling over one bare shoulder. Her eyes were dark and soft, her lips curved in a small smile.

"Hey," she whispered, her fingers tracing lazy patterns across my skin—over my ribs, down my sternum, circling my navel. "Didn't mean to wake you."

"I'm not complaining," I said, my voice rough with sleep. My hand found her hip, thumb stroking the soft skin there. "What time is it?"

"Late. Or early. Not sure which." Her hand drifted lower, more purposefully now, and I responded despite how thoroughly we'd worn each other out earlier. "Couldn't sleep."

"No?" I reached up to tuck a strand of hair behind her ear, let my fingers linger on her jaw. "Something on your mind?"

"You," she said, leaning down to kiss me. "Just you."

Her mouth was soft and slow against mine, the kiss languid and unhurried. We had time now. All the time in the world.

I rolled her onto her back, settling between her thighs, and she welcomed me with a sigh that sounded like contentment. Everything felt softer in the moonlight—the edges blurred, dreamlike. Her hands moved over me slowly, tracing the planes of my back, the curve of my shoulders, like she was memorizing me by touch alone.

"Max," she breathed, and my name had never sounded like that before. Like a prayer, like coming home.

I kissed her jaw, her neck feeling the slow-building warmth, this gentle pull toward each other. When I finally slid inside her, we both exhaled, eyes locked in the dim light.

It was different this time. Slower. Deeper. Each movement was deliberate and measured, like we were savoring every sensation. Her legs wrapped around my waist loosely as I rocked into her with long, rolling thrusts that had her arching beneath me, her breath catching on soft moans.

"God, you feel so good," I murmured against her lips, barely coherent. Sleep-hazed and drowning in sensation, I worshiped her body with mine. She tightened around me with each stroke, making little gasps as I hit just the right spot.

Her fingers tangled in my hair, nails scraping lightly against my scalp, sending shivers down my spine. "Don't stop," she whispered, though I had no intention of stopping. Ever.

Time seemed to stretch and blur. Minutes or hours, I couldn't tell. Just the two of us moving together in the moonlight, skin sliding against skin, breath mingling. Her hands roamed my shoulders, my back, gripping my ass to pull me deeper, and I lost myself in her heat.

"I'm close," she whispered, grinding against me.

"Me too," I admitted, though I wanted this to last forever. This perfect, drowsy intimacy.

I shifted slightly, changing the angle, and she moaned, her whole body tensing beneath me. "Right there. Oh god, right there."

I kept the rhythm steady, consistent, feeling my own release building slowly at the base of my spine. Her breathing quickened, her fingers dug into my shoulders, and then she was coming with a long, shuddering exhale and a soft cry against my neck as she pulsed around me.

The feeling of her unraveling beneath me pushed me over the edge. I buried my face in her neck as I came, groaning her name, pleasure rolling through me in warm, languid waves that left me boneless and spent.

We stayed like that, tangled together, neither of us moving. Her fingers traced lazy circles on my back. I pressed sleepy kisses to her shoulder, her collarbone, anywhere I could reach without moving too much.

“Love you,” she murmured, half-asleep again.

"Love you back," I promised, rolling to the side and pulling her with me. She curled into my chest immediately, one leg thrown over mine, her hand resting over my heart.

Within minutes, we'd both drifted back to sleep, wrapped up in each other and the moonlight.

Chapter 30 Emma

SATURDAY MORNING SUNLIGHT filtered through Max's bedroom curtains, turning everything golden and hazy. I woke slowly, awareness returning in stages—the warmth of his body behind me, his arm heavy across my waist, his breath soft against my neck.

"You awake?" he murmured, his voice rough with sleep.

"Mmm. Maybe."

His arm tightened, pulling me closer. "Good. I was starting to think I'd have to use more persuasive methods."

I turned in his arms to face him, taking in the sight of him—hair mussed, stubble shadowing his jaw, eyes still soft with sleep but warming as they met mine. "What kind of methods?"

"Those which involve my mouth and significantly less clothing."

"We have no clothing," I pointed out, very aware of every point where our bare skin touched.

"Then I'm already halfway there." He kissed me, slow and thoroughly, and I melted into it, into him, still marveling at the fact that I could do this now. That I was allowed.

His hand slid up my spine, gathering me closer, and I went willingly, pressing against him until there wasn't an inch of space between us. The sheet slipped lower, pooling around our hips, and his palm was warm against my bare back, his touch reverent and possessive all at once.

"I'm never going to get tired of this," he murmured against my lips. "Touching you whenever I want."

"Whenever *you* want?" I pulled back enough to raise an eyebrow. "Pretty sure I have some say in this."

"Do you?" His mouth curved into that smile that never failed to make my stomach flip. "Because from where I'm sitting, you seem pretty agreeable."

"That's because you haven't given me anything to disagree with yet."

"Challenge accepted." He rolled us over in one smooth motion, settling me on top of him. I gasped at the sudden shift, at the feeling of him between my thighs and his hard cock nestled next to my heat.

"Max," I breathed, as his palms cupped my butt, fingers digging in deep.

"Tell me to stop," he said. "Tell me you're tired of this already."

"Never." My hands slid across his chest, feeling the flex of muscle under warm skin, and I leaned over to kiss him, whispering against his lips. "Never, never, never."

His eyes were dark and warm and full of love. "Good. Because I plan on spending the rest of my life proving you made the right choice."

"The rest of your life?" My voice came out breathless. "That's a pretty long time."

"Not long enough." He cupped the back of my head and kissed me, deeper this time, and I lost myself in it. Lost my heart in the taste of him and the impossible reality that he was mine.

His other hand traced down my body—breasts, waist, hips—like he was committing every curve to memory. I arched into his touch, already wanting more, always wanting more when it came to him.

"You're so beautiful," he murmured against my lips. "Do you have any idea what you do to me?"

"Show me," I whispered and felt him shudder.

He took his time, kissing me with the kind of focused attention that made my breath catch and my toes curl. Every touch was deliberate, reverent, like he was worshipping me. His mouth found my breast, tongue circling, and I gasped, fingers tightening in his hair.

"Max, please—"

"Patience," he said, but there was strain in his voice now, that same desperate edge I was feeling. "I want to savor this. Savor you."

But patience had never been my strong suit. I rocked against him, feeling him hard and ready beneath me.

"Emma—" His voice broke on my name, hips lifting to meet mine. "You're going to kill me."

"What a way to go," I murmured, and took him inside me in one slow, deliberate movement that had us both groaning.

For a moment, we just stayed like that, joined completely, foreheads pressed together, breathing hard. Then I started to move, finding a rhythm that had his fingers digging into my hips, his head falling back against the pillow.

"God, yes," he breathed. "Just like that. You feel so perfect."

I braced my hands on his chest, riding him harder, faster, chasing the building pleasure. His hands roamed my body like he couldn't decide where to touch, like he wanted to touch everywhere at once.

"Look at me," I said, and his eyes snapped to mine, dark and dazed. "I love you."

"I love you," he groaned, and then he was sitting up, wrapping his arms around me, changing the angle so that every movement hit deeper, harder. "I love you so much."

We moved together, desperate and synchronized, chasing release. His mouth found mine, swallowing my moans as the pressure built and built until I couldn't take it anymore.

"Max, I'm—"

"I know. Let go, baby. I've got you."

And I did, crying out against his shoulder as pleasure crashed through me in waves that seemed endless. He followed seconds later, my name on his lips, holding me so tight I could barely breathe—like he was afraid I might disappear if he loosened his grip even slightly.

We stayed locked together as the aftershocks faded, neither of us willing to let go. My legs trembled where they wrapped around him, my skin slick with sweat everywhere we touched. I could feel his heart hammering against my chest, as wild and unsteady as my own. His hand stroked up and down my spine, soothing, grounding, while his other arm banded around my waist, keeping me anchored to him.

I pressed my face into the curve of his neck, breathing him in—that mix of sleep and sex and something uniquely Max that I was already addicted to. His pulse jumped under my lips when I kissed his throat, still racing.

I lifted my head to look at him, taking in his flushed face, his kiss-swollen lips, the dazed happiness in his eyes. "That was—"

"Yeah." He grinned, boyish and beautiful. "It really was."

I shifted, and we both gasped at the sensitivity. He was still inside me, softening now, but neither of us made a move to separate. Instead, he guided me down until we were lying side by side, still connected, our legs tangled together in the sheets.

"Coffee?" he murmured, pressing a kiss to my shoulder, then my collarbone, then the swell of my breast.

I laughed, boneless and satisfied, my fingers playing idly with the hair at the nape of his neck. "In a minute. Or ten. Or twenty."

"Take all the time you need," he said, his hand cupping my face with such tenderness it made my throat tight. "I'm not going anywhere."

"Promise?"

"Promise." He kissed me softly, sweetly, so different from the desperate passion of moments before. "You're stuck with me now, Emma."

"Sounds perfect to me."

We lay there in the golden morning light, wrapped around each other, the rest of the world forgotten. Eventually we'd get up, make that coffee, shower, start our day. But for now, this was enough. More than enough.

This was everything.

We made our way to the kitchen wrapped in sheets like teenagers, laughing when I tripped over the trailing fabric. Max started the coffee while I perched on the counter, the same counter where we'd been significantly less dressed on Friday night.

"So, I've been invited to a conference in Rome in July. Cutting-edge research in education, networking opportunities, really incredible speakers." His thumbs traced circles on my skin. "I was planning to go alone, but now... I want you there with me. We could stay a few extra days. See the city. Enjoy ourselves."

"Max—"

"I know it's only a month from now, and I don't know what your summer plans are—" He gestured vaguely between us. "—but, Emma, I don't want to go without you. I don't want to pretend this is casual or take it slow because that's what we're supposed to do. I want you with me. In Rome, and everywhere else."

I set down my coffee mug and framed his face with my hands. "Yes."

"Yes?"

"Yes to Rome. Yes to all of it." I kissed him, tasting coffee and possibility. "I don't want to take it slow either."

His smile was brilliant, relieved. "Thank God. I was prepared to be significantly more persuasive."

"Save it for later," I said.

We moved to the couch, tangled together with our coffee. I told him about the fellowship with SHAPE AMERICA that I'd been eyeing for months but had been too scared to pursue.

"Emma." Max pulled out his phone before I'd even finished explaining. "You're applying. End of discussion."

"It's competitive—"

"You're brilliant."

"The application is extensive—"

"We'll work on it together." He was already pulling up the website. "What's the deadline?"

"End of June."

"Perfect. That gives us time." He looked at me seriously. "You deserve this. You deserve every opportunity, every success. And I'm going to make sure you believe that."

My throat tightened. "How did I get so lucky?"

"Pretty sure I'm the lucky one." He pulled me into his lap, and I went willingly, wrapping my arms around his neck. "You and me, Em. Italy in July, fellowship applications, whatever comes next. We're doing this together."

"Together," I agreed, and kissed him to seal the promise.

We spent the rest of the morning on the couch, laptop open between us, working through the fellowship application. Max was relentless in the best way, pushing me to articulate my research goals more clearly, challenging vague statements, celebrating every strong paragraph with enthusiastic kisses that kept derailing our progress.

"Stop distracting me," I said, laughing as he nuzzled my neck.

He shifted closer, one arm sliding around my waist like it belonged there, his thumb tracing lazy, absentminded circles through the fabric of my shirt. "I'm motivating you."

His breath was warm against my skin as he dipped his head, not quite kissing—just enough to tease—his nose brushing along my jaw. I tried to refocus, straightening in my chair, but he followed the movement, chin resting on my shoulder, a soft hum of amusement vibrating against me.

"You're making it impossible to think."

I shot him a look, but he only grinned, eyes bright, rocking gently, as if he had all the time in the world and zero intention of giving me my concentration back.

"Good."

His phone buzzed on the coffee table, and he ignored it, more interested in the spot below my ear that made me shiver.

It buzzed again. Then again.

“Max,” I said his name with a warning edge, lifting my head to look back at him, one eyebrow already arched.

“It can wait.” He waved a hand dismissively, lips brushing my temple as if to underline the point, though his eyes flicked, just once, toward the phone lighting up on the table.

“It seems like a *lot* of notifications.” I leaned back slightly, folding my arms, watching him now.

He groaned, rubbing his face with one hand before reaching for it. The moment his fingers closed around the phone, his posture changed, shoulders locking, breath catching mid-exhale. He stared at the screen, jaw tightening.

“Emma.” My name came out low and careful, all the playfulness stripped away.

Something in his voice made my stomach flip. I straightened, uncrossing my arms, my chair scraping softly against the floor as I leaned closer. “What?”

"It's... it's the grant committee." He stared at the screen, then at me, eyes wide. "They're trying to reach me."

"Answer it!"

He fumbled with the phone, nearly dropping it, and I had to press my hand over my mouth to keep from laughing nervously. He put it on speaker.

"This is Dr. Harrison."

"Dr. Bennett, this is Carla Jenkins from the National Science Foundation grant committee." The woman's voice was warm, professional. "I hope I'm not catching you at a bad time."

"No, not at all." Max's hand found mine, gripped tight.

"Wonderful. I'm calling with some very good news. The committee met earlier than expected, and I'm pleased to inform you that your application has been approved for full funding."

The world seemed to stop. Max's eyes locked onto mine, both of us frozen in stunned wonder.

"Dr. Harrison? Are you still there?"

"Yes! Yes, I'm here. I'm—" He laughed, the sound unsteady. "Thank you. Thank you so much."

"Congratulations. You should receive the formal notification via email within the hour, along with next steps and funding disbursement details. Your research proposal and STEM Field Day were exceptional. The committee was particularly impressed with the collaborative approach and the potential applications to take this to other schools in your district. Well done."

They spoke for a few more minutes about logistics and timelines, but I barely heard any of it. The words blurred together, fading into background noise as I watched Max instead.

His shoulders lowered, inch by inch, as the tension left him in real time. The tight line between his brows smoothed, and something in my chest loosened with it. I hadn't realized how used I'd gotten to that look on his face or how much I'd been worrying with him until I saw it disappear.

He let out a breath that sounded almost like a laugh, and relief washed through me, warm and dizzying, followed by a sudden, aching pride that made my eyes sting. I wanted to reach for him, to touch him just to make it real, but I stayed still, afraid of breaking the moment.

When the call ended, he let the phone drop into his hands, then settled it between his knees, elbows braced on his thighs. He sat there for a second, staring off into nothing, that soft, disbelieving smile still on his face, as if he were afraid that if he moved too fast the moment might vanish.

Only then did I move.

I wrapped my arms around him, pressing my cheek to his shoulder. His arms came up tight around me, pulling me in, squeezing hard enough that it stole my breath in the best way. He buried his face in my hair and kissed it, once, then again, lingering there as he breathed me in, his grip tightening like he needed the contact to make it real.

I could feel the tremor in him now, the aftershock of months of waiting and worrying finally breaking loose. He rocked us slightly, forehead resting against the side of my head, one hand splayed between my shoulder blades, grounding us both.

When he spoke, his voice was rough, low, and thick with emotion: “We got it.”

"You got it."

"We got it." He pulled me to him, lifting me off the couch and spinning me around, both of us laughing and maybe crying a little. "We fucking got it, Emma."

"We got it," I repeated, and then his mouth was on mine, the kiss desperate and joyful and full of everything we'd been working toward.

When we finally broke apart, both of us breathless, Max kept his forehead pressed to mine. "We have to celebrate."

"Absolutely."

"Dinner out. Somewhere that isn't this couch or kitchen counter."

"Revolutionary thinking."

He grinned. "I have my moments."

BARREL WAS PACKED, warm and loud with conversation and laughter. His hand was firm on my lower back as we followed the hostess, just light enough to be comforting and make my stomach flutter. We'd been doing this all day—fingers intertwined, stolen kisses, casual touches—and somehow, it never got old. Every brush of his hand felt electric.

Halfway to the table, I heard a familiar voice.

“Max? Emma?”

I looked up to see Jen, Thalia, Dante, and Eli at a large table near the window. All of them were watching us with a mixture of surprise, amusement, and that knowing look I recognized too well.

“Hey,” I said, stepping away from Max, still glowing from the simple fact that he was there, and hugged my friends immediately.

They crowded around me, hands on my back, shoulders, hair—tight hugs and whispered words. I laughed softly at their low, excited chatter, my head tipped toward Jen and Talia. Every so often one of them glanced at Max, eyebrows lifting, little smirks playing at the corners of their mouths. I caught their looks but tried not to smile too widely.

Another whisper, another look. One of them stared straight at him, smirked, then ducked their heads back into the huddle. I laughed again at something Jen said and shook my head, shaking off a blush, then glanced at Max. His eyes found mine, and I squeezed his hand under the table.

Dante nudged Eli with his elbow, and Eli clapped Max on the shoulder with a satisfied grin. Max caught my look, and I knew exactly what it meant. *About time.*

Talia and Jen loosened their hugs, stepping back slowly. Talia's hand lingered on my shoulder, and Jen's fingers brushed against my arm. They were still whispering, still smiling, but their attention turned to the table.

"Join us," Talia said, signaling for chairs. "We just ordered appetizers."

I glanced at Max. He grinned down at me. I squeezed his hand again. "Sure. Why not?"

As we settled in, Jen leaned forward, a sharp, delighted edge to her smile. "So, how was your weekend?"

"Jen," Talia warned.

"What? I'm just saying—Emma and Max look very... relaxed." She waggled her eyebrows, and Talia snorted into her wine.

"Leave them alone," Eli said, laughing, but I could hear the warmth in his tone. "Though I *will* say, about damn time."

"We've been taking bets," Dante added, smirking. "I said you'd crack before Field Day. Jen said after. Looks like she won."

"You've been betting on us?" I asked, laughter rising despite myself.

"Everyone's been betting on you," Talia said. "The tension was unbearable. We were all suffering secondhand."

I buried my face in my hands. "I hate all of you."

"No, you don't." Jen reached across the table, squeezing Max's arm. Her expression softened, and I saw it—not teasing, not just fun—but genuinely happy for us. "We're happy for you. Both of you. It's about time you two figured your shit out."

Max leaned in, voice low. "Speaking of figuring shit out... we got the grant. They called today."

The table erupted. Congratulations, demands for details, Eli ordering more beers despite Max's protests. I felt the warmth of the moment—the ease of being here with our friends, Max beside me, hand on mine under the table.

"This calls for a toast," Eli said, raising his bottle. "To Max and Emma. For the grant, for finally getting together, and for putting us out of our misery."

"Cheers," everyone chorused.

I clinked bottles with Max, smiling into his eyes over the rim, feeling love settle in my chest. This was real. This was *us*. And everyone knew it.

The conversation rolled on, Eli telling one ridiculous story after another. I laughed, but I couldn't help noticing the smaller, sharper rhythm at the table—Jen and Dante.

"Seriously, Dante?" Jen elbowed him lightly.

"Someone's got to have taste around here," he replied, shrugging with a teasing grin.

"Taste for disaster, maybe," she shot back, smirk flickering.

He leaned toward her, teasing. "Come on, admit it—you'd be lost without me."

"I survive despite you," she snapped, but the laughter in her voice made it clear she didn't mean it.

Their banter threaded through the conversation, under the radar but electric. Eli paused mid-sentence, smirking, and Talia shook her head in amusement. Dante's hand brushed Jen's as he reached for the appetizer plate, and she froze for a moment. Subtle—but I noticed.

Even while she laughed at Eli's story or nodded at Talia, her attention always snapped back to Dante, and his eyes followed her every move. It was quiet, playful, sharp, and charged all at once—a storm tucked under the casual chatter.

Dinner stretched late, the conversation getting louder, sillier, more ridiculous. I fit perfectly against Max, his hand finding mine under the table, grounding me, reminding me that this was real.

Eventually, Thalia checked her phone. "I should probably get going. Lots of laundry and lesson planning tomorrow."

"Same," Eli agreed, signaling for the check.

We gathered coats and bags. Jen pulled me into a tight hug. Dante shook Max's hand, congratulating him.

"You good?" Max asked.

"Yeah. Fine," Dante said, but his smile didn't quite land. "See you Monday."

Walking to the car, tucked under Max's arm, I thought about Jen and Dante—the way they'd circled each other all night, pretending everything was fine when it wasn't.

"Did you notice—" I started.

"Jen and Dante? Yeah," Max said.

"Think they'll figure it out?"

He pulled me closer, pressing a kiss to my temple. "Eventually. Everyone does, if they're lucky."

"Are we lucky?" I asked, tilting my head up to him.

"The luckiest people alive." His voice was soft, warm, steady. The streetlights hit his face, and I was struck again by how much I loved him. "I love you, Emma."

"I love you too." I rose onto my toes, kissing him. "Take me home?"

"Already there," he said, because anywhere with him *was* home.

Windows down, cool spring air rushing in, hand in his on the console—everything was possible.

Acknowledgements

FIRST AND FOREMOST, thank you to my amazing readers—without you, this journey wouldn't be nearly as much fun. You all bring the magic to my words, and I'm so grateful for each of you.

To my incredible family: Jim, you've been my rock, my sounding board, and the one who gets why I'm always talking to myself (I promise, it's all for the plot!). A special shout-out to Miles and Megan, who have to say "mom" ten times before I surface from whatever scene I'm in.

To Liz: Thank you for reading late into the night, for your endless support, and for always being my favorite sister. I'm lucky to have you by my side.

To Lauren: Marchfield wouldn't exist without you. Thank you for answering my endless questions and always pushing me to be better.

To Suzanne: My accountability partner in writing and crime— you keep me on track, even when the words aren't flowing Thank you for always being there with a kind word, a pep talk, and a good laugh.

To Nancy: Thank you for asking me how it's going at least once a week and listening to me vent with such patience and kindness.

And finally, to all the teachers and educators out there who inspire everything I write. Your passion, humor, and heart make a difference every day, and I can only hope my characters reflect even a fraction of the amazing work you do. Thank you, thank you, thank you!

About the Author

M. JAYNE LADOW COMBINES her love of storytelling with her background as a longtime educator. When she's not creating fictional worlds where coffee is plentiful, snowstorms are romantic, and teachers always have a happy ending, you can find her at the beach, spending time with her family, or being distracted by her cats. She lives in Virginia Beach with her husband, kids, and a bunch of furry and reptilian friends.

Stay Tuned for:

BOUND AND HEXED

Fifty Feet and Falling

By M. Jayne LaDow

Rowan Mira has a problem. A six-foot, annoyingly calm, Bureau-badge-wielding problem.

When a routine spell goes sideways, Crystal Hollow's most chaotic witch accidentally tethers herself to Elias Delancy—a Magical Compliance investigator with sharp eyes, sharper cheekbones, and one very inconvenient superpower: he's immune to magic.

All magic. Including hers.

Now they're stuck within fifty feet of each other until Rowan figures out how to break the bond—which would be a lot easier if the bond itself wasn't apparently rooting for the two of them. Or if Elias would stop being so *infuriatingly* competent. Or if her cat would stop taking his side.

Breaking a spell that shouldn't exist, between a witch and a man magic can't touch, was never going to be simple. But as the tether pulls tighter and the line between frustration and something warmer gets harder to find, Rowan starts to wonder: is she trying to break the bond because she wants to—or because she's afraid of what will happen if she doesn't?

A sparkling paranormal romance about accidental magic, forced proximity, and the one person your heart tethers itself to whether you asked it to or not.

Stay Tuned for:

MASQUERADE OF BROKEN Truths

Book 2 in the Tides of Truth Series

By M. Jayne LaDow

English teacher Dani Jones was finally settling back into her ordinary life in the fall of 1997 after barely escaping her last brush with murder. When an anonymous caller whispers a name into her boyfriend's microphone—Clara Hammond, a girl who vanished after prom in 1975—Gavin Larkhurst does what any good radio host would do with a fifty-year-old cold case.

He tells all of Virginia Beach that his girlfriend can solve it.

He has no idea who's listening.

Somewhere in the city, a man has carried his secret for fifty years. Patient. Careful. Certain he'd never be found. Now Dani is asking questions, and Gavin's voice is carrying every word straight to him.

Some secrets don't stay buried. And the most dangerous thing Gavin Larkhurst ever did was say her name on air.

Featuring beloved Virginia Beach, Virginia landmarks: The Cavalier Hotel, First Landing Lighthouse, The Jewish Mother, The Duck Inn, Peabody's, and the Oceanfront.

Books by M. Jayne LaDow

The Marchfield Series

ONE NIGHT STANDS AND Lesson Plans

Learning Goals and Dancing Poles

Pop Quizzes and Stolen Kisses

Tardy Pass, No Questions Asked

Budget Cuts and Midnight Lust

The Tides of Truth Series

A Pilgrimage of Whispered Truths

A Masquerade of Truth (Coming Soon)

The Magical Bonds Series

Bound and Hexed (Coming Soon)

www.ingramcontent.com/pod-product-compliance
Lightning Source LLC
LaVergne TN
LVHW100521110826
845146LV00002B/723
* 9 7 9 8 8 9 8 6 0 7 5 5 5 *